Second Chances: Romance & Mysteries

Three Romantic Suspense Novellas

Trinity Sands Beach Club

Jen Dodrill
Sharon H. Carpenter
Deborah Sprinkle

Scrivenings
PRESS
Quench your thirst for story.
www.ScriveningsPress.com

Published by Scrivenings Press LLC
15 Lucky Lane
Morrilton, Arkansas 72110
https://ScriveningsPress.com

Printed in the United States of America

Paperback ISBN 978-1-64917-476-5

eBook ISBN 978-1-64917-477-2

Editors: Erin R. Howard and Linda Fulkerson

Cover design by Linda Fulkerson - www.bookmarketinggraphics.com

SeaBreeze
Obsession

Jen Dodrill

Scrivenings
PRESS
Quench your thirst for story.
www.ScriveningsPress.com

Chapter One

I stepped onto the weather-worn porch of the beach cottage, and a rush of memories flooded my mind. This time last year—Memorial Day weekend—Gage and I vacationed here, neither realizing it would be our last trip as a couple. How fast life changed.

The front door lock stuck, but I shimmied the key back and forth until it turned. I wiped sand off my shoes on the doormat and stepped inside. Returning alone never crossed my mind. The weight of sorrow in my chest almost took me to my knees.

"I refuse to stay sad the whole summer." Squaring my shoulders, I resolved to confront the ghosts of my past. Maybe find a glimmer of solace amidst the familiar sights and sounds of the island. If my counselor were here, she would ask, "What do you want this summer?"

If I were honest, my answer would be "Peace." It's what I longed for and yearned for in this place I've always loved.

Then, she would ask me what I meant.

Ugh. Details, details.

Loud meowing drew my attention back to the car. "The windows are down, boy."

My well-fed, fluffy orange cat Rusty complained again.

"Let's get you out of this heat." Using both hands, I lugged his extra-large carrier to the door. We entered the cottage, and I groaned at the sight in front of me. What a mess. Gage was the last person here. When we met thirty years ago, his messy ways tickled me. He told me he once thought my ability to talk to anyone was cute.

Both of our perceptions altered over time.

I kicked the door closed, lowered the cat carrier to the floor, and slid my blue paisley fabric purse off my shoulder and onto the kitchen bar.

"All right, Rusty, go check out the place." Once free, he zoomed into the living room, stopped, and licked his back as if he had been tormented on the eight-hour trip from West Tennessee to the Florida Gulf Coast. I guessed he'd forgotten the times I stopped to pet him and how I sang old country and western songs. He meowed along with me, so I assumed he liked it. Or maybe that was the tortuous part.

"Silly boy." I scratched his head twice. That's all he allowed. Friends who disregarded my warnings learned that the third scratch resulted in antibiotic ointment and a minimum of three bandages.

With my hands on my hips, I surveyed the open floor plan of the kitchen, living, and dining rooms. "Karah,"—I shook my head—"your work is cut out for you. You better get started."

Talking to myself had become second nature. Gage moved out of our home the night I went on a rampage about his many faults—a.k.a., the night I lost my mind, according to him. We didn't see each other again until we signed divorce papers.

Too often, I couldn't even remember why we divorced. It happened quickly. At least, I thought so. Things changed, we changed, and then, we were over. I couldn't point to just one incident or wrongly spoken word. It was more a conglomeration of a lifetime of living together. I think we forgot how to love each other well.

Reminiscing and resentment wouldn't get the place cleaned. I checked the two bedrooms and bathrooms and called Ursula. She would clean it in no time for a reasonable price, even though I'd have to put up with her nosiness. After I changed the sheets on the king-sized bed in the master bedroom, I gathered dirty towels and stray bathroom items and deposited them all in the spare room.

I walked through the house, recalling the good times Gage and I shared there. The time we painted our bedroom, when we picked out beachy furniture for the living room, and the day he played air guitar with the toilet brush while I used a can of air freshener as a microphone. Once, I accidentally sprayed my mouth and breathed "Tropical Hawaiian" on him.

A smile tugged at my lips.

I shoved the thoughts to the back of my mind and returned to the car for the rest of my things. A large rolling cooler and a heavy tote sat in the back seat. First, I dropped the canvas bag on the table with a thunk, and then I unloaded the cooler into the refrigerator, leaving a soda on the counter. My mouth watered at the thought of the cold drink, but the top wouldn't budge. I narrowed my eyes, got a firmer grip, and twisted another time, grimacing as pain shot through my hand.

Reason number four on my "I miss being married" list.

It took me several minutes to find a non-slip rubber jar opener. After I opened the bottle, I found a pack of disposable cups in the pantry and filled one with ice—my favorite way to drink soda. One of my other quirks Gage found attractive at first.

Why was I spending so much time obsessing over my ex-husband? Thinking about him wasn't part of my summer plans. I settled at the table and opened my laptop. "No more Gage." I could do this and be the person I wanted to be. Alone.

Navigating to my new website, I admired the sea-green and pale blue SeaBreeze Designs logo with my initials in the center. When my friend designed my brand, she asked me if I would keep my last name, but I couldn't imagine taking back my maiden name after being Karah Halyard for over a quarter of a century. Plus, our daughter Nikki would have pitched a fit. She sided with her dad and only communicated with me if necessary. I tried to keep the peace in any way possible.

I reminded myself why I was here—to get my new business up and running. Forcing all thoughts of my daughter and ex from my mind, I got to work. I'd uploaded pictures of several handmade items, but each decoration took time to describe. Finding enticing keywords and putting them together in a way that made sense and drew buyers was a struggle. Making beach décor wasn't new to me, but operating a website and everything that entailed was uncharted territory.

I was deep into work, considering each descriptive word for the seashell coasters I needed to list, when Rusty rubbed against my ankle. He responded to my yelp with a loud meow.

"How are you, big guy?" He stretched up and put his paws on my knee. "Are you hungry? Sorry, fellow." I set out his food and water bowls and tucked the litter pan under the bathroom sink in the spare room. On my way back to my computer, I rubbed his head. He looked up, green eyes glittering. "You're a good boy." I was pretty sure he grinned.

My fanciful ideas made me chuckle. "Okay, let's get this one done." Before I sat, I glanced out the sliding glass door. Fifteen years before, the view of the sparkling Gulf across the street sold us on the cottage. Gage and I enjoyed many romantic strolls along the gleaming white sand beach, sea oats waving in the breeze and seagulls crying out, begging for food.

Except what I noticed wasn't the gorgeous beach view. No, it was a man. Tall, slim, with a runner's lean build—a lot like Gage's—dressed in embarrassingly short shorts and a clingy tank top. I stepped closer to the door. It wasn't my ex. The man stared at me as he grabbed one foot behind him and stretched. He repeated the same action with his other leg, then put his hands on his hips and leaned side to side. He took off with a wink.

"Did you wink at me? He did. He sure did. Rusty, did you see him?" I turned, but the cat was nowhere in sight. "I can't believe he did that."

Why did he stare at my house? Was he flirting with me? He couldn't have been stretching for me. I opened the door, walked to where he had been, and looked back across the road. Yes, he could see straight inside. I never realized how vulnerable I was in my little cottage. A shiver skittered down my spine.

Back in the house, I pulled the vertical blinds over the door, tipping them for privacy while still getting ambient light. Then I moved my chair to the other side of the table. Now, he couldn't see in, and I wouldn't be tempted to look out.

I spent another hour uploading and positioning my favorite designs, refusing to allow myself to turn around. I didn't have time for some strange man doing odd things.

Sunset had come and gone when I finished for the day. I stretched my neck side to side and rubbed the cramps in my fingers. Most of my work was done with real shells, handmade candles and soaps, and anything natural I could find for accent. It was all hands-on except when I used my vinyl-cutting machine, which I'd left behind in Tennessee. Maybe Nikki would bring it if she came to Florida.

That was a big if.

Chapter Two

Someone pounded on the door, and Rusty sprang off the bed, leaving behind deep scratches on my leg. "It's not even morning," I whined. My phone read six-thirty.

"Coming!" I tugged my faded purple-and-white-checked sleep shirt down around my knees, limped to the door, and peeked through the peephole to find Ursula on my porch. I opened the door and stood behind it so no one else saw my ratty pajamas.

"Mrs. Karah! The sun is rising, and you're still in bed?" She threw her arms around me and patted my sides. "You've grown a little, dear." She was not talking about my height.

She let go, and I drew a deep breath. "Thank you for coming on such short notice." And before the rest of the island woke up. "I appreciate it."

"Of course, anything for my favorite couple. Oh, here you go. These were on your doorstep." She handed me a gorgeous bouquet of yellow and white carnations. A card stuck out of the green wrapper. "Must be from your handsome hubby." Her eyes twinkled.

Hmm, no one here knows we're divorced? I took the flowers and opened the note—not a typical florist's card but more like a folded piece of construction paper. It read: "Did you like what you saw yesterday?"

Ursula leaned over my shoulder, her corkscrew gray curls tickling my cheek. "What does he mean?" She nudged me. "Maybe I shouldn't read it?"

Warmth crept up my neck. I understood what she was implying. Best to stop her ideas before anything started. "These aren't from my hubby ... husband. Mr. Gage and I, well, we are no longer married." Which wasn't the point right now. Who left me these flowers? I checked both sides of the handwritten note, but there wasn't a signature.

"What?" Her arms flew upward, the expression on her face comical. "No, no, no. That couldn't be true." She peered into my eyes. "Did he beat you? I bet he did. My fourth husband beat me. What a scoundrel." Her mouth and nose wrinkled in disgust.

"No." I barked a laugh. Gage, one of the gentlest men I ever met, would never hit me. I didn't want her spreading untruths to her other customers. "No, not at all. We grew apart, that's all." I dropped the bouquet and note inside the trashcan. Surprise gifts, especially from random, unknown people, made me uncomfortable. My hands trembled, and I forced the threatening tone of the card from my mind.

"Humph. If you say so. He doesn't know what he's missing out on. How could he let you go? He made a big mistake." She smoothed her bandana, gathered her cleaning supplies, and marched inside. "This place is dirtier than I've ever seen it. I'll start in the back. You rest."

But I didn't want to rest. I had goals and ambitions and wanted to move on with life. My homemade beach décor business was my new focus. I slipped into the bathroom, dressed, and bandaged the scratches on my leg. "I'm going to the beach for a while," I called out.

Ursula peeked her head out of the spare room. "I had a thought. If those flowers aren't from Mr. Gage, then you, my dear, have a secret admirer."

Maybe, but that note seemed kind of creepy. The mysterious runner from the day before crossed my mind. No, they couldn't be from him. More than likely, he'd stared at the wrong cottage. I closed the door and trekked across the road. My feet sank into the powdery, sugar-white sand on the other side. The day might be early, but sunbathers had already staked their claim on the beach.

Our little island wasn't a touristy area. Most families with young kids stayed on the mainland to enjoy the variety of restaurants and attractions. Trinity Sands Island was populated by what everyone called old-timers, or the people who inherited bungalows and cottages from their families. Or by some residents like us who managed to grab and fix up a foreclosure.

I glanced back. Our little aquamarine and peach cottage would be spotless in a few hours.

My cottage. Mine. Besides alimony, it was all I asked for.

A half-hour later, I finished combing the beach, my pockets and arms full of pretty shells and washed-up driftwood. I set my loot on the kitchen counter and found Ursula in my bathroom, fussing at Rusty, who hid behind the toilet. "Who's winning?"

She slapped her hand against her chest. "You scared me! I didn't hear you. This boy of yours won't move, and I need to clean right there."

I scooted past her and shooed the cat out of the room. "He's a stubborn fellow." The bathroom sink and tub gleamed. "Thank you for coming today."

"No problem, but I've never seen *your* house this dirty." She emphasized *your* like it was all my fault. "Did you figure out who left you the flowers?"

"Nope. I think they had the wrong address. I did see a man outside yesterday."

"A man?" She wiggled her eyebrows. "Handsome, rich? Does he have a brother?"

"Funny woman. I didn't talk to him. He watched me from the beach. It was … odd. He stretched like he was showing off." I mimicked what he'd done. "Then he ran off down the beach."

She rubbed her hands together. "A mystery. I love them. Tell me what he looked like. I know everyone here."

I described him, and she nodded. "That's Barney. Barney Cobb. He's fine. He lives somewhere on the island." She eyed my outfit. "If you want to catch him, you might consider a cute sundress. And cut back on the cookies."

Okay, then. Way to punch a woman when she was down. I forced a placid smile and headed for the kitchen to wash my new collection. It's not like I didn't know I'd put on a few pounds since the divorce. I didn't start out skinny. And apparently, I was a stress eater. Who knew?

My counselor advised me to focus on my emotional and spiritual well-being first and then worry about how much I ate.

"Not that they don't all work together," she said. "But as your emotions and spiritual life get healthy, I think you'll find you're more able to take better care of your body."

She helped me talk things out. The little white pill I took every day worked in my brain. I also read my Bible and intentionally focused on God throughout each day. Contrary to Ursula's words, I didn't always eat cookies, but I liked some ice cream after dinner.

I rinsed the driftwood under warm water and cleaned it with a soft-bristle brush. Then, I submerged the pieces in a bleach and water solution. While they soaked, I washed and scrubbed the shells. In between a search for tools and a bottle of baby oil to use on the shells, movement caught my eye.

There was Barney. Outside, across the road and standing in the sand. He waved, a broad smile on his face. I lifted a hand. "Why are you watching me?" I whispered.

He stretched and took off, this time without a wink. Why would he put on such a show? Was it for me or someone else? Maybe my neighbor knew him.

Ursula bustled into the room. "I'm finished. Let me know when you need me again."

"Wait." I pointed to the sliding glass doors. "He was there again."

She turned, but the beach was already empty. She looked at me, eyebrow cocked. "You feeling okay, Mrs. Karah?" Her lips turned up into a grin. "Maybe you've been out in the sun too long." She shook her head and left, muttering about crazy old women.

Chapter Three

Ursula was gone for only a minute before she burst back in the front door. "I forgot the trash." She slapped her palm on her forehead. Before she emptied the kitchen can, I dug out the notecard. She might think it was from a secret admirer, but I wanted to investigate further. I tucked it in my pocket as she entered the kitchen with the bathroom garbage cans.

"Hey, don't worry about Barney," she said. "If you get a chance to talk to him and can't think of anything to say, ask him about his pinky ring. It's a huge, silver one with an elaborate outline of a pirate ship inlaid with turquoise. Pretty strange looking and quite flashy, but he's proud of it. It's an antique thing that covers most of his finger." She checked her watch. "Oh, I have to run. Call me when you need me."

My current craft inventory was uploaded and labeled, and I needed a break. I massaged my hands while deciding how to spend the afternoon. Typing stressed my joints, but I refused to give in to the diagnosis the doctor handed to me a few months ago. How could I be old enough or have the time or energy to deal with degenerative arthritis? I dry-swallowed my pain medication and reached for the tube of prescription cream, working it into my fingers.

A peek in my refrigerator confirmed it was time for a grocery store run to Maude's Market, the Beach Club's version of a quick-stop shop, complete with live bait and fresh-from-the-Gulf seafood.

Large plastic tubs in front of the store held pool noodles and beach toys. I picked a pink noodle and grabbed a blue plastic sand bucket for fun. If nothing else, I'd use it when searching for shells.

Inside, Maude greeted me with a holler and a wave. "Mrs. Halyard, how are ya? It's hot out already, isn't it?"

I found a non-wobbly buggy and added my noodle and bucket. She sat at the customer service desk where large glass jars full of old-fashioned candy lined the rustic wooden counter. My mouth watered, and I picked out a cherry stick and a handful of caramels. "I'm doing well, Maude. How are you?" I wiped the sweat from my upper lip. "Yes, it's hot. Summer started early this year."

She patted her outdated hairdo. Her fingers, swollen and curling inward, made me cringe as I pictured mine like that in several years.

"I hear you and the mister split the sheets." She leaned forward, an eager expression on her face.

Gage would cackle over her old-fashioned saying. It didn't have the same effect on me. "Yes, we are divorced now."

"Who got the cottage? You?"

Her momma never taught her to keep her nose to herself. I repeated the words over and over and managed a polite smile. If I told her, everyone in the Beach Club who shopped here would know. If I didn't, everyone on the island would find out from Ursula.

"Yes, the cottage is mine. How much do I owe for this?"

She bagged the candy and instructed me to pay at checkout. I turned toward the store's interior. "I need to stock up. Talk to you later."

"Later 'gator." She laughed at her joke.

Maude manned the sole checkout lane when I finished shopping. I unloaded my groceries and braced myself for her commentary. She reviewed each item before she scanned and bagged it. She held up the noodle. "Going to the pool? It'll be busy since tomorrow is Memorial Day."

"Maybe the day after, then." I was done for today. Shopping and unloading groceries when I got to the cottage would steal the last of my energy.

Next, she gave her opinion on the frosted cookies I found. She lifted the package and turned it around. "Someone requested these. Let me know if they're any good, okay?"

"I will. They look yummy."

She grabbed my blue bucket. "You gonna make sandcastles?" Her brows drew together in consternation. I imagined her picturing fifty-one-year-old me playing in the sand.

I chuckled. "No, but I do collect seashells and driftwood for my new business making beach décor."

"Oh, like the little hula girls made from shells? Those are cute." She held her flappy arms out to each side and wiggled her hips.

Not exactly, but I didn't think she cared what I had to say. She lifted the carton of chocolate ice cream and cocked an eyebrow.

"Is this why Mr. Gage left you?"

It was late afternoon, and my medicine had kicked in, so I was slow on the uptake. "What do you mean?"

She scanned the frozen dessert and bagged it by itself.

"You've grown a bit," she said, echoing Ursula's earlier comment.

My mouth dropped open. I swiped my credit card and snatched my bags. "Thanks." Not. Ice cream had nothing to do with my marriage ending, but I wouldn't tell this woman anything else. I stomped to my car, deposited my food in the back, and slammed the hatch.

* * *

The short drive home gave me time to calm down. What Maude, Ursula, or anyone else thought didn't matter. After stowing my groceries, I headed for the front porch, lowering myself into the white Adirondack chair. It had seen better days. I kept a firm grip on the armrests and prayed it would hold my weight. What a day. The sun began its descent while I attempted to relax. Summer on the Gulf Coast of Florida meant long, hot days and warm nights, but being next to the water had its perks.

Waves lapped against the shore, and the soothing rhythm calmed my mind and spirit. I tasted the salty tang of the sea air. Seagulls cried in the distance. My world felt safe, and I liked it. It's why I came here this summer.

"Long day?" A familiar voice sounded from my left.

I vaulted out of the chair and ended up in the flower bed.

"What are you doing here?" My screech raised a flock of gulls who took off in a flurry of feathers. My ex-husband stood on the driveway separating my cottage from the next-door rental.

"Gage, why are you here?" I repeated as I picked my way out of the flowers.

"I'm staying there." He thumbed toward the bright yellow

townhouse. "I thought about asking to use the cottage, but I didn't think you'd let me."

I wanted to say, "Duh," but settled for, "Good call." I crossed my arms. "*Why* are you on the island?" How often would I have to ask before he told me his plans?

He shrugged. I recognized the gesture. The man had a shrug for every circumstance. This one included a lift of his left eyebrow.

"Work," I said. Nothing new there.

"Yeah. I got in last night." He scuffed his foot against the driveway. "I saw your car, but I've been gone all day."

Together close to thirty years, and here we stood—me in my tiny yard and him twenty feet away at a rental house. Close but not too close.

I recalled how it felt to be in his arms. My gaze went to his mouth. I still thought about his kisses.

"Karah?"

Warmth spread up my neck and across my cheeks. It started as a subtle tingling before it intensified. I feared my eyes mirrored the emotions stirring inside me—embarrassment tinged with a hint of irritation at him and myself.

I checked my bare wrist. "Well, it's late. I need to feed the cat." I hustled inside, locked the door behind me, and leaned against it. Who would have thought I'd live next door to Gage? My calm, peaceful summer imploded.

* * *

Rusty didn't leave my side all night, and in the morning, it took me several minutes to unkink my body and climb out of bed. I refilled his chow and gave him fresh water before I dressed. Ursula's words mocked me as I chose blue Bermuda shorts and a white tank—no cute sundress for me. I wasn't here to catch a man, especially Barney.

I poured a cup of dark roast coffee and stepped onto the porch, my gaze fixed on the ocean. Gage was no longer a part of my life, and I refused to keep up with his comings and goings for however long he stayed next door.

Clouds gathered in the distance—some fluffy and white and others darker, full of rain yet to come. Even through the humidity, I felt the breeze the storm would bring, along with the familiar scent of salt and seaweed. I set my cup inside, slipped on my sandals, and scooped up my bucket. I'd see what treasures I could find in the sand now and go again after the storm ended to discover what it washed ashore.

Leaving my sandals at the top of the beach, I headed to the water and turned toward the less populated area. As I scanned for shells, I sensed a presence close behind me. I whipped around to find my mystery man less than five feet away.

"Hello?" I would be polite until he stated his purpose for watching me.

He tugged his Hawaiian-print swim trunks up his skinny hips. "Hi, how are you?"

"Fine." I stepped back and scanned the empty beach, then wiggled my sand bucket. "I think I'm finished. Heading home now. My husband is waiting for me." My *ex*-husband, and he had no idea I was at the beach, but whatever worked.

He smiled and stepped closer. I moved farther up the beach, toward the road. He kept pace with me. Finally, I stopped and dug my toes into the sand.

"What do you want?" I asked, my tone firm and all business.

"To get to know you." He shaded his eyes with one hand. "Did you like the flowers?"

"Barney, right?" Maybe he'd leave me alone if I called him by his name.

He offered a toothy smile and stuck out his hand. "Yes, Barney Cobb. And you are?"

I was smart. That's what I was. He wouldn't get close enough to shake my hand or touch me. I stumbled in the sand and fell to my knees. When I stood, I held the piece of driftwood I had tripped over.

"Look, Barney." I shook it at him. "I don't want to know you. Understand? Don't watch me or leave anything at my house."

"Me? No, I'd never do such a thing." He held his palm over his chest, a smarmy, innocent expression on his face. The ring Ursula told me about covered his entire pinky. "I think you've misread my intentions, Karah."

He was lying—he asked if I liked the flowers—but a tiny seed of doubt tickled my brain. "Fine, but you have to stop watching me." Then it hit me. He knew my first name.

My body went on high alert. The hair on my arms and the back of my neck stood on end, and my legs trembled. I ran out of there, but sprinting in the soft sand wasn't easy. Before I got two feet away, I felt a tug on my collar, turned, and swung my arm, whacking him with the driftwood. He collapsed.

"Barney!" Was he okay? I meant to stop him, not hurt him. My hands trembled so hard I had trouble finding his pulse. When I did, it beat in a steady rhythm. Then, I caught another glimpse of his ring. Gaudy, just like Ursula said. With no plans to ever ask him about it, I picked up my bucket and ran.

I reached the road about a dozen houses down from my cottage and crossed into a neighbor's yard to keep my feet from burning on the hot asphalt. I leaned over and tried to catch my breath, one hand on my knee, the other gripping the bucket handle. Did I need to call someone? Report what happened?

A black SUV pulled up beside me. "Karah? Karah, what are you doing? What's wrong? Have you been running?" Gage's incredulous tone would have tickled me if I could breathe. He loved to run for fun. And he knew I didn't.

"Running away, yes. Running for pleasure, no." I used my forearm to wipe my hair back.

"Is someone chasing you?" He jumped out of his car and rushed to me. He reached out a hand but pulled it back when I glared at him. "Who is it? Are you all right?"

I drew a few more deep breaths, my fear draining away. Barney was harmless, like Ursula said, and I overreacted. "Yeah, I'm fine. I got spooked."

Thunder boomed in the distance, and dark clouds rolled closer.

"Let me take you home. I was heading to my place anyhow."

I climbed into his car just as the raindrops started. By the time we reached his driveway, sheets of rain battered the ground in a relentless cascade. He pulled into his garage and closed the door behind us.

"Come on inside. Once it slows down, you can go home. If you go now, you'll look like a drowned rat."

"Thanks for the visual."

He chuckled.

I stood at the window of his townhouse, watching the rain pound against the glass, distorting everything outside. The storm matched the turmoil in my heart. I hadn't been this close to Gage in months. He tapped my shoulder and handed me a cup of iced soda.

"Thanks." He remembered how I liked it, and he had it on hand. Hmm.

Chapter Four

Gage busted my bubble with his next words. "It's Nikki's favorite."

Oh, yeah. Our daughter got me hooked on the brand. "How is she?" I hated having to ask. A mother should know what was going on with her child.

"She got a new job."

"Another one?" The words came out in a screech. I cleared my throat and repeated them in a kinder tone. Nikki could do anything except stick to a job.

His jaw tightened. "Yes."

I held up my hand. "Sorry, forget I asked." I needed to go home, downpour or not. Nikki and her strong-willed ways had been a bone of contention between us for years.

"Come on, sit down and wait a few minutes. This is supposed to blow over."

He knew the weather better than any weatherman. With his PhD in biology—specializing in marine life research—he stayed current on local storms.

I curled up in the corner of the couch, sipped my soda, and searched for safe topics.

"Who were you running from? You never said." He sat in an armchair, elbows resting on his knees, his blue eyes filled with concern.

Not exactly what I wanted to discuss, but I explained how Barney watched me several times and left flowers. "At least I think he sent them?" My words ended in a question, even though Barney had asked if I liked them.

He held up his hands. "Not me. Besides, I know better than to bring you rinky-dink carnations. You're a daisy girl all the way." His grin reminded me again what attracted me to him all those years ago.

Besides his intelligence, Gage was drop-dead gorgeous. I never understood why he chose me, but I enjoyed his attention. My self-esteem took a blow when he left.

I shifted on the couch. "I didn't think you left them. But I saw him on the beach today, and he sort of threatened me."

His brows drew together. "Threatened?" He growled the word.

"Yeah. I guess I blew it out of proportion." I didn't mention hitting Barney. I gestured to the window. "The rain is slacking up, so I'll head home. Thanks for rescuing me today."

He held the door for me. "You're welcome, Karah. I'm glad you're all right."

His tender tone and the look in his eyes drew me toward him. I pulled back before making a fool of myself. Once inside my cottage, I leaned against the closed door and shook my head.

"Seriously, woman, you still have feelings for him? Even after the divorce? I thought we worked through all of that. You will not go over there again," I scolded myself. "Not even if he rescues you from a murderer." I pushed off the door and set my bucket, which had far fewer shells than before I whacked Barney, in the sink.

Yesterday's beach finds were ready to use. Being creative would distract me from both Barney and Gage. I picked several of the same size shells and carried them to the table. After mixing paint colors until I got a blue closest to the morning sky, I painted the shells. Once they dried, I would attach each piece to a picture frame. While I waited, I worked on the description.

I logged onto my website and started writing. By the time I finished, the sky had darkened again—this time, not from rain. I closed my laptop, stood, and stretched.

"Rusty? Come here, fellow." Where was that cat? I checked for him throughout my tiny cottage, searching under both beds. Then I opened the front door and hollered his name. Where had the rascal gone?

"Rusty!" I checked under my car, but he wasn't anywhere. He didn't like going outside, especially in the Florida heat. As much as I hated to, I'd have to ask Gage for help.

He opened the door dressed in gym shorts and a sweaty T-shirt. "Hey, what's up?"

I held his gaze, consciously avoiding looking at how the tee clung to his lean, muscled frame. "Rusty got out."

"Rusty?"

"My cat," I said.

"Your cat?"

At this rate, the conversation would last until morning. "I got a cat after"—I tipped my head—"you know."

"Hmm. And he got out?" He waved me inside and wiped the sweat off his face with a kitchen towel before tossing it onto the counter.

It took everything in me not to pick it up and find the dirty clothes basket. *Not your problem anymore, Karah.* "I guess so? He's not inside. I don't understand how he got out."

"Let me put some dry clothes on, and I'll come help you."

Dry clothes would help me. Maybe he'd add a parka? I closed my mouth. Get it together, girl.

Back at my cottage, we searched the rooms one more time. How had the cat escaped? All the windows and the door were closed when I'd arrived home earlier.

"I don't understand." I crossed my arms. "He hates being outside."

"He's little, so he might be tucked up somewhere, and we can't see him."

I giggled. "He's not little." I found a picture of Rusty on my phone and showed it to Gage. "I adopted him from the shelter. He's about five years old and a pretty big guy."

"He sure is. He's not anywhere inside, or we would have spotted him." Gage handed back my phone. "We'll check out front again, and if he's not there, I'll help you look tomorrow."

One thing—one more thing—I always liked about Gage was his willingness to help in any situation.

We couldn't find Rusty anywhere. We stood out front and hollered for him. Gage checked around his rental and returned to my yard.

"I'm sorry, Karah. I don't see him."

I opened my mouth to respond, but a Trinity Sands Island police car bleated its siren and flew by, lights blazing. It startled me, and I stumbled into Gage, who caught me and held me tight. We stayed that way and watched the car squeal to a dramatic stop about a quarter mile up the road. When I realized I still stood in his arms, I turned and pushed away from him.

"Sorry ... I'm sorry." I stepped back.

He ran his hand through his hair. I resisted brushing it into place and linked my hands behind my back to keep them away from him.

"Weren't you in that area when I picked you up yesterday?" he asked.

"More like where I came out onto the road. But yeah. Want to go check?" We walked down the road, moving into the sand, when an ambulance roared past. "Someone got hurt if they called for EMTs."

Gage nodded his agreement. Several neighbors joined us, and we crowded around the police car until one of the patrolmen waved us back.

"Who got hurt?" called out a bystander.

"It looks like Barney Cobb," someone else said. The crowd shifted as people passed the news around.

"He's missing a finger," another person yelled. The woman beside me gagged. My stomach flipped.

Gage grabbed my hand and pulled me back from the crowd. "Think he threatened someone else?"

"And they cut off his finger?" I broke out in a sweat, and not because of the temperature. The sun dipped below the horizon, the beach now shrouded in deep twilight. Dark clouds swirled overhead, their heavy masses flickering with occasional bursts of distant lightning.

What if it was Barney? Did I hurt him when I whacked him with the driftwood? But if I had, I hadn't removed any body parts. I tugged on Gage's hand. "Can you see him?"

He shook his head. The atmosphere was thick with anticipation as if the crowd held its collective breath and waited for something to break the eerie stillness around us. Then came a "Meow," and something brushed against my ankles.

Rusty. It was my fluffy orange cat, except for his paws. The front two looked like he was wearing red gloves dipped in sugar, and when he stood up and placed them on my Bermuda shorts, they left red paw prints—blood red.

Chapter Five

"Oh no." I pulled Gage's hand again and pointed.

"You found your cat." He leaned down to pet him. I didn't have a chance to warn him about the two-pat limit. He stood back up in a second like a jack-in-the-box, eyes unfocused. "There's blood. He has blood on him. Blood."

I forgot he didn't handle injuries well. I picked up Rusty, something only I could do, and brushed the sand off his paws, examining the bottom of them. "He's not hurt. Looks like he stepped in ..." My words trailed off. Gage and I stared at each other.

"Does he go to the beach?" he asked.

At the same time, I said, "Let's go home." I turned and sped toward my cottage.

I didn't know why Rusty had blood on him or if it was Barney Cobb out there, but one plus one equaled three right now. "No way I killed him," I muttered.

Gage stopped so fast his sneakers squeaked. "Wait, what?"

I took off again, and he followed me as I filled him in on the whole fiasco with Barney. "But I just smacked him with the driftwood," I finished.

"It's possible he tripped and hit his head. Head wounds bleed a lot," Gage said. He opened my front door and followed me inside.

"That doesn't explain his finger if that part is true. I need to clean Rusty's paws. Can you hold him?" Not in full control of my faculties and forgetting my unfriendly kitty's ways, I handed the chubby feline to my ex. Rusty nestled into his arms and rubbed his head against Gage's chin. I frowned. "He never acts like that."

Gage adjusted his hold on the cat. "Maybe the right guy never held him."

I ignored the challenge in his words and wet a dishtowel. I didn't know what to expect when I cleaned Rusty's paws, but it was not the docile animal I encountered. "You're the cat whisperer."

The cat touched Gage's cheek with his now-clean paw.

And Rusty seemed to be a Gage-whisperer. In our marriage, I cleaned up any blood, whether it was Nikki's scraped knee or when I accidentally peeled the top of my thumb with a potato peeler. And as Gage said, head wounds bleed a lot. He had his fair share of them the time he decided to enclose our basement in Tennessee. It didn't take long before he hired a contractor and returned to his blood-free life as a biology professor.

"All clean, fellow," he crooned to the cat. He set him down, and Rusty sauntered off, leaving small wet paw prints on the tile floor. "He's a good kitty."

"Yeah. He's helped me a lot." Oops. Shouldn't have mentioned that to my ex. Obviously, I still had feelings for Gage. Love? Maybe. Attraction? Always. I definitely wouldn't say any of that to him though.

Gage raised his eyebrows.

"Well, I'm going to get ready for bed," I said.

"Oh, sure, no problem. Maybe we'll find out tomorrow what happened on the beach." He opened the front door to find Sandi Ronald, fist raised to knock.

"Hi, Gage. I didn't know you were here," she said in a sultry tone.

"I'm leaving. Night, Karah, Sandi." He winked behind her back and mouthed, "Have fun."

I scrunched my nose and turned to my other next-door neighbor with a forced smile. Sandi—with an "i," you know, Captain Ronald's widow—is how Gage and I described her every time we ran into her. "Nice to see you. What brings you by this evening?"

"Did you hear the news?" She held onto my arm. She had been deep into the cocktails already. I resisted fanning my face to disperse the smell.

"What news?" I led her to my couch before grabbing two water bottles.

She accepted hers, unscrewed the top, and gulped until the bottle was empty. She swiped her hand across her mouth and hiccupped. "Excuse me."

"You wanted to tell me something," I prodded.

Tears filled her eyes, dimming her usual sparkly blue gaze. "It's Barney. They found his dead body on the beach."

I froze at her words. It was him. Dear Lord, what should I say? "Did you know him well?"

"He was my man. He is ... was precious." She drew out the word and waved her hand, long, blood-red nails catching my attention. She leaned toward me on the couch and gripped my shoulder to steady herself. Tears tipped over her lashes and trailed down her cheeks.

Precious isn't how I described Barney. Lecherous, maybe. Stalkerish, for sure. "How did you meet him?"

She giggled and hiccupped again. "I didn't. He found me." She yawned. "I need to go. Will you tell me if you hear anything else?"

She'd gone from crying to giggling. What a night. "Sure." I watched her until she reached her doorstep to ensure she didn't fall. What did she mean by saying that Barney found her? Was she the one he stretched for and waved at? But he lunged for me on the beach. My shock at finding out who died gave way to questions.

So many questions.

I dreamed of Barney and bloody cat paw prints all night long. My morning started like it had two days earlier, with someone pounding on my front door long before I wanted to get out of bed. Rusty jumped down, this time avoiding my leg.

"I'm coming." I ran my fingers through my hair. "Please don't be Gage."

Sandi waited on my front porch. She pushed her way inside and plopped onto my couch. "You won't believe it." She shook her head. "I can't fathom what's happened."

I covered a yawn and shuffled into the kitchen, thankful I'd set the coffee on a timer, and it had already brewed. "Believe what?"

She turned and eyed me. "You sleep in that?"

I tugged the bottom of my nightshirt, which barely covered my behind. "Yes." Why did people feel the need to criticize what I ate and what I wore?

"It's cute," she said.

"Oh, well, thanks." Guess I read that wrong. "What did

you want to tell me?" I poured coffee into two mugs, handed Sandi one, and joined her on the couch.

"They think someone murdered Barney. They found a piece of wood beside his body, and it was covered in blood."

For the first time, I understood the phrase, "My blood ran cold." A shiver ran through me, and I rubbed my arms. I couldn't have killed him. It wasn't a big piece of wood. And I wasn't very strong. Wouldn't I know if I killed him?

"Have you heard anything else?" I prayed he wasn't really missing a digit.

Sandi placed her mug on the coffee table and stood. "No, not yet. I'm going to go find out about a memorial service for him and if he has family here on the island." She pulled the door shut behind her.

I sat, frozen on the couch, trying to recall specifics from the day before. Question after question ran through my mind. I inhaled, forced it out, and allowed my shoulders to drop. I was sure of one thing: Barney was alive when I left him.

Or at least, I thought so.

Chapter Six

Sandi left, and I ate my bagel, which I smothered in more cream cheese than usual. With another cup of coffee in hand, I settled into a dining room chair. My day's agenda included working on social media. It took everything in me to stay on task. Worry crept in as I waited for word from Sandi or Gage.

At lunchtime, I grabbed my bucket and headed for the beach, hoping the sun and sand would distract me. But first, I ensured Rusty was safe inside the cottage and locked the door behind me. The sky had cleared and was now a brilliant blue. A soft breeze brought mingling scents of salt and warm sand, washed clean by the storm. Sea oats swayed, and here and there, the shoreline bore the marks of the storm's fury. Seashells lay scattered with bits of driftwood and the occasional piece of sea glass.

Barney's murder was the talk of the beach, and everyone I spoke to mentioned a list of possible suspects. It surprised me how many names people bantered about.

I asked one man how many murders there had been on

the island. He leaned back on his elbows, knobby knees and vein-lined feet stretched before him on a blue-striped beach towel. "I don't know, young lady. I can't remember any at all." He squinted. "I've been here since the Beach Club opened, but you should ask Maude. She would know for sure."

True, but I wasn't ready to return to Maude's Market. I'd been there two days before, and her comments still stung.

I thanked him and headed for the section of beach where they found Barney's body. The area was cordoned off with crime scene tape fluttering around a misshapen rectangle. I scanned for Rusty's bloody prints. No one had mentioned cat prints or seeing him. But if someone had ...

I shut down the thoughts. Rusty couldn't be the lone feline on the island. I turned and walked back to my cottage.

* * *

After a quick lunch, I knocked on Sandi's door, hoping she knew where Barney lived. If I went inside his place, I might figure out who killed him, although I had no idea what to look for. Hopefully, I'd know when I saw it. Something had to exonerate me.

Sandi answered her door, and I explained my thoughts, minus what I'd done to Barney. "Hang on one minute. I'll take you there." She darted back into her bungalow.

While waiting, I admired her flower bed, thinking I'd ask her advice on what to plant for the fall. I leaned down and peeked at some soil that appeared freshly turned over. She rushed outside, grabbed my arm, and yanked me up. "No time to waste. Let's go." She took off down the front sidewalk while I struggled to catch up.

"He lived a few blocks this way." She gestured ahead of us.

"Did you know he served as captain of the tennis team? For three years. Such a kind and talented man."

She beamed, and I forced a smile. This man watched me and grabbed at me. Then he was murdered. I wasn't interested in his attributes, although being murdered might not be his fault.

"Tennis?" What else could I say?

She stopped, gasped, and covered her mouth. "You don't think ..."

We walked inland, away from the ocean breeze. Sweat dripped down my back and face. "I don't think what?"

She spoke through her fingers. "He and Pete Chandler hated each other. They competed all the time, and Barney often beat him." She stopped in front of a baby blue cottage, a little bigger than mine. It was freshly painted with crisp white trim.

"Pete Chandler?" Did she think he killed Barney over a game?

"Yes. He threatened him the last time they played."

I tucked the information in the back of my mind and pointed to the cottage. "Is this Barney's? Wonder why the police aren't here?" There was no crime scene tape either.

"Yes, follow me." She pulled a set of keys from her pocket and sorted through them until she found a bright yellow one with white flowers. "He gave me this." She cupped it in her hand and nestled it against her chest. "Such a good man."

I nudged her toward the front door. "Have you ever been here?"

"No, why?"

I struggled to keep a blank face. I had a bad feeling but gestured for her to unlock the door. She inserted the key. It went in but wouldn't turn.

"Hmm." She removed it and tried again.

"Can I?" I held out my hand

She passed me the key. I held onto the doorknob and wiggled it while trying to unlock it. Nothing happened.

Until someone on the other side opened the door.

"What are you doing?" the man boomed. He was no shorter than six and a half feet, with broad shoulders and brown eyes full of suspicion and anger.

Sandi stepped back onto my toes. "Who are you?" She clenched her fists.

I pushed her off my foot. "We thought Barney lived here."

"Ma'am, I've lived here for over fifteen years," he said, a stern expression on his face. "Do you always go around trying to break into people's houses?"

Sandi shook her head. "But he gave me the key. I don't understand this."

"Well, it's not his place. This is my home." His face softened. "Are you talking about Barney Cobb, the one they found murdered yesterday?"

"Yes." Her voice cracked. "Barney Cobb. He was my boyfriend. Or I thought so." She trembled, and I put my arm around her.

"Come on, let's go back home." I turned to the man. "Do you have any idea where Barney lived?"

He shook his head and slammed the door.

That didn't help us at all. Sandi and I walked toward home.

"I can't believe it wasn't Barney's key," she wailed. "He told me he lived there. He pointed it out to me one time."

Words failed me. Barney was a liar as well as a stalker. When we arrived at my cottage, I invited her in for ice water and handed her a damp paper towel. She wiped the sweat off her face and held her glass against her forehead.

"Do you have any tissues?" she asked.

I handed her several. After she blew out a loud honk, she returned them to me.

"Thanks." I picked them up between my thumb and forefinger, tossed them in the trash, and washed my hands.

Sandi plopped onto the couch and closed her eyes, leaning back with a loud groan.

While she rested, I prepped fresh coffee, and when I set down a mug in front of her, she stirred.

"I think I fell asleep." She sat up and ran her fingers through her hair.

"I thought a pick-me-up would help."

"Thank you, Karah. You're a lovely friend."

I settled into the matching armchair and sipped my coffee. "Do you think Barney lived on the island? Or on the Beach Club property?"

"I don't know." She blew out a deep sigh. "I'm beginning to doubt *everything* he told me."

Something niggled in my brain. "Do you remember when you said Barney picked you or found you? What did you mean?"

"It happened several months ago. I was in my living room reading a magazine." She glanced around my cottage. "My place is the mirror opposite of yours, I think. I'd opened the blinds over the sliding glass doors and saw him on the beach. He stretched, and I thought he was going for a run. He was the most handsome man ..."

The coffee burned its way down my throat. Handsome? Not the word I would use. He didn't compare to Gage.

"He waved at me, so I waved back," she continued. "The next day, he did it again. By the third day, I opened the door and went to talk to him." She tipped her head, eyebrows drawn together, and one finger tapping her lip. "You don't think he was using me, do you?"

What should I say? Should I tell her what he did to me? Before I opened my mouth to answer, my doorbell rang.

36

Chapter Seven

Gage stood on my front porch, his hand propped against the door frame. "Is she here?" he mouthed.

I waved him inside. "Come on in. We're talking about Barney. We've had an adventure."

Gage sat on the couch, and Sandi scooted beside him, grasping onto his arm. Her tears flowed again. I passed her more tissues while, at the same time resisting the urge to push her away from him.

Jealousy reared up in my mind. I gritted my teeth and forced it back down.

"What's wrong?" he asked.

"Don't you know? Barney is dead!" Sandi flopped against his shoulder.

"Yes, I knew." Gage's eyes grew wide. "Um, do you have any other news? Did something else happen?" When she looked away, he wiggled his pinky at me.

I shook my head. "We went to his house. Sandi had a key. But it wasn't his place. Someone else opened the door. We don't have any idea where Barney lived."

He shifted away from Sandi. "I had an idea."

"What?" I hoped whatever it was would get Sandi away from him.

"We should talk to Maude. She knows everything about everyone."

Sandi perked up. "You're right. Good idea." She leaned closer to him. "You're incredibly smart." She rubbed her hand up and down his forearm.

My jaw hurt. I wanted to yell at her to take her hands off him, but I didn't have that right anymore.

Gage cleared his throat. "So?" he said.

I must have missed something. I raised my eyebrows.

"Maude?" His lips twitched.

Oh, yeah. I didn't want to see Maude with or without my ex-husband and neighbor. "I have some things I need to do this afternoon. Can you two go talk to her?" An icy shower might calm me down.

Sandi jumped up and held out her hand, wiggling it until Gage took it. "Let's go."

Gage turned to me, brows drawn together, and mouthed, "Help me." I wrinkled my nose. Learning what happened to Barney might be necessary, but I wasn't up to the Beach Club's gossip brigade. Even if it meant Gage was once again in Sandi's clutches.

When they left, I gathered my shells, driftwood, and other materials and sat at the table, thinking about what to do next. I picked up a shell, and Barney Cobb's face appeared in my mind. I tried a frame, but Barney was still there. He consumed my thoughts, especially how he lunged at me.

"Ugh. Woman, get a grip." I paced the living room. Rusty sat at the sliding glass doors. "What do you think, buddy? Any ideas?"

Rusty had been there that night. The blood on his paws

had been fresh. If only I had a video camera on his collar. I grinned at the thought of my chubby feline trotting along the shoreline and peeking into places he didn't belong.

"Okay, boy, I'm not getting anything done today." I switched my shoes to flip-flops and headed for the crime scene. Maybe seeing it in person would exorcise Barney from my imagination.

The yellow police tape was gone, but footprints from the officers and EMTs remained. Who killed Barney? And why? Sandi said he talked to her. And it sounded like they were together for a while. What would make him change from seeing her to attacking me? Had I mistaken his actions?

How could I have killed him unless he had a heart attack or something? I used a stick to sift through the sand but found nothing. Maybe I did kill him—although how, I didn't know. But I sure didn't cut off his finger. I gave up and walked home.

If Gage and Sandi got any other information from Maude, they would be back soon. We'd sit down and piece our clues together, and I could ask Sandi about the ring. And the finger.

By the time I arrived at my cottage, my shirt was stuck to me, and sweat dripped down my face. I hopped into the shower to rinse off but jumped right back out when a knock sounded on the front door, and someone hollered my name.

"Coming!" I grabbed the first clothes I found and pulled them on. I opened the door to Sandi and Gage. "Come on in. I'm surprised you're back already. Want some water?" We settled on the couch with our glasses. "What did you find out?"

"Maude hasn't heard anything besides what we already know." Gage gulped his water and rose to get himself more. "She had lots of questions, though."

"Nosey old biddy," Sandi grouched.

I pinched my lips together to keep from laughing. That was

a case of the pot calling the kettle black. I cleared my throat. "I guess we're back to square one?"

Gage nodded, but Sandi leaned toward me, eyes squinted.

"What's that?" She pointed to my Bermuda shorts.

I looked down. A paw print showed on the upper thigh of my shorts—a bloody one.

* * *

To say the doorbell saved me would be an understatement. I hopped up, praying for anyone to be there, anyone to distract Sandi from what she'd seen. I flung the door wide without checking the peephole.

My daughter stood before me. "Nikki?"

"Is Dad here?" She peered over my shoulder, brushed past me, and walked straight into Gage's arms. I closed my eyes and counted to ten in an attempt to hide my hurt feelings.

When I turned around, Gage's eyes held so much sympathy my knees almost gave out. He understood what the loss of my relationship with our child had cost me. His feelings weren't helpful, though. I wished he would stand up for me. But he insisted Nikki had to make the change.

I was about to offer her something to drink, anything to make her talk to me, when shouting came from outside. "Sandi Ronald. Open up."

"Uh oh." Sandi slunk down on my couch.

"Who is it?" I opened my door again and peered outside. "Sandi, some man is at your place."

"Yeah," she drew out the word. "Pete, Pete Chandler. He played tennis with Barney."

Nikki sat on the couch beside Sandi. "He sounds mad."

"Yeah," she repeated.

"Hey, Pete, over here." I waved at the angry man. This

sitcom-slash-murder-mystery-slash-soap-opera had turned another corner. Clues were piling up, and I needed answers.

"No, Karah." Sandi whimpered.

Pete stomped to my cottage. "Is she here? Sandi Ronald? If I get my hands on that woman ..."

His words trailed off when Gage stepped in front of me. At least forty pounds lighter than Pete and six inches shorter, Gage gave off a "don't mess with me" attitude in a way his former middle school students and now his college-aged ones respected.

He raised his hands, palms out. "Hold up there, buddy—no need to call names or threaten people. You can come in, and yes, Sandi is here. But you have to *talk*, man. No yelling."

Pete narrowed his eyes. I imagined puffs of anger released from his nostrils like one of those mad cartoon bulls on TV. Gage and I exchanged glances. His said to wait. You can't be married to someone as long as we had been without learning to read their expressions.

I had never met Pete, but I knew he competed against Barney. Sandi suggested his name as someone who might have killed Barney, and it hit me why Pete was so furious.

"Sandi, did you accuse him of murdering Barney?"

She made a face. "Yes."

I closed my eyes. This day had gone from difficult at best to worst-case scenario. Why, oh, why, had I gotten involved with her and her schemes?

Gage set a chair in the living room for Pete, then settled on the couch beside Sandi. "Pete, can you tell us why you're here?" He emphasized the word tell.

Pete shuffled his feet, ran a hand over his bald head, and cleared his throat. He pointed a thick finger at Sandi.

"No finger-pointing." Gage's command had Pete dropping his hand in an instant.

Pete clicked his tongue, hands flat against his knees. "Sandi, did you tell the police I might be a person of interest in Barney's murder?"

"You did that?" I asked, amazed at the woman's audacity.

She didn't deny it. "The police asked me who knew Barney."

Pete inhaled. His huge barrel chest filled, and I waited for the explosion. He forced the air out. "Did you accuse me?"

Sandi cowered against the couch. Gage put his arm around her and squeezed.

I held back a gag. He never knew when he was being played—case in point, our daughter—who chose right then to participate in the conversation.

"Dad, who is this man? Who's Barney? What is Mom doing here?"

Chapter Eight

"I live here." Resisting the urge to stomp my foot, I turned to Gage. This girl, my daughter, was something else. "She didn't know?"

Nikki scoffed. "I *knew*. I didn't know you'd be here *now*. Cindy and Jasmine are going to be in town any minute." She glanced between me and her dad. "Dad? What am I going to do?" She crossed her arms and tapped her foot.

Gage groaned. "Karah ..."

I forced a sweet expression on my face and thought about when she was ten, all freckle-faced with crooked teeth. Now, not a freckle in sight and a beautiful smile.

"Nikki, dear, you and your friends are welcome here." I gritted my teeth. "If your dad hasn't told you, this is my cottage now." My words came out in a staccato fashion. "He is staying next door and has a huge townhouse. In case y'all want to spread out." I left the words dangling and prayed she would jump at the chance to stay at Gage's. This summer was mine. My time to recoup, start my business, and find out what I wanted to do next. I hadn't planned on spending it with my ex and my bitter, resentful daughter.

Were my feelings selfish? Maybe. Or maybe not. I raised my child. Gage and I were no longer married, meaning I could make my own decisions.

Gage jumped up. "Yes, you three should come stay with me." He waved for her to follow him, and I breathed a sigh of relief. I loved my daughter, but she tested every ounce of patience in my body.

As he reached for the doorknob, someone knocked. "Mrs. Halyard, it's Sergeant Spencer. I have some questions."

We all froze in place, reminding me of an old black-and-white comedy—Gage mid-reach, Nikki on his heels, Sandi's and Pete's eyes and mouths wide open.

I stepped around my ex and opened the door. "Come in, please. The more, the merrier." He didn't pick up on my sarcasm.

Gage and Nikki tried to leave, but the police officer motioned them back. "I need to talk to all of you," he said.

Gage dragged another chair into the living area, and everyone sat. Nikki crowded in beside her dad, and I claimed the armchair, crossing my legs to hide the bloody paw print and praying Rusty would continue to stay hidden. And for Sandi to forget what she'd seen.

Spencer introduced himself and flipped open his notepad, his gaze roaming over us. "I'm glad you're all here together." He stopped at Nikki. "Wait a minute, who are you?"

Gage spoke up. "My daughter."

I cleared my throat.

"Our daughter," he corrected.

He nodded. "I'm one of the police officers assigned to investigate Barney Cobb's death."

"Murder," Sandi said.

He cocked an eyebrow. "Alleged murder." He turned to Nikki. "Were you here when Cobb died?"

"I don't even know who he is." She studied her nails.

"You can leave." He dismissed her with a wave of his hand.

"You can wait in my room, honey," I offered.

She turned to her dad. "Can I have your keys? We'll wait over there for you."

I slumped in my chair. Why did I try? Gage handed over his keys, and Nikki left.

"Who does she mean by *we?*" Spencer asked.

"She has a couple of girlfriends coming into town for a few days." No way would I let him go after my daughter. Even if she wasn't nice to me. "She just got here."

The officer pointed from me to Gage. "Y'all are married and live in two different places?"

Gage shifted on the couch. "No, we're divorced."

Spencer's eyebrow twitched.

I had to move things along. Once he completed his interview, Sandi, Gage, and Pete would leave, and I could go to sleep. I yawned, thinking about my comfy bed.

"I won't keep you all long. Mr. Chandler, we'll need a formal statement tomorrow. But can you tell me where you were"—he checked his notebook—"yesterday? Memorial Day."

Pete rubbed his chin. "Yeah, some of us on the tennis team had a cookout. I invited Barney, but he never showed."

Spencer pulled a pencil from his shirt pocket and scribbled for a minute. "You say Barney never came?"

"Right."

"Hmm." He tapped the pencil against his chin. "Where'd you have the cookout?"

"At my place."

He wrote for another minute. "But you expected Mr.

Cobb? I thought you two didn't get along." His gaze shifted to Sandi.

Pete's neck broke out in red splotches. "Not true. We're all pals. Playing a game. Friendly competition." He bit out the last words while he glared at Sandi.

"You can go, Mr. Chandler. I'll see you at the station tomorrow. Let's say ten?"

"Sure, yeah, no problem." Pete hurried out the door.

The officer turned his attention to Sandi. "You talked to someone today, right? At the station?"

She nodded.

He leaned forward. "I'm curious. You said Mr. Chandler might have hurt Mr. Cobb?"

"Yes." Sandi picked at the hem of her shirt. "They were both very competitive, you know? They didn't like each other. Lots of arguments. I thought it was possible ..."

"You *thought*? With no reason or evidence?" Spencer's voice rose.

Her face fell. "I just wanted to help."

Gage stood. "Could she meet you tomorrow too? Mrs. Halyard and I can come in around eleven and give our statements. We're all tired."

Spencer snapped his notebook shut. "Fine, but don't be late."

I released another yawn right on cue.

* * *

"Well, this has been an evening." Gage shut the cottage's front door. "First time I've had to talk to the police."

"Me too." I uncrossed my legs, stood, and headed for the kitchen, except my feet had fallen asleep, and I tumbled straight into Gage.

He caught me and set me back upright with a chuckle.

"What's so funny?" I wiggled my legs until the feeling came back.

"This is the second time I've caught you in the last few days. If I didn't know better, I'd think you were making a play for me." He winked.

"Wait, what?" Heat climbed my neck.

"Calm down. I'm kidding." Gage put the chairs back at the dining table and turned to leave. "I need to check on the girls. I'm sure they're hungry. See you tomorrow morning."

I locked up behind him and turned out the front porch light. When I stepped out onto the patio, I found the sun had set, leaving the sky a rich, velvety indigo studded with countless stars.

A gentle breeze carried a faint salty smell and the rhythm of the soft crash of waves on the shore. The moon hung low, casting a silvery glow that danced across the water's rippling surface.

"God, I don't know what's going on here or what You want me to do. I thought this summer would be about me finding peace and healing. But now I'm stuck with Gage as a next-door neighbor. And Nikki." Tears welled in my eyes and rolled down my cheeks. "It breaks my heart to see her hurting and so angry." I hung my head. "I'm going to bed. I hope You know what You're doing."

Chapter Nine

My brain wouldn't turn off. After tossing and turning, I tried praying, singing worship songs, and reevaluating the last thirty years of my life. Nothing helped. I fell asleep as the sun peeked over the horizon and woke up in a rotten mood. When I stomped into the kitchen and scared Rusty, I stopped, took a deep breath, and bowed my head. "What I said last night? Well, it was very prideful. I want You to lead me. I will trust You, and I'm not giving up on following You."

Gage arrived at my door a few minutes before eleven. "Want a ride?"

"Sure, hang on." I checked my hair in the bathroom mirror and said another prayer for the right words to speak to the police. I hadn't decided whether to tell them about Barney stalking me, which seemed like an essential piece of the puzzle. But then I would have to confess to hitting him with a piece of driftwood. I studied my hands. Could they get fingerprints off driftwood? How much trouble was I in?

Gage hollered my name, and I hurried out to him. "Ready." I locked my front door and followed him to his car.

"You nervous?" he asked.

"I've been thinking about what all I should say." I buckled my seatbelt for the short ride to the Trinity Sands Island Police Station, an old, refurbished one-story Florida beach house. "If I confess to what I did, they might arrest me."

"Yeah, I wondered too. I heard Sandi's question about the blood on your shorts."

I chewed on my lower lip. "I threw them in the wash this morning."

Gage winced but didn't comment.

We arrived at the station as Sandi exited the building, Pete Chandler on her heels. The two of them were in the midst of a heated discussion. When Pete got in Sandi's face, Gage jumped from the car and rushed to them. I followed, staying a few feet away. Pete had a temper, and he frightened me. I had no problem believing he might have hurt Barney.

"Whoa, what are you doing, Pete? You can't threaten her." Gage pushed himself between the two.

"Stay out of it, Halyard. Not your business. This ... woman accused me of murdering Cobb." Pete shifted back and forth, hands opening and closing, his face a dark red.

"I didn't." Sandi grabbed Gage's arm. "I suggested they should investigate him." She turned to me. "I told them about your shorts too."

Uh oh. Was I supposed to thank her for ratting me out?

Gage disentangled himself from her grip and took my arm. "Let's go in. It's time for us to make our statements."

* * *

There was no "us" or "we" about giving our statements. Gage was directed to a room while I waited in what was once the house's living room. The tiny kitchen served as the front desk, and the scent of fresh-brewed coffee came from behind the counter. I considered asking if they'd give me a cup.

While I waited for my turn, I sorted through my purse, caught up on social media on my phone, and filed my fingernails. My stomach roiled when a door down the hall opened, and Gage emerged.

"Your turn." He dropped onto the seat beside me and shoved his fingers through his hair.

I studied his face. "What did you tell them?"

"The truth, of course." Gage rubbed his hands on his blue-jeans-clad thighs.

"Oh, Gage, what did you say?" My stomach clenched, imagining the worst.

Spencer poked his head out of a doorway. "Mrs. Halyard? I'm ready for you."

I shook my ex-husband's arm. "Gage?"

His beautiful blue eyes held the saddest expression. "It's all going to be okay, Karah." He patted my hand. "Trust me. Go along with everything he says."

Walking down the hall to the third door on the left—what used to be a child's bedroom, judging by its size—felt like it took days. Voices in other rooms sounded distorted. It was like a fog settled around me.

Spencer held the door and gestured to the small wooden table in the center of the room. I sat, squirming to get comfortable on the hard chair. He pulled up the second chair and folded his hands on the table.

"I've heard some interesting things today," he said.

What should I say? "Oh?" My voice squeaked. If he mentioned the missing finger, I'd claim honest ignorance.

"Yes." He stared at me.

I waited. Did I need a lawyer? Had I broken the law when I defended myself against Barney's attack? Would they think I was guilty because I washed my shorts and pretreated the stain?

What did Gage tell him?

Spencer cleared his throat. "Would you like some water?"

"Coffee, maybe? It smelled pretty good."

"Sure."

When he left the room, I checked my surroundings. Dull beige wallpaper with a thin blue stripe covered the walls. No one-way mirror anywhere in sight. Then I spotted it. A tiny camera mounted in the far corner, its green light flashing.

Spencer brought my coffee in a dark blue mug with the Trinity Sands Island police department logo.

"I expected a paper cup, thanks." I sipped, enjoying the strong, dark roast.

He smirked.

Duh. Paper cups don't show fingerprints. Or at least from what I've seen on cop shows. I set down my mug.

"What do you need from me?" I asked.

"Your husband ..."

"Ex."

He settled into his chair, hands resting on his stomach. "Yes, sorry, your ex-husband told us what happened. Tell me your version."

Gage, what did you say? "Of course. Well, Barney, Mr. Cobb, kept watching me."

He nodded. "Yes, go on. Did you tell Mr. Halyard?"

"Yes, but ..."

"Don't defend him, Mrs. Halyard." He held up his hand. "Can I call you Karah?"

"Yes." What did he mean don't defend Gage? "I think you may have the wrong impression." I rubbed my hands. My whole body hurt between the stuffy room, the humidity, and the stress.

"Why do you say that?"

"Sandi Ronald said she implicated Pete Chandler. And—" I lowered my head— "she told you about the bloody paw print."

Spencer leaned forward. "She did."

I stood, sweat beading on my forehead. "Do I need a lawyer?"

He raised his eyebrows. "Do you?"

"Arrgh! What am I supposed to say? Okay, here's the truth. I hit Barney with a piece of driftwood. It wasn't a big piece, and he tried to grab me. I think he was alive when I left him. What else could I do?"

I closed my eyes and held out my hands. "Go ahead, cuff me. Throw me in jail." At his chuckle, I opened my eyes. "What?" I stomped my foot.

He placed the coffee mug in front of me. "Please sit down. I'm not arresting you." He stood and gestured to my chair. "Here, I think you need the caffeine."

I did as he suggested. The hot drink soothed me, and I sighed, my shoulders dropping in relief.

"It's not every day a divorced couple takes the fall for each other." He let out another chuckle. "First time I've seen it, anyhow."

I set down the mug. The coffee, which calmed me, now burned a trail down my throat and churned in my stomach. "What do you mean?" Please don't let it be what I think it is.

He tipped his chin toward the door. "Your ex. He confessed to it all. Said he still loved you, and he killed Barney for stalking you. Then your cat walked in the blood, and Mrs. Ronald noticed the print on your shorts. Mr. Halyard explained everything. He asked us to wait to arrest him until you entered the room. He's being booked right now."

Chapter Ten

"He still loves me?"

Spencer frowned. "That's all you got from what I told you?"

I couldn't process what he said. *Gage loved me?* And he confessed? But I didn't kill Barney. I checked to make sure he was alive. "He had a pulse."

"Who? Cobb?"

"Yes, Barney. He was alive. I checked, and his pulse was strong." I touched my fingertips together, still able to feel his heartbeat.

Spencer sat back and tapped his pencil on the table. "So, you're saying you killed Cobb?"

"What? No, no, no. I didn't kill anyone. Gage didn't either. I'm saying I *whacked* him."

Spencer grimaced.

"I mean, I swung the driftwood, and it tapped his head." I stood and demonstrated the move. "He must have tripped or something. But he *was* alive when I left the beach."

"And you didn't think to call the police?" His eyebrows reached his hairline.

How could I make him understand? I sat and leaned forward, maintaining eye contact. I wasn't sure he comprehended the depth of my fear at being attacked. "He tried to grab me. Yes, I hit him. No, I didn't think to call you. I thought I handled the situation." My words came out husky.

He shoved back his chair and stood. "You're free to go, Mrs. Halyard. Mr. Halyard will be held until we confirm his information." He dug in his pocket and pulled out Gage's key ring. "Here."

I stayed on his heels as we walked to the front of the police station. "I know he confessed, but he didn't do it. He's trying to protect me." Dread filled me. How could I convince this police officer of the truth?

He turned. "You're confusing the issue, Mrs. Halyard." He opened the door and held it for me. "Have a good day."

The next thing I knew, I was standing on the front step of the police station. Spencer's words about confusing the issue didn't make sense. When did telling the truth obscure anything?

I drove Gage's vehicle back to the Beach Club and parked in the driveway of his rental. Nikki and her friends weren't anywhere in sight. Did she know what happened to her dad? I winced, anticipating telling her. Not a conversation I wanted to have. I pocketed his keys and entered my bungalow.

"Home, sweet home." I appreciated this place, my home, more than ever, whether Gage loved me or not. Rusty rubbed against my ankles.

"Hey, boy. Are you hungry?" I filled his food and water bowls. "You wouldn't believe the day I've had. Your da ... I mean Gage, said he killed someone I'm not sure he ever met." I scratched Rusty's head. "He didn't do it."

Rusty meowed. I imagined he agreed with me.

I paced the kitchen, wondering what to do next and feeling lost. Every ache and pain in my joints made themselves known. First things first. I rummaged in my purse and found my medication. I grabbed a soda from the fridge and wandered out to the front yard. Knowing Gage was behind bars was agonizing. Everything that happened piled up and overwhelmed me.

I lowered myself into the porch chair. Despite our separation, Gage had been a friend these last few days. His kindness and true character were a rock for me.

Grappling with the reality of the situation left me in shock and disbelief. Gage was in jail and would go to prison if I couldn't find a way to exonerate him. How did he feel? Could I take him anything? Even as I thought about going to visit him, I fought the urge to scream. Compassion and concern mixed with frustration and helplessness at the injustice he faced. He did not kill Barney, but no one would listen to me. And I couldn't make them.

I closed my eyes and forced my shoulders down. Drawing deep, measured breaths and blowing them out quieted my mind and helped me concentrate. Talking to my daughter was tricky on a good day. I wasn't sure how to explain what happened, and I didn't look forward to the conversation. *Lord, be with Gage, please. Help me to help him. Keep him safe. And guide me when I tell Nikki.*

The rhythm of the waves, the warmth of the afternoon sunshine, and the cries of the seagulls lulled me into a light doze. Car doors slammed next door, and I opened my eyes to see Nikki and her friends.

"Hey, honey." I waved. "Can you come over for a minute?" I ignored the face she made.

She sent her friends to her dad's place and joined me.

"What do you need?" She stood in front of me, hands on her hips.

I straightened up in my chair, smoothed my hair, and cleared my throat. "Your dad and I had an interesting morning. The police asked us to give our statements about Barney Cobb. Someone killed him." *What do I say next, Lord?* "Nikki, I didn't do it, and neither did your dad." I swallowed. "But he confessed."

My words must have hit her like a punch in the gut. She collapsed onto the grass and held her head in her hands. I reached forward to stroke her hair. "I'm sorry, honey. I didn't know how to tell you."

She grasped my hand. I thought she would push it away, but she leaned against it. "Oh, Mom." She glanced up, tears filling her beautiful eyes. "What are we going to do? Dad wouldn't kill anyone. Why did he confess?"

The corners of my mouth lifted. What should I say? She'd be mad if I said he still loved me and was protecting me. Of course, she'd be angry with anything that came out of my mouth after this. "I have a few people I want to talk to."

"Like suspects?" She straightened up.

I wiped my eyes. "Yes, pretty much."

"How can I help?" She sniffled and wiped her face. "I'm sure Cindy and Jasmine will help too."

Warmth filled me. This might be the turning point in our relationship. "Can y'all come over for dinner? We can make some plans."

"Sure. I'll let them know." She stood and brushed grass and sand off her shorts. Pain lined her face, and she swiped more tears away. "Mom, how did this happen?"

"What do you mean?"

"Why would the police question you and Dad? How were you suspects?"

"Oh." I chewed my lower lip, thinking of all the ways to word this. "He, Cobb, came after me, and I whacked him."

She froze. "Wait, what?" Her expression turned cold.

"Yeah. Barney Cobb ... he sort of stalked me. And he tried to grab me. I hit him with a piece of driftwood. I told the police."

"And Dad confessed to killing him when you did it." She blinked. "So, it's your fault Dad's in jail?"

Oh, boy. Here we go again. I didn't have the energy for this. "I repeat, I did not kill him, and I don't know why your dad confessed. I'm making grilled chicken and coleslaw. You and the girls are welcome. If you're ready to discuss this like adults."

I went inside, shut the door, and drew the blinds.

That girl. I never knew what would happen next when it came to her. She was Team Gage all the way. She wouldn't believe me even if I explained everything.

Good thing I didn't tell her he still loved me.

Chapter Eleven

I fired up the grill. Even if the girls didn't come over, I needed to eat. Rusty followed me onto the porch, and I reminded him to stay close by with a shake of my finger. He didn't look my way but curled up on the warm cement and kept an eye on the seagulls and other water birds, flipping his fluffy tail this way and that.

"Dad could name every kind of bird out there," Nikki said.

I'd been so focused on grilling the meat without burning it that I hadn't heard her approach. "Oh, yes, he sure could." I shaded my eyes and gazed out at the water. "He used to make fun of me because I can identify seagulls and pelicans, and that's about it." I flipped the chicken. "The girls coming too? There's plenty here, plus a huge bowl of slaw and some sliced tomatoes."

She shuffled her feet and avoided my eyes. "Cindy said I'm wrong." Her voice was husky, and a peek at her face showed she'd been crying.

"Hmm." I wasn't interrupting whatever this was.

Nikki squatted and called to Rusty. He flicked his tail,

ignoring her. He was Team Karah. "Silly boy." She turned to me. "Mom, I want to help. We have to get Dad out of jail."

Was this the olive branch I'd prayed for? If I rejected her offer, would that end any relationship with her? Of course, there wasn't much there right now, anyhow.

"I'd love help, honey." I playfully snapped the tongs at her. "Can you run in and grab a platter for the food?"

When she went inside, I told the cat, "You need to help, boy. Can you warm up to Nikki?" He gave me the side eye.

She returned with a ceramic platter I made years ago. It was bright blue with a cheerful sunflower in the middle. "That's one of my favorites." I stacked the chicken on it.

"Me too." She shoved her hands in her shorts pockets. "Cindy and Jasmine should be here by now. I'll go get them."

Returning inside, I laid yellow-and-white-striped placemats on the table and placed the chicken, slaw, and tomatoes in the middle. I was pouring glasses of iced tea when Nikki opened the sliding door. Her friends both hugged me before we all sat to eat. Having the girls here felt good, like old times back at home. I caught Nikki's gaze and smiled.

"Mrs. K, Nik said we're going to help find a killer." Cindy rubbed her hands together. The wild child of the three, I never expected her to grow up and become a kindergarten teacher. Nikki explained the kids liked her because she was a child at heart.

"Mr. Gage didn't hurt anyone." Jasmine, always the encourager, patted my hand. "And Cindy, it's not like an adventure. This is real stuff."

Cindy spooned a large helping of coleslaw onto her plate. "I know that. I was trying to lighten the mood. So, do we have any suspects?"

Good question. I relayed the story of Barney watching me and then grabbing my shirt. They each chimed in with encouragement, saying I did all I could. Even Nikki conceded she would have lashed out if someone tried to take her.

"Nobody else to blame, though?" Cindy sipped her tea. "How could the police arrest Mr. Gage without searching for other suspects?"

"He confessed." I shrugged, not knowing what else to say.

"Mom, you said you had people you wanted to talk to? Suspects." Nikki took a bite of her chicken.

"Yes. Sandi Ronald. Remember her? She lives next door. And Pete Chandler. He played tennis with Barney."

"Why them?" Jasmine asked.

I explained Sandi's prior relationship with Barney and added how she thought he gave her a key to his house.

"You never figured out where he lived?" Cindy added more chicken to her plate. "If we could find his place, we could investigate."

Jasmine cocked an eyebrow, and Cindy grinned.

"No, but I haven't had another chance to ask around," I told them, adding that Sandi had accused Pete.

Nikki got out her phone and tapped something into it. "I'm making a list. Sandi and Pete. Means, motive, and opportunity, right mom?"

I chuckled. As a little girl, Nancy Drew was one of her favorite characters. We read the books together at night and tried to solve the mysteries, but Nancy always beat us to it. I lifted my glass of tea in a salute. "True!"

Her smile reached her eyes. I bit the inside of my mouth to keep happy tears at bay.

"Anyone else?" Jasmine asked.

"Not that I can think of." I cut my chicken into bite-sized pieces, then dropped a tiny bit for Rusty. "Oh, but one more thing. Barney is missing a finger. They didn't find it with his body."

"What?" Jasmine made a face like she smelled something rotten.

Cindy gagged, and Nikki's face paled.

"That's what I've heard." I shrugged.

"Missing finger or not," Nikki said, narrowing her eyes. "We have to look at who might have done it. Does Mrs. Sandi still drink a lot?"

"Yes, I think so. But that doesn't give her means." I grabbed the pitcher of tea and refilled our glasses. "I don't know Pete at all."

"I thought the alcohol might lower her inhibitions."

It did that. I thought of how Sandi played Gage. "What would be her motive?"

Nikki cocked an eyebrow. "Jealousy?"

"Jealous of what?" Jasmine asked.

"Of Mom." Nikki winked at me. "You're way prettier and younger than Mrs. Sandi."

Whoa, where did that come from? "Aww, thanks, honey." I fanned my face in mock embarrassment.

"She's right, Mrs. K," Cindy said.

"You've never met her." Nikki laughed.

"Maybe not," she said. "But your mom is way cooler than most moms. I'm sure she's prettier too." She clinked tea glasses with me.

"Thanks, kiddo." These girls were building up my sagging ego.

Jasmine pursed her lips. "If this Sandi lady was jealous, why would she kill the guy? Wouldn't she go after your mom?"

A chill ran through me, and I rubbed my arms. Time to change the subject. "Are y'all too full for ice cream? There's a half gallon of chocolate in the freezer." I stood and began stacking plates. Jasmine followed me into the kitchen and opened the dishwasher.

"I didn't mean to scare you," she said.

"It's okay. You made a good point." Even if it wasn't one I wanted to think about.

She loaded the dishwasher while I scooped ice cream. The girls settled onto the couch, and I curled up in the armchair, savoring the cold, chocolatey dessert. When we finished, Nikki carried our bowls into the kitchen. I was chatting with the girls when something rattled. Nikki came and stood beside my chair.

I reached for her hand, but she jerked hers away. "What's up, honey? Is something wrong?"

She held up a pill bottle. "Why are you taking pain pills? What is going on, Mom?"

Chapter Twelve

"Where did you find those?" Was she accusing me of using drugs?

"Were you hiding them?" Her superior expression and accusing tone stabbed me in the heart. Why would she think I would misuse medicine? She should know me well enough to realize I wouldn't do that.

Cindy stood. "Nikki, stop. Give that to your mom." Her teacher's voice and command worked, and my daughter handed me the medication.

I shook the bottle. "I haven't told you or your father yet, but I have degenerative arthritis disease." After I explained what my diagnosis meant and how it affected me, realization hit her. I saw it in her eyes. Would she back down or continue to be in my face about this? In our short time this evening, I thought some wounds were healing. Apparently, I was mistaken.

Her shoulders drooped, and tears filled her eyes. "Oh, Mom. Dad told me you started a new business. Can you still do it?"

"So far. I have these pills and some cream."

"I'm sorry." She leaned over and hugged me. "For everything."

I accepted her apology, but I learned something. She still held plenty of anger inside. My good standing was on shaky ground. One step or wrong move in either direction, and she would be back on her Dad's side. How I wished there weren't sides, only Team Family.

Three raps on my door startled us all. Cindy jumped up and opened it before I could caution her.

"Hello?" She stepped outside, checking both ways before coming back in. "No one is there."

"You shouldn't answer the door without looking." Jasmine scoffed. "A murderer is running around, after all." She leaned over the back of the couch and pointed. "Something is on the ground by your foot."

Cindy picked up the item. "Flowers? There's a card." She plucked it out and brought me the bouquet.

I couldn't breathe. Barney left the flowers the first time. But he was dead, so who left these? Were both bouquets from the same person, and Barney hadn't been involved? But he asked me if I liked them. He had to have left the first set.

"Who are they from?" Jasmine grabbed the card from Cindy and read it out loud. "Dear Karah, I know these are your favorites. I'm watching you."

Thankfully, I was sitting down. The flowers, white with a yellow center, were daisies. Gage knew they were my favorite, and he couldn't have ordered them from jail, let alone written a note like that.

"Who sent those?" Nikki scowled. "Aren't they what Dad always got for you?"

"I don't know who left these." My voice cracked. "And yes, they are." I leaned forward in my chair and rubbed my temples as dread weighed me down.

Jasmine kneeled beside me and rubbed my back in slow circles. "Deep breaths. Nik, get your mom some water. Take your time, Mrs. K."

Someone placed a water bottle in my hand, but I couldn't unscrew the top. Jasmine opened it. I drank half and returned it to her. "Thanks." I sat up, holding the arms of my chair until the room stopped spinning.

"Mom, do you need any medicine?" Nikki pointed to the bottle she had argued with me about a few minutes before.

Funny how perspectives change. I shook my head.

Cindy sat on the floor in front of me. "Why did that scare you so bad?"

I barked a laugh. I hadn't told them about the flowers. "Nikki, will you bring me my purse?" When she did, I searched for the first note. I put it beside the new one. "The first one says, 'Did you like what you saw yesterday?' Same handwriting as today's. How could that be?"

"Where did the other one come from?" Nikki asked.

I explained about the first bouquet and how Barney asked if I liked the flowers. Each girl studied both cards and agreed the handwriting matched.

"Did Barney say anything about the note?" Nikki stood and paced the living room.

I thought back. "I don't think so. Not that I can remember."

"Hmm," she said.

"What does that mean?" Cindy asked.

She nibbled on her thumbnail. "What if ... what if he didn't write the note? Maybe he left the flowers the first time, but not the card." She shrugged. "It's just an idea."

"It's a good idea." I agreed with her. "One we need to consider."

"What do we do now?" Jasmine asked.

"Go to the police." Cindy regarded me. "You know we have to."

I did, but I sure didn't want to.

* * *

Jasmine drove us to the station. I stared out the car window, watching the gorgeous sunset, the sky filled with shades of pink and blue. Usually, the sight would calm me, but tonight, it directly contrasted with the fear filling me. I couldn't wrap my head around what had happened—with Barney, Gage, or the flowers. None of it made sense.

I sat forward in my seat. "Can you pull over? Fast?"

Jasmine jerked the car to the side of the road and slammed on the brakes. "What? Do you need to puke?"

"I'd be puking if I were you." Cindy patted my shoulder.

These girls. "No, no puking. But I have a question." I caught Nikki's eyes. "Hear me out, please. Do we *need* to tell the police?"

The three girls began arguing with me, insisting we put it all in the police's lap.

"They have experience with this, Mom." Nikki grimaced. "Why would we not tell them?"

"Because from what the police officer told me, they believe your dad killed Barney. I don't think they'll search for anyone else. But we could check into Sandi and Pete."

"As long as we don't turn over the cards?" Cindy asked.

"Right."

Jasmine made a quick three-point turnaround and drove back to my cottage. "Let's write this all down on paper. There must be other suspects. And I think we need to find this Barney guy's house." She parked in Gage's driveway.

"Mom, will you stay with us tonight?" Nikki opened her door. "Please?"

"The flowers scared me, but no one wants to hurt me." I got out and headed for my house.

"How do you know, Mrs. K?" Cindy called. Jasmine shushed her.

I approached my place and dug out my keys. "Why would they?" I realized my door stood ajar, and I backed up. "Uh-oh."

"Mom?" Nikki walked toward me. "I really think you should get Rusty and your PJs and come over." She reached for the doorknob, but I grabbed her arm and pointed.

"You're sure you locked it?" she asked.

I nodded.

She took my hand, and we hurried back to the other girls. "Inside, now," she commanded.

"What's wrong?" Cindy asked.

Nikki grabbed her arm. "Shush, come on."

We hurried inside Gage's rental. Nikki locked the front door and the door to the garage.

"What is going on?" Cindy asked in a demanding tone.

"Someone's been in my place." I crossed my arms.

Jasmine pulled her phone out of her shorts pocket. "I'm calling the police."

It looked like we had to talk to them whether I wanted to or not.

Chapter Thirteen

A female officer showed up, said they were short-staffed, checked my place, and left without saying much or seeming concerned. The girls accompanied me into the cottage. While I packed a bag, they found Rusty and gathered his supplies. I didn't want to be alone. Rusty explored Gage's townhouse, then curled up on the sofa and slept. He didn't appear particularly upset.

"It makes me wonder if anyone went inside or if the door didn't catch when I closed it."

"Mom, I don't think you can judge what may have happened by how your cat acts. Look at him." Nikki pointed at my fluffy feline, who was sound asleep, his head hanging off the edge of the couch cushion.

I sat beside him and scooted his head up. He curled a paw around my hand. "I'm glad he's okay." I stroked his fur.

"He's a sweet boy," Cindy said.

Jasmine held out her hand. "Do you have the florist cards, Mrs. K?"

I rustled around in my purse until I found them. "Can we make copies of these before we do anything else?"

Cindy held up her phone. "I took pictures."

Nikki cleared off the dining table. Per Gage's norm, folders and paperwork covered the surface. "Let's sit here and discuss what we know."

Exhaustion filled me. I wanted to go to bed, but the girls wanted to help. I headed for the kitchen. "I need some decaf. Anyone else?"

We settled at the table, mugs in hand. Jasmine found blank paper and wrote "Suspects" on the left and "Details" across the top. I showed her the cards, and she numbered them.

"I wonder how we could find out who wrote these," she said. "I think it's a woman's handwriting."

"How can you tell?" Cindy held out her hand. "Jas, pass those over." She examined each side of the cards and held them up to the light.

"Okay, Inspector, what do you think?" Jasmine giggled.

She shrugged. "No idea. Here, Nik, you take a look."

"Without something to compare them to, we can't tell anything. They might be from a woman. I don't know." Nikki handed them back to me.

"That was productive," I said. "The only suspects I can think of are Sandi and Pete."

Jasmine wrote their names. "Why?"

I blew on my coffee and took a sip. "Sandi, because she loved Barney. That doesn't make her a murderer. Put a question mark by her name."

Jasmine marked it. "And Pete?"

"Because Sandi brought him up?" I raised my hands. "She said they competed, and Pete threatened him."

"Did Pete have a thing for Sandi?" Cindy asked.

I shrugged. "No idea, but she never talked about him like that."

Nikki groaned. "Murder is from three things." She held up three fingers. "Money, love, or power. Mrs. Sandi has money, right?"

I nodded.

"But she loved Barney according to you, so she's a definite possibility. We need to find out more about Pete," she said.

"This conversation is going in circles." I stood. "We all need sleep."

Exhaustion weighed me down as I thought about everything I needed to do. One, hire a locksmith to change the locks on my doors. Two, check into a security system. And three, figure out how to spring Gage from the Trinity Sands Island jail.

I crawled into Gage's bed, but the pillow smelled like his shampoo. I switched to "my" side but found that pillow held the faint scent of the cologne he used—my favorite. That made me think all kinds of things until I finally slept. Thunder woke me early the following day. I opened the blinds, and lightning flashed over the water. Rusty, who typically stuck to me like glue in a storm, was nowhere in sight.

Downstairs, someone had started a pot of coffee. I poured myself a mug and curled up in the corner of the couch. At the next thunder boom, Rusty scampered up beside me, and I scratched his head.

"Where have you been, big fellow?"

He twitched his tail and burrowed his face into the couch pillows. I checked the weather app on my phone and found that a tropical storm originally aiming for Texas had switched its path overnight and was now swirling our way.

Nikki wandered downstairs.

"Morning, honey. Looks like we'll be wet for a while."

She poured coffee and joined me in the living room. "I saw that on the news this morning. I woke up early."

"Worried about your dad?"

She nodded. "I thought we could show the cards to Maude today. She's been on the island forever. She might recognize the handwriting."

"Good idea. I've got some phone calls to make." I shifted to make room on the couch. We sat together, drinking our coffee and enjoying the quiet. Did she understand how precious this time was? Us being together and not arguing was a balm to my soul.

Cindy bounded down the stairs. "Hey, y'all. What's the plan for today?" She scooted in beside Nikki and peered over her shoulder. "Whatcha looking at?"

Nikki rolled her eyes and passed her phone to her. "You're like the nosy little sister I never had."

"Maude's Market? We going there?"

"Yes, we are." Nikki stood and pulled her friend up. "Go find Jasmine and get dressed. We have some investigating to do."

I chuckled at Cindy's salute. "Okay. I need to get moving too." I loaded the dishwasher and turned it on before getting ready for the day. Rusty was still snuggled on the couch when I left for my house. "First stop, make those phone calls."

"Mornin,' Karah."

Sandi's words startled me. I looked up to find her standing on my front porch. "Hi." I reminded myself she didn't know she was on our list of suspects. "What's up?"

She tipped her head, her lips pulled down in a frown. "You stayed at Gage's last night?"

Oh, boy. What to say? I didn't want to tell her someone broke into my place. "I was keeping the girls company." That wasn't a lie.

"I came to tell you about the pop-up craft sale. Have you heard about it?"

"No." I unlocked my door, and she followed me inside. "Can you hang on for a minute? I need to make a call."

She stood by the back sliding glass door while I found a number for a locksmith and placed the call. When I hung up, she turned.

"You're changing your locks?"

She was nosier than Cindy. "I thought, you know, with Barney's murder and all, that I needed to."

"Yeah, that makes sense. I should change mine too." She plopped down on the couch. "I thought you might want to sell some of your crafts in this pop-up sale."

"Where's it at?" I had heard of pop-ups before, but they were usually food trucks.

"Inside the clubhouse. It's too wet to hold it outside with the storm coming through. I can help you take some things there."

"The locksmith said they'd fit me in this morning." I hated to miss this chance to sell some of my creations. Somehow, I needed to tell locals about my business, and word of mouth was one of the best marketing tools.

"That's okay. I can wait for him." She waved her hands and shooed me toward the door. "Go on. I'll be fine here."

Could I trust her? I wasn't sure. "Just a minute." I hurried into my room, shut the door, and called Nikki.

"Are y'all busy? I need a favor," I said in a low voice.

"We're going to see Maude, remember?" she said.

"Oh, yeah. No problem." I hung up and went back to the living room. "If you're sure you'll be okay ..."

Sandi waved her hands again. I didn't think she killed Barney. What could she really do? Against my misgivings—and there were several—I thanked her, loaded my car with as many items as I had made, and grabbed my business cards. On the short drive, I dreamed about hitting it big in the beach décor business. Money wasn't the driving force. But I wanted to prove to myself that I could do this. I pulled close to the clubhouse's curb and hurried inside.

A young man headed my way. "Hi, ma'am. Can I help you?"

"I'm here for the sale. I mean, I have things to sell. How can I get involved?" Nice start, Karah. Now he'll think you can't talk.

He questioned me about my items and then showed me to a table, explaining I would share it with a woman selling handmade cards. Between rain showers, I unloaded my things and arranged them on my half of the table. While I waited for customers to arrive, I called the girls to check in.

"We showed Maude the cards. She's searching her memory." I could almost hear Nikki rolling her eyes.

"I'm at a pop-up craft sale at the clubhouse. Stop by when you're finished there." The three of them could pass out my business cards and help promote sales. As I hung up, the card seller arrived. I introduced myself, and she stopped and jerked around to face me.

"You're Gage Halyard's wife?" Her eyebrows, thick and bushy, slid up under her bangs.

"Ex."

"He's in jail for murder." Her voice shook. "I can't share a table with you. Hey!" She yelled to the young man who had helped me. "I need a different table. She's married to a murderer."

Chapter Fourteen

Her words sliced through me. How could she say that? Gage didn't kill anyone. Did people think of me that way—a killer's wife?

"But, but it's not true." I stepped back.

She furiously packed up her cards. The man came over and offered her a different spot. While he helped her carry her things, she turned and shot me another hateful glare. What was I going to do? I slumped onto the folding chair behind me. I had to prove Gage wasn't guilty for many reasons. Never did I think it would be to also clear my name.

"Karah," Sandi stood before me with a confused expression. "What's going on? Why is everyone staring at you?"

She was right. People clustered together, whispering and glancing my way. Tears welled up and spilled down my cheeks. "They think Gage killed Barney."

Sandi stepped into the middle of the room, hands on her hips, and raised her voice. "Mind your own business. Gage Halyard is not a killer, and you shouldn't say he is. What happened to innocent until proven guilty?" She raised her hands and huffed.

I couldn't stay after this. I began packing up.

"You can't give into them," she said.

Yes, I could. I couldn't battle the entire island's gossip. Not right now. "I'm going home." And going to bed with a hot pack. I remembered why she stayed at my house. "Did the locksmith come?"

"Yes, here's the key." She passed it to me. "He said he'd bill you."

I was so engrossed in getting to this pop-up sale that I forgot to pay him. "Good. Thanks so much." She took one tote, and I grabbed another. On my way out, I slid my business cards into my purse—no need to leave them behind.

The girls pulled up beside me as I prepared to leave the parking lot. Nikki rolled down her window. "Where are you going?"

More tears came. "Home." I sniffled and wiped my face.

"Mom?"

"Follow me, please." The card woman's wicked words repeated in my head the entire drive home.

The girls tried to comfort me, but I wanted to be alone. After promising to check in with them once I got up, I used my new key to unlock the door and headed for bed. Today had taken a chunk out of my self-esteem. I spent time praying and thinking about what happened.

I hadn't originally planned to attend the pop-up. So, it shouldn't keep me from pursuing my business. This was a tiny blip in the grand scheme of things. And I couldn't control what people said or thought. Once we'd proven Gage innocent, everything would be fine.

At least, I hoped so.

Before I closed my eyes, I remembered something that had

nothing to do with beach décor but everything to do with the murder. If Barney lost a finger, it couldn't have been from my hitting him with the driftwood. I knew I hadn't killed him, but now the fact that I wasn't a murderer sunk in. And Gage found out about it at the same time I did.

"Where is his finger, and what did the person use to cut it off?" I waited for Rusty's reply, but he was still with the girls. I hopped off the bed and hurried to Gage's townhouse.

Jasmine opened the door. "Hey, Mrs. K. How are you? I'm sorry about today."

"Excuse me, Jas." I slipped past her. "Where are Nikki and Cindy? I have an idea."

Jasmine called for the girls. I wandered into the kitchen.

"Do y'all never pick up?" I unloaded clean dishes, reloaded the dishwasher, and wiped down the counters. Keeping busy calmed me.

"Mom, what's up?" Nikki hopped up onto the counter, which I'd just wiped. "Yuck, this is wet."

"It's clean," I said.

She got down and dried herself with the kitchen towel. "That's Cindy's job. She's not very good at it."

I shooed her out of the room. "Let's go sit down."

Once the girls were seated, I said, "When we saw the ambulance at the beach where Barney died, someone said he was missing a finger." Cindy's face paled. "I haven't heard anything about it since then. The police officer didn't mention it to me either. Only that Gage confessed." I chewed on my lip. "So, where is it?"

Rusty jumped into my lap and curled up. I waited for a response, and finally, Nikki said, "How do we look for a ... um ... missing finger?" She gulped.

"I'm not sure. I checked the sand where they found his body, but I didn't see anything. Did I ever tell you about

Chapter Fifteen

The old grocery store was from the last century or maybe the one before. Several older gentlemen sat out front in rocking chairs, the wooden porch creaking under their weight. I loved the market's weathered fishing village charm. Considering how Maude used to do business, according to the girls, the place was ancient. It fit right in with the island vibe.

After I climbed the stairs to the porch and nodded to the men, I spied a cooler of ice-cold sodas beside the bucket of pool noodles. I grabbed one and popped the top, enjoying the icy taste, refreshing in the June heat. A sign on the cooler read 'pay inside,' so I entered the store. Maude stood at the customer service counter.

"Hi, Mrs. Halyard," she said in her usual booming voice. "Your girl came in earlier. She sure is all grown up. Quite the beauty."

"Yes, thank you." I hurried to her, speaking quietly, hoping it would make her keep her voice down, not wanting the whole store to hear my business. "She's a wonderful young woman." Nikki and I were still wary of each other, but things were improving. "Any luck on the handwriting they asked you about?"

She shifted through some paperwork and handed several pages to me. "Here ya go. I don't think these exactly match, but that's what I've found so far. I thought I remembered the handwriting until I started looking through the papers. Now they all jumble together in my mind."

I glanced at the names. One I didn't know, but the other two I did. Sandi Ronald and her husband, the captain, had signed one form and Pete Chandler the other.

"Can you make copies of these for me?" My hand shook when I passed the pages back to her.

Maude shrugged. "Sure, I don't use them anymore anyhow. Everyone pays with a card nowadays." She walked to a desk behind her, which held a laptop with a copier beside it. "I can't believe how everything is all technology today. The kids don't even glance up from their phones when they come in." She shook her head. "They can pay with those phones too. I don't get it." She returned with my copies. "You don't think either killed old Cobb, do ya? Sandi Ronald is a maybe in my book, but Pete Chandler? I don't think so."

I didn't know what the girls told her, and I didn't want to discuss Barney's death right now. "We're following up on some things. Thank you." I grabbed the papers and was in my car when I remembered I hadn't paid for the soda. "I'll pay her next time. I'm not going back in there today."

No cars were in Gage's driveway. After parking at my place, I headed inside to study the signatures, hoping one of the girls would return soon since the cards were at Gage's. I wanted to hold them side-by-side with the forms for comparison. It made no sense that my neighbor or Pete killed Barney.

A car pulled in at Gage's as someone knocked on my door. I needed to catch whichever girl was home and grab those notecards. Sandi stood on my doorstep, and my stomach churned. Could I trust her?

"Hang on," I said. "I'll be right back." I jogged to Gage's and caught Jasmine and Cindy on their way into the townhouse. Cindy retrieved the cards for me.

"I'll explain about these later. Y'all want to come over for dinner?"

She nodded.

I hurried back to my place and found Sandi sitting on the couch in my living room.

"What do you have?" she asked.

"Oh, nothing." I shoved the papers and cards into a kitchen drawer. She didn't need to know what I was up to, especially since one of the signatures was hers. I joined her on the couch.

"How are you?" She reached out and patted my arm. "I'm checking on you. You were so disappointed earlier. I hate what happened. Now your little business won't have any sales." She thrust her lower lip out in a pout.

Why would she think that? "It should be okay. I wasn't depending on that sale anyhow."

"Oh, no." She shook her head. "Now, now, it's all right to face facts. It's not good for you to keep your feelings bottled up."

Why was she being so sappy? I wanted her to leave so I could compare the handwriting. "The girls are coming over soon for dinner. I need to start on it."

She followed me to the door and gave me a long, tight hug. "I'm worried about you. Call if you need me. And keep an eye on the weather. They're predicting this tropical storm to turn into a hurricane." She squeezed me another time and left.

I was standing in front of the open refrigerator, wondering what to make for dinner, when someone knocked again. Prepared to send "Sunny Sandi" back to her house, I jerked the door open. Nikki stood there, Cindy on one side and Jasmine on the other. Tears streamed down my daughter's face.

"What's wrong?" I waved them in. "Nik, what happened?"

She fell into my arms. "It's ... Dad ..." Her words came out between sobs.

"Okay?" I sent a questioning look to the other girls. They shrugged. "Here, let's sit, honey. Will one of you get her some water?" We sat on the couch, and I rubbed her back. Jasmine handed her a glass, and she sipped until her breathing slowed. "Feeling better?"

She shrugged.

"Take your time." I pulled her close and waited, cherishing the chance to comfort her even while images of what could have happened to Gage flashed through my mind. Nikki was often dramatic, but I felt her heart beating wildly and knew whatever happened was bad.

She swiped her tears and leaned against the couch.

"Can you tell me now?"

She drew a deep breath and exhaled hard. "Dad got beat up. Bad." Her last word came out in a wail.

"Oh, honey." I wanted more details, all of them, but she couldn't stop crying. Was Gage okay? Was he still in jail? "Tissue, please." Cindy handed me the box, and I passed several to Nikki. When she quieted, I asked, "Do you know why he was beat up?" I gritted my teeth, waiting for her answer. Who hurt my husband? The thought stopped me in my tracks. *Ex*, Karah, I reminded myself. Ex-husband.

"They arrested Pete Chandler," Cindy said.

"What? Why?" What was going on and what did Pete have to do with it?

Nikki blew her nose in a loud honk. "Maude told them he might have killed Barney."

"She mentioned Ms. Sandi, too, I think," Jasmine added.

Oh, my, what had we done?

* * *

After a long, disjointed conversation, in which Nikki revealed Gage sported a black eye and Pete hadn't fared much better, I still had lots of questions.

"Why in the world did they put those two in the same jail cell?" Gage wouldn't have started the fight, that much I knew.

Cindy gasped. "You don't think they'll put Ms. Sandi in there with them, do you?"

I rose and headed for the kitchen. We all needed food before we went off on tangents. "I have no idea, but I hope not after what happened." I filled a pot with water and set it to boiling. "Mac and cheese okay with y'all?"

Cindy and Jasmine nodded, but Nikki followed me. "Shouldn't we go check on Dad?"

"Let's eat and talk about it." I didn't know what to do. Comfort food would help. At least I hoped so.

We ate quietly, Rusty begging me for a bite. Jasmine placed one cheesy noodle on a paper towel for him. He sniffed it and walked off, tail high.

"He's a strange cat," she said.

"He's something else." I thought about how he enjoyed it when Gage held him. "Your dad loved him," I told Nikki.

"A cat?" She giggled. "We never had a cat. I didn't think he liked them."

"Me either. People change." I didn't mean that as a dig against her, but she cocked an eyebrow. It was true. People did change. My feelings for Gage were changing. I thought I still loved him, maybe even more than ever before. And Nikki? She had come a long way in just a few days.

Chapter Sixteen

Nikki took our dishes into the kitchen while Cindy, Jasmine, and I discussed Sandi and Pete. I didn't know Pete Chandler well enough to label him a murderer. But I couldn't imagine Sandi being involved. She wasn't that kind of person. Besides, she loved Barney. She said so.

I proposed another walk on the beach. We all needed a few minutes of peace. We kicked off our shoes when we reached the sand and headed for the water's edge. The sun descended, and the sky transformed into an expanse of soft oranges, dark pinks, and faded purples. The colors blended seamlessly.

"I wish I could paint," Cindy said. She held up her hands like a frame. "I'd hang this in my living room so I could see it every day."

"It would be beautiful," Jasmine said.

Waves gently lapped at the shore, washing over our feet. I breathed deeply and released some of the stress and worry of the last few days. Yes, we still needed to solve the murder, and yes, Gage was still in jail. But God was refreshing my spirit and soul out here by the water.

We walked along the harder-packed sand. The beach was quieter than usual, with an occasional seagull gliding gracefully overhead. A heron stood nearby in the shallow water, watching us with his small, dark eyes. The ocean reflected the sky's colors, shimmering as the sun set deeper. Finally, as the horizon faded into twilight, I suggested we turn back, ready to face the next step in our investigation.

Inside my cottage, Cindy curled into the corner of the couch. She stretched and tucked one foot between the cushions. "Ouch." She jerked out her foot and rubbed the side of it. "What do you have in here, Mrs. K?" She wiggled her hand down and pulled out a large knife.

With blood stains on it.

"Oh, oh no, no, no." She dropped it with a clatter onto the coffee table and scrambled as far back on the couch as possible.

Nikki hurried into the living room at her friend's cry. "What in the world? What is that?"

I found a clean napkin and picked it up. "This might be the murder weapon." I held my arm straight, but my hand shook so hard I had to support my elbow with my other hand. "Jasmine, will you call the police, please?"

How did this knife get in my couch? Who had been in my cottage? Then it hit me. "Sandi. It had to be her." My legs trembled, thinking of how I trusted her.

"Mrs. Sandi?" Nikki's face paled. "But Mom, how? Are you sure?"

She "met" the locksmith and gave me the new key. I laid the weapon on the coffee table, searched my purse for my original house key, and compared it to the supposed new one. "These are the same." I turned to the girls. "She didn't give me a new key."

I dialed the local locksmith, feeling sure he had an after-hours number. We chatted briefly, and he confirmed my suspicions.

"She was here. Sandi. She sent the locksmith home and made a copy of my original key. She had to be the one to stick the knife in the couch." I was sure of it now.

Cindy covered her mouth. "She wants to frame you," she said through her fingers.

"Yeah ..." Words escaped me. All this time, I lived next to a murderer. Why didn't I know? I collapsed onto the couch, my breath whooshing out.

Nikki sat beside me and held my hand. "Mom, we have another problem."

I stared into her lovely eyes. "Not sure I can handle anything else, Nik."

"Ms. Sandi might be arrested soon like Pete was." She grimaced. "She doesn't need to be in Dad's cell."

Would they put the three of them together? We couldn't take a chance. Jasmine sat in frozen silence. She hadn't moved to call the emergency line.

I motioned to the girls. "Get your things." I slipped the knife into a plastic zippered bag and stuck it in my purse. "We have to go to the police and show them the weapon."

It was pitch black outside when we arrived at the police station. Thunder rumbled. The storm sounded much closer now. Another band of heavy rain started, and Sandi's words about the possible hurricane ran through my mind. Lightning struck so close that the hair on my arms stood up. I shivered in the gloomy night.

Once the rain let up a bit, we hurried for the porch and shook off like a pack of wet dogs. I turned the doorknob and pushed the front door open. Lightning flashed again, and the electricity popped, throwing the police station into complete darkness. Without any moonlight, I couldn't see in front of my face.

"Hello?" The girls huddled behind me, and we stepped into the lobby as one mass.

"Stay right there," a female voice said. Light flickered. The police officer held a long, black flashlight in one hand, and she shined it our way. "Can I help you?"

"Yes. I think?" I cleared my throat. This wasn't the time for indecision. "My husband. Ex, I mean, is here. Gage Halyard? I need to talk to him. And to you." I stumbled over my words.

She tipped her head. "My husband is home, and I need to see him." Her sarcasm wasn't lost on me.

Nikki elbowed her way in front of me. "Mom, let me handle this." She approached the policewoman. "Can I see my dad, please?" She used the softest tone I'd ever heard and wiped an imaginary tear from her eye.

"Oh, honey, I wish I could let you." She spoke in a similar quiet voice. Then she jerked her flashlight to the side and growled, "Go back over there. I don't know who you are, but as you can see, we've lost power."

My snarky side wanted to say, "No, we can't see," but I bit my cheek to keep my mouth shut.

"I've got my phone," Cindy said. She pulled it out of her back pocket. "No. It's dead." She grunted. "I forgot to charge it."

"I left mine at home," Jasmine said.

"Me too." Nikki turned to me. "What else can we do?"

I held up my hands. "No cell phone here either." I had my purse but never thought to grab my cell.

A gust of wind blew the door wide open. Thunder pounded outside, followed by lightning and a sharp cracking sound. In the seconds following, we waited, hearing a roar of rushing wind building.

"Come over here." The policewoman barked her command, her eyes locked on her cell phone. "The Coast Guard sent a message. The tropical storm sped up, and they're saying we need to watch for tornadoes and waterspouts." She lifted the half door that blocked us from the hall leading to the rest of the building.

I'd been down this hallway. Was that two days ago? I shook my head. No, it was yesterday.

She waved us in front of her with her flashlight. The roar grew louder. Sticks and limbs slammed the roof and sides of the police station. Rain sliced sideways and poured through the front door. A harsh snap rang through the night. We all froze in place. I recognized that sound. When the tree hit the ground with a heavy thump, I breathed a sigh of relief. This old house had likely survived many storms, but if one of the tall pine trees beside it uprooted and hit the building, there would be massive damage.

"Where is my husband?" I asked, raising my voice over the storm.

She hurried us down the hall and turned into the first room. "Jail cell. I'll get him and Mr. Chandler. You guys stay here." She shut the door behind her, pitching us into darkness.

We waited. I was afraid to move, not knowing what was in the room. The door flung open, and Gage hurried in, the cop behind him, her flashlight lighting the way. We threw our arms around him.

"I'm so glad you're all okay." He kissed me so quickly that it almost didn't register.

Almost.

I touched my lips and then lightly traced his black eye. "Ouch."

He cocked an eyebrow and stepped aside. Pete Chandler looked worse than Gage. His lip split when he grinned, and he winced. "Maybe next time I won't swing first." His eyes, the little showing through the black and purple surrounding them, twinkled.

"I guess y'all worked out your misunderstanding," I said.

Gage turned to Pete. "For now, anyhow. We have more important things to do." He called out to the police officer. "We need to shelter in place. Is this the safest room?"

She nodded.

He held up his handcuffed hands. "Can you unlock these? We need to move fast."

She hesitated briefly, then shook her head. "No can do. Sorry."

The room was more storage space than office, so we cleared an area to sit on the floor and wait out the storm. Another *whomp* shook the building.

"That's the second tree to go," I said, wondering how much more damage we'd get.

Chapter Seventeen

"Where's everyone else?" I asked. Surely she wasn't the only officer or staff on duty.

"Spencer went to find Sandi Ronald. Detective Young is off island at the moment." The policewoman shuddered at another round of crashing thunder and flashes of lightning. "Is it always this nasty here?"

I shifted on the hard floor. "You're not from Trinity Sands?"

"Nah. I come from up in Virginia. I imagined tropical island life. You know, palm trees and fishing. Not this kind of weather." She pointed to Gage and Pete. "Not a murder either. Or these two yahoos."

"Never been called a yahoo before," Gage said. "You, Pete?"

He shrugged. "I've never been arrested before." He leaned toward the police officer. "It wasn't me, ma'am. Wasn't him either." He thumbed in Gage's direction, his cuffs jingling against each other.

"I'm pretty sure Sandi Ronald killed Barney." Everyone

shifted to stare at me. The police officer blazed her bright flashlight in my face. I opened my purse and grabbed the bag containing the knife. "Look. This is the murder weapon, I think." I gently placed it on the ground and pushed it toward the police officer.

She picked it up with two fingers and examined it the best she could in the dim lighting. "Where did you find this?" She blinded me again with her light.

"Please lower that." I held up my hand until she did. "It was in my couch. Cindy, tell her how you found it."

Cindy told her the story.

"Down in the cushions?" the police officer asked. "Wow. What some people will do." She continued questioning us. Finally, she stood, brushing off her pants. "Everyone up."

She opened the door and gestured for us to go ahead of her. "You all are going in the jail cell. I need to help Spencer with Mrs. Ronald. He hasn't checked in, and if she's as tricky as you say, he might need me."

I couldn't believe what she said. "We're *all* going in the cell?" My stomach clenched. How could this be happening?

"Yup." She waved her hand for us to hurry.

Gage caught up to me and interlaced his fingers with mine as best he could with his handcuffs still on. "It'll be okay." He pulled me closer and kissed my forehead.

How could he be sure? We were all sitting ducks in the storm. I tried telling the police officer, but she ignored me and pushed us into the cell.

"You'll be fine. I'll be back. You can use this flashlight until then." She pulled out her phone and shook it. "No service anymore. We must have lost a tower." She gestured to the two men. "Hold your hands out." She uncuffed them and turned. Her footsteps echoed down the hall, and the front door slammed.

"Gage, how can this be all right? We're locked in here in the middle of a storm." My words ended in a wail. Another round of thunder and lightning caused the girls to huddle in a circle, arms around each other. Pete stood to the side.

"She didn't lock the cell." Gage tapped the bars, and the door swung wide.

"But you didn't know that before when you told me everything would be okay."

He ran his fingers down my cheek, brushing his thumb over my lips. "I didn't want you to be scared."

"PDA," Cindy called out. "Gross."

Pete cleared his throat. "Can we go now?"

Using the bright flashlight, we navigated through the sticks and limbs in the front yard and piled into my car. I maneuvered around a large, downed magnolia that must have been one of the thumps we'd heard. The darkness amplified every noise as rain lashed the windshield and wind buffeted the vehicle. Even with the windshield wipers on high, I struggled to see. I clamped down on the steering wheel, aware of the storm's power, and made my way down the debris-littered streets.

My headlights barely penetrated the sheets of rain while thunder rattled the car, causing the girls to gasp and squeal. I prayed my place was still safe. Rounding the corner to my street, we saw two police cars, lights strobing through the darkness, sitting in front of Sandi's. I pulled into my driveway and jumped out, heading for her house.

"Hold on there." Gage rounded the car and held onto my arm. "This woman is dangerous."

Sandi's front door burst open as he spoke, and she ran out into the storm. She saw us and pulled up short.

"They're the guilty ones," she said, waving her arms and pointing at us. "Arrest them."

Lightning lit up the area, and thunder boomed. Her face, full of anger and fear, scared me, but I approached her.

"You lied to me." I shook my finger. "You told me the locksmith came, but he didn't. *You* hid the murder weapon in my couch."

If looks could kill, I'd be flat on the ground. She got nose-to-nose with me. "I didn't do it. *You* did." She put her hands on my shoulders and shoved me. "You hit Barney." Her face scrunched up, and her tears flowed faster than the rain. She pushed me again, and I tripped, landing on my backside.

Gage rushed to help me up, Nikki at his side. "Mom, are you okay?"

Another round of lightning and thunder clapped. The storm was directly overhead. I brushed off my pants, although a bit of dirt or mud didn't make much difference, considering I was soaked through.

"I'm fine," I said.

Sandi stood before us, chest heaving. "It's her. She hurt Barney. She killed him." Her eyes were unfocused and wild.

The female police officer and Spencer approached her.

"Ma'am, you need to come with us." Spencer read her rights as the other police officer wrestled her arms behind her and slapped cuffs on.

They led her toward the police car but stopped at the sound of rushing water and a low roar. We all turned as lightning spotlighted a waterspout. I froze as the swirling column of water shot up into the sky. Snakes topped my greatest fear list, and tornadoes were right up under them. I knew a little about waterspouts, but I'd never seen one before.

Gage grabbed my hand and yelled over the sound, "Go inside. Now! It might come on land."

Sandi's was the closest place, and we all hurried inside her cottage. Gage watched the funnel cloud through her blinds, giving us movement-by-movement updates. Seconds later, he said, "Bathroom, now!" We ended up in a logjam, trying to get into the room. Spencer stepped back and waved the women in first. Then he, Pete, and Gage crowded in, and he shut the door.

Gage gathered the three girls and me in his arms as best he could. He mumbled prayers while the spout-turned-tornado roared overhead. Crashing and banging above us made the girls squeal. Sandi cried out. Before the tornado passed, I felt the air change in the bathroom. Someone had opened the door. I counted heads.

"Sandi's gone," I hollered.

"That woman is an escape artist," Spencer said. He ran after her. From the noises I heard, he either captured her, or the spout was still on land.

I tiptoed into her living room. Through the open door, lightning illuminated Sandi struggling in Spencer's hold.

Then I spotted Rusty.

Chapter Eighteen

My cat sauntered into Sandi's house with something that looked suspiciously like a finger hanging out of his mouth. The female officer shined her light at him. It reflected off of Barney's silver ring.

"How did you get out of the house?" I asked as if that was the most crucial question of the night.

Rusty stopped before me, dropped the finger at my feet, and meowed.

"Good boy." I stroked his head, trying not to gag at the sight. "Girls,"—I warned them—"stay where you are."

Gage scooped Rusty into his arms. "Well, how about you, Mr. Detective? What a good fellow." He crooned lovingly into the cat's ear, brushing dirt off his paws and whiskers. Loud purring came from my chubby kitty.

Nikki and I exchanged glances. My ex-husband was the only person Rusty had allowed to pet him more than twice. She peeked over my shoulder, ignoring my earlier warning.

"Is that a finger?" She gagged. "Where did the cat find it?"

Where had he found it? Sergeant Spencer entered, Sandi squirming in his arms. She whined at the top of her voice.

"Let me go. I didn't kill anyone." She saw Rusty and then spotted the finger and ring. Her face paled. "I want a lawyer. Now."

* * *

We stayed at Sandi's until the storm passed. The female police officer, who finally introduced herself as Cheryl White, placed Barney's finger and ring into an evidence bag. Spencer handcuffed Sandi to a dining table leg. She complained about how uncomfortable she was, and we all ignored her.

Once the wind died, the officers helped a sullen Sandi into the back of one of the police cars and took off for the station. I checked the area in her flower bed that had been disturbed a few days earlier. It looked like she'd buried the finger there. That close, and I never knew. Of course, with all the rain, we couldn't prove the finger had been there, but I was sure of it.

I took Rusty from Gage and told him and the girls good night. It had been a crazy day. It was after midnight, and I was beat. My entire body ached from the weather and the long hours I'd spent at the police station and then at Sandi's. My front door stood open. I assumed from the wind pressure. Now I knew how Rusty escaped. I'd call the locksmith in the morning to replace the lock. It was too late tonight. I fixed a quick snack and took my medicine before changing and crawling into bed.

As exhausted as I felt, I couldn't settle. Barney's murder had been solved, but why did Sandi kill him? Supposedly, she loved and adored him. She called him precious. Why did she cut off his finger and bury it in her front yard? Such an extreme thing to do, even for her. None of it made sense to me.

Had she killed anyone else? Had I lived beside a serial killer? A bitter taste filled my mouth, and my throat burned. I was being ridiculous. There wasn't any evidence Sandi killed anyone except Barney.

The question remained—why *did* she do it? One of the girls suggested Sandi was jealous. If so, she didn't know me well. I was still hung up on Gage. Even if I wasn't, Barney was not my type. A shudder ran through me at the thought of being close to him.

Gage. The final loose end. What would I do about him? He indicated he cared about me through his actions, like the near kiss. Plus, he told Spencer he still loved me. But he hadn't said the words to me. I wondered if he said it to convince the officer he was guilty.

Lying in bed, I imagined getting back together with Gage. We never really figured out what went wrong the first time around. I wasn't sure our reconnecting was the best idea, especially under these circumstances. Too much had happened in such a short time.

I couldn't survive another divorce.

I turned over and shoved my pillow under my neck. "No more Gage. Not tonight."

* * *

My morning began like always, with coffee and a bagel. The old Adirondack chair was still wet, so I opened the sliding glass door but sat inside. The sky was clear, and the air was fresh. Birds called from the ocean. I couldn't wait to go down there to see what treasures I could find.

When I finished eating and downing my morning meds, I grabbed my trusty blue bucket, told Rusty goodbye, and closed the door tight. I'd call the locksmith when I returned to the cottage. I would meet him this time and ensure things were done correctly.

The sand wasn't hot yet and was packed hard from all the rain, making the search for shells and driftwood easier. I added more sea glass to my bucket and considered what to use it for. I had plenty of ideas for creations, but I liked variety and always looked for more ways to incorporate what I found. I was lost in thought when someone called my name.

"Karah? Mom?" Nikki stood at the water's edge, her arms crossed. Her defensive body language set my stomach roiling.

"Hi, honey."

"Did Dad tell you he's going home?" She shaded her eyes. "I thought he would stay."

"I didn't have any idea. He hasn't talked to me about his plans." I wanted to be alone. Hearing Gage was leaving from someone besides him hurt. "I thought he came down for work."

"Yeah, me too." She scuffed the sand with her toes. "I'm not mad at you, Mom. Not anymore." She held out her hand. I stepped forward and took it.

"I'm glad. I've missed you." I drew her into a hug. "You are always my daughter. No matter what. I love you, and that never changes."

She sniffled and leaned back. "I'm sure you haven't liked me much."

I wouldn't admit that, but I couldn't stop my lip from twitching. She grinned and kissed my cheek.

"I'm going to stay on for a while. Dad rented the townhouse for the whole month of June. Maybe we can go for coffee or dinner?"

It took everything in me not to question her about the new job in Tennessee. From what Gage said, she just started it. Stay in your lane, I reminded myself. This was Nikki's life, not mine.

"I'd love that. Anytime." I squeezed her tight again. "Look at what I've found this morning." I showed her my treasures and explained how I wanted to use them. After several minutes, someone called both of our names. Cindy and Jasmine stood at the top of the beach.

"What's up?" Nikki asked.

Cindy waved. "Y'all gotta come here. Quick."

Nikki and I rushed up the sand. I could barely catch my breath thinking of all the horrible things that might have happened. Was Rusty okay? Did the lock not hold again, and he got out? We reached the street. I grabbed Cindy's arm. "What happened? Is it my cat?"

She tipped her head. "No, he's fine. But you have to come to the townhouse. Follow me."

Chapter Nineteen

Cindy opened the door, and we followed her and Jasmine inside. Gage stood in the middle of the living room, dressed in a suit and my favorite dark blue tie, more handsome than ever. His cologne, woodsy and masculine, reached me. I'd always loved the scent.

"What's going on?" I ran my hands down his lapels. "You look great. Are you on your way to work?"

Gage got down on one knee. Behind me, Cindy, Jasmine, and Nikki gasped.

"What are you doing?" I reached for him. "Gage?"

He held out a small box wrapped in silver paper. "Karah, I've never stopped loving you. I knew it before you were going to be arrested, and I know it now." He shook his head, tears welling up in his eyes. "I knew it when we got divorced too." His voice was husky.

My legs trembled. I still loved him. If we actually talked then, we might not be here now. "Gage?" I repeated.

He handed the gift to me. "Open this."

I tore off the wrapping and lifted the top from the box. Inside, nestled in a bed of green tissue paper, lay a beautiful silver band covered in tiny diamond chips. "Gage." I couldn't think of anything else to say.

He stood, took my hand with one hand, and held the ring with the other. "This is a promise ring, Karah. A promise to stay by your side. To support you with love and be your best friend. I promise not to give up or be lazy."

I cocked an eyebrow.

He chuckled. "Okay, I'll work on picking up after myself. I promise. If you'll have me?" Worry lines crossed his forehead.

I smoothed them with my thumb, relishing the chance to touch and be close to him. "Yes." I hesitated, and his worry lines reappeared. "We need to do some things differently."

He released a huge sigh, and his shoulders drooped with relief. "I agree." He led me to the couch and slipped the ring on the fourth finger of my left hand. "I thought we could date?"

"Nikki said you're going home."

"Only to get a few more things. I still have several weeks here at the townhouse. I hoped we could spend time together and ..." He shrugged. "Get to know each other again."

The love in his eyes filled me with warmth and peace. We could do this. I was sure of it. "I'd like that." I turned to where Nikki stood with her friends. "Come here, honey."

She joined us, perching on the edge of the coffee table.

"This is y'all's relationship, not mine." She fiddled with her hair.

"That's true," I said. "I would like to prevent it from becoming one side or the other. I think we have a lot to work on. As a family."

"I'm willing to do that," she said.

"Me too," Gage said. "You two are my life." He put one arm

around me and one around Nikki and held us tight, whispering a prayer of hope, love, and commitment.

THE END

102

About Jen Dodrill

Jen Dodrill is living out her dreams on the pages of her books, bringing readers compelling stories of inspiration and hope for good times and bad.

As a mother of five, she cherishes the time she has now to tell her stories in between her honored role as Grandma, her passion for reading, and her adoration of all things coffee.

Her first book, *Birds Alive! An Empty-nesters Cozy Mystery* released in 2024. Book 2 in the series, *Where's the Quetzal*, came out in February 2025. Book 3, *No Egrets*, will be published in 2026.

For information about Jen, her books, and more, check out her blog: https://jendodrillwrites.com.

Trinity Sands Treasure Hunt

Sharon H. Carpenter

Chapter One

"Everything you brought to the curb needs to go back where it came from."

At the sound of the deep, chipped-ice voice, Claire Anderson tugged a bit too hard on the oversized box and landed on her rear when the cardboard gave way. She tried to blow her hair from her eyes, but strands of it stuck to her forehead. Sweat rivers ran through the wrinkles around her eyes like tributaries off a major waterway. Great. Just how she wanted to meet the neighbors.

Claire had spent half the day and too much energy getting out-of-date canned goods, stale pasta, beans, and unidentified frozen food out of the kitchen and into boxes to be taken to the curb. No way was she taking the stuff back inside.

"Excuse me? Are you trying to make me break a hip?" Claire craned her neck to see the man disrupting her progress. With the Florida sun behind him and shades covering his eyes, she couldn't make out his face, but he was wide in the shoulders, lean in the hips, and wearing a pristine white shirt and khaki slacks. Who dressed like that in the dripping Florida heat and humidity?

"Not hardly, ma'am. But you cannot leave garbage out in your driveway. It is unsightly and attracts animals. You don't want raccoons and gators in your yard. Not to mention, no one is coming to pick it up."

The icicle voice had melted a bit. As she stood, Claire could see his squared jaw, dimpled chin, and abundant greying dark hair. And the smirk that crossed his face.

"Who do you think you are? The trash police? Besides, I was told the garbage truck is coming this afternoon."

"Ma'am, I am exactly that, among other things. Ben Hastings. Director of Security and enforcer of the homeowners' covenants for Trinity Sands. The truck does pick up this afternoon, but not on the street. Didn't you notice the dumpsters?"

Claire looked at her neighbors' driveways and saw the lack of bins. She realized that somewhere in all the paperwork was pertinent information she might need to read. Oops. She wasn't in suburban Louisville anymore—nor in New York City or any of the other myriad places she had lived. Looks like life in a Florida beach community would be totally different from anything she knew.

"Ooh-kay. Looks like I may have missed a few details about living here. So, trash day is Thursday, but take it to the dumpster at any time, right? I guess Saturday's yard sale is a no-go?" Claire glanced at Ben to see if she'd hit a nerve.

"I just hope you didn't waste your time and money advertising it, because yard sales are a definite no." Ben peered at her over his shades. "Have you even read the covenants, Mrs ...?"

"It's Claire. Claire Anderson. And the title is *doctor*. I

haven't had the time—" She crossed her fingers behind her back. "—but I'll get around to reading them soon."

"Well, Dr. Anderson, see that you do." Ben smiled, and his tone defrosted a bit more. "Are you setting up a practice here in Trinity Sands? And what does Mr. Dr. Anderson do?"

"I earned a doctorate in Art History and taught all over the Pacific Northwest, New England, and even Kentucky until I retired. And, no. There is no 'Mr. Dr.'" Claire glared at the nosey rule enforcer for pressing a sensitive spot in her psyche.

"Whoa. Sorry. I didn't intend to offend." Ben took his glasses off and looked her in the eye. "Let's try again. My name is Ben. Welcome to Trinity Sands. It's very nice to meet you."

"I guess I was a bit thin-skinned. Yes. Let's start over." Clair rolled her eyes and smiled at the absurdity. "It's nice to meet you as well, Ben. My name is Claire, and I think I am going to like it here."

Relaxing his stance, Ben admired the front porch. "I didn't realize Marty Olsen's bungalow had gone up for sale already."

"Oh, I didn't buy it. I inherited it. Marty is—was ... my uncle." She had a hard time remembering he was gone. "His death was such a shock. The suddenness of it made me realize it was time to retire and do the things I've always wanted to do. Uncle Marty was so vibrant and full of life. Then, gone." Claire snapped her fingers. "All because he fumbled his feet and hit his head on the edge of the fireplace. Who even needs a fireplace in Florida? It was so senseless. But that's the short version of why I'm here."

"Marty's death shocked everyone," Ben said. "We had plans to go fishing the next day. He said he wanted to discuss a problem with me. He wasn't one to complain about the neighbors. I don't know what was on his mind."

"Huh. Uncle Marty called me and left a message referring to his new project. But he didn't give me any details. I'm not sure which project he was talking about. He had so many things going on. He was getting new pieces ready for an exhibit in January."

"Can't help you with that. He didn't talk art with me. When it comes to art, I'm just a guy who knows what I like but can't really tell you why." A slow grin appeared on Ben's face.

Realizing she had been chatting long enough to turn pink-shouldered, Claire moved toward the porch, confused by Ben's look of interest. Surely, she was mistaken. How could Mr. Perfect be interested in her? She looked and felt like an overheated goat. And not the "greatest of all time" kind, either.

But Ben stepped onto the porch with her, reaching to open the door and let her pass. A real live Southern gentleman.

Ben chuckled as he unloaded bags of garbage from his golf cart into the dumpster. The prominently placed, large steel container was visible to all who lived in the neighborhood, if they bothered to look. Or at least read the signs. The pretty, silver-haired lady might have a doctorate, but it wasn't in common sense.

Oof. That wasn't very kind. Since giving his life to Christ, he was working on WWJS—what would Jesus say? Claire arrived after dark last night, so it stood to reason she hadn't seen the dumpster.

Zipping back to her bungalow to see if she needed anything else, Ben parked the golf cart and climbed out. He took the porch steps two at a time and spotted her watering her potted plants. "Hey, Claire! How about a quick tour of the Beach Club? I don't want to fine or ticket you because you didn't know something."

"What? Can you do that?" Claire's turquoise eyes widened.

"Of course, as the de facto law enforcement for Trinity Sands Beach Club, I can give tickets and assess fines. If we take a ride, you can get better acquainted with the property and the amenities." *And me.*

"I guess I'd better go with you, then Officer." She chuckled. "I can't afford a ticket now that I'm retired."

Claire put on a ball cap and pulled her hair through the back loop. On the front was embroidered a multicolored "Hang Loose." Ben looked forward to finding out if it was just a logo, or was it a motto for the pretty, silver-haired lady?

Chapter Two

The Florida morning sun peeped over the rooftops as Claire finished breakfast beside her pool.

"Mm." She sighed and sipped coffee from her favorite mug.

Yesterday's golf cart tour of the property revealed vibrant landscaping and a naturally beautiful island. The Gulf was captivating, and the onsite restaurant, tennis courts, pool, and spa made Trinity Sands Beach Club luxurious. But who would have thought the most interesting amenity, by far, was her tour guide?

As she went inside to clean her dishes, she smiled, thinking about the handsome Director of Security's dry wit and thought-provoking observations. He wasn't just a pretty face and a fine form—he had an engaging mind that made him dangerously attractive. She had to keep reminding herself she had been burned before and even when trust was earned, it wasn't always reliable.

"Halloo! Halloo! Are you home?" The strident voice jerked Claire from her musings.

"Coming!" She yelled while muttering, "Hold your horses,"

under her breath. The backyard oasis of garden, porch, and pool had already been earmarked "private" in Claire's mind. Whoever was at the French doors needed a sign to read. That could be arranged.

Claire opened the door, but the hot rebuke she had planned evaporated as her jaw dropped. Standing in front of her was a misplaced model sporting a black bikini and flowing cover-up that covered little and accentuated a lot. Long dark hair fell below her shoulder blades. A pair of sunglasses used as a headband kept it from getting in her eyes. Nary a laugh line was found around kohl-shaded blue eyes that looked past Claire into her living area and kitchen.

Red lips parted to reveal beautiful veneers. "Hallo. I wanted to be the first to welcome you to our little piece of paradise. I'm Rene Harrington, and this is my husband, Vic." She pointed her perfectly manicured hand toward a man standing by the pool. He nodded but kept his face averted. Rene slid past Claire into the kitchen and set a turquoise bakery box on the counter. "We brought you a little welcome gift. I hope you like key lime. Maude's macrons are to die for."

Claire stumbled back into her home, leaving an opening for Vic to stride right in. She hadn't even had a chance to say hello, much less ask her visitors to use the front door instead of coming around the back, and they were already in her house. "Well, um, thank you, but ..."

"Oh! No need to thank me. What are next-door neighbors for if not to make you welcome? We want you to come for dinner tonight so we can introduce you around," Rene gushed while walking to the bookshelves and trailing her red nails across the book spines.

"Again, thank you. But I'm just moving in ..."

"All the more reason to come for dinner," Vic said.

Claire jumped. She had been watching Rene, so she hadn't

noticed Vic was in the living room. What was he doing all the way over there?

"No." She hardened her voice yet tried to remain polite. "Thank you. I am not ready to meet neighbors yet, but maybe later. Where did you say you live? Next door?"

Rene and Vic exchanged glances as she moved to join him by the French doors. "Ours is the house with the pink bougainvillea on the front porch. You can't miss it. And we'll be sure to have our little soiree another time since you're busy. Ta-ta." And they bulldozed out of the house just like they'd entered.

Claire let out a deep breath. They hadn't even asked her name.

The sound of the birds greeting the morning soothed Claire's nerves after the strange encounter with her neighbors and a restless night. Uncle Marty's aesthetic for his bungalow almost perfectly matched Claire's taste. She nestled into the pillows of the porch swing and breathed in the coastal air as she sipped her coffee, thinking they had been cut from the same cloth. He was so much more than her mother's brother. Oh, how she missed him.

Claire watched Ben's golf cart zip down the lane and stop in front of her porch. His long legs unfolded as he ducked to get out of the vehicle, whistling a vaguely familiar tune.

"Hi, Ben. Nice morning, huh?"

"Hey. Just dropped by to see if you needed anything. I see you have the essentials." He pointed to her cup of coffee. His smile showed off white teeth, the front two a bit crooked.

"Can I offer you a cup? It's good. I learned how to brew it during my time in Seattle." Ben nodded and requested it black.

She went inside to get his cup. When she returned to the porch, she tried in vain to place the song he was whistling.

"Are you always so cheerful in the mornings?"

"Before I get my day started, I look at the beauty of this place. It makes me thankful for another day. The birds remind me to praise the One who made me, the ocean lets me know He is holy, and the sunrise tells me of His faithfulness." Ben ducked his head and sipped his coffee.

"Wow! And I thought you just got up in a good mood." Claire walked to the other side of the porch, uncomfortable with the conversation. At one time, she believed all those things, but time and circumstances had eroded her faith—faith in men and faith in God.

"So ... what's on the agenda today?" Ben's question jolted her from her memories. "Coffee's good."

Claire smiled at the compliment. "Thanks."

She closed her eyes and breathed deeply to settle her mind and focus. It was the first step in her ritual to devise a logical plan. She opened her eyes to see Ben's questioning face, green eyes twinkling as they met hers.

"You know, I'm not sure I even have an agenda yet. I haven't been exercising like I should, so I am going to start today with a walk on the beach before it gets too hot. Since you aren't wearing your spiffy uniform from yesterday, do you want to come?"

"Spoken like a native." Ben looked down at his white golf shirt with the Trinity Sands logo, khaki shorts, and tennis shoes, then slanted a teasing smile at Claire. "You think I'm spiffy? Those were my class A's—the ones I wear to impress. Looks like mission accomplished. These are comfortable and utilitarian. Great for patrolling the beach." With a grin he gestured toward the sidewalk that led past the lagoons toward the beach access.

Uh-oh. His pearly whites were dangerous. She ignored the

tingle of awareness and walked past him toward the sand and water, reminding herself they weren't even friends yet, which was probably all they would be. She learned her lesson about handsome men years ago and wouldn't be so gullible again. "I said your uniform was spiffy, not that I was impressed."

* * *

Ben silently thanked God for the breeze. Sweat trickled down his spine, and he attributed it to the heat of the day even though it was still early. He pushed his sunglasses up by the nosepiece, cutting his eyes toward Claire. He wanted to mention sunscreen because he would hate for her shoulders to go from sun-kissed to sunburned, but he valued his head and their burgeoning friendship.

As they approached the bridge over the lagoon, Ben scanned the water's edge to see if Annie, the resident alligator, was sunning herself. She was in the water, eyes and nose out, slowly swimming.

"Claire." Ben reached out and touched her arm. She jumped. Did she feel the sizzle too? "Look to your left, about ten o'clock. I want you to meet Annie."

Claire gasped. "An alligator? Are you going to call animal control and get it out of here? That's a dangerous animal."

Ben leaned back against the rail, not trying to contain his amusement. "Yep, Annie could be dangerous. The fence around the lagoon encourages her to stay in her area, but even more to keep people from encroaching. The no-feeding signs are so she doesn't think of humans as breathing vending machines. Just be aware and give her space."

"The Nature Preserve protects the island's wildlife, right?"

Ben's brows raised in respect. The lady knew her stuff. "Yeah, they do. Getting people to abide by the no-feeding rule is tricky. People don't realize that if the animals start seeing them as breathing vending machines, the animals will start searching them out. Especially gators. Annie may be part of the community, but she isn't a pet, so people can't treat her like a dog."

"Well, I'm glad you waited to introduce me in the daytime. I don't think I would have enjoyed meeting her on a moonless night."

"Gators' eyes glow in the dark." He grinned at her shudder.

"Let's head to the beach. Dolphins are more my style."

Ben was surprised at how much he enjoyed Claire's company. Her sharp wit and intelligence made conversation fun, and she wasn't hard to look at either. As they passed other tenants he stopped and introduced Claire. He saw the looks of curiosity and admiration that she got from many of the men, but she didn't seem to notice. Why wouldn't they admire her? She was lovely. Silver hair and sparkling turquoise eyes set off a face that might not launch a thousand ships, but it sure would be a beautiful sight to come home to. Whoa ... where did that thought come from? He reminded himself that she was a new owner, and he was only helping her get settled in.

Chapter Three

Claire pulled herself out of the small lap pool in her back garden. Thank you, Uncle Marty, for splurging on such luxury. The walk to the beach and back hadn't been great exercise because she and Ben kept stopping to chat and meet neighbors.

He seemed to know everyone and was anxious to introduce her, but he was unnaturally quiet on the walk home. He had been very easy to talk to ever since they met, but suddenly, he had nothing to say. Proof that she was wise to ignore the sparks between them. He probably didn't even feel them. She was just part of his job, and he was a nice man, if a bit of a flirt.

Mentally settling Ben safely in the friend zone, Claire changed out of her swimsuit and put on a cool sundress she could work in. It was time to tackle the studio.

She climbed the wooden staircase and leaned against the doorway of the upstairs room. Thoughts of the sunshine-filled room melted the icebox where she had stuffed her emotions, and the tears began to fall. She hadn't been able to face the workspace since her arrival.

Claire remembered this beautiful space—the entire second floor with a closet tucked into one corner and a bathroom into another. Sliding picture windows on each wall filled the area with natural light, and there were copious inset ceiling lights for the times natural light wasn't enough. Shelves with glass jars filled with myriads of trinkets occupied the rest of the wall space.

Even though she and Uncle Marty were both mixed-media artists, Uncle Marty used mostly recycled goods, baubles, and artifacts, along with paint and other traditional mediums. Claire's style was more earthy, so she tended to use natural materials. A large worktable with storage drawers for supplies underneath it was in the middle of the room and held unfinished projects, drawings, and various supplies. It really was the perfect studio. She had shared it with Uncle Marty on her infrequent visits—at his invitation. The reality of his death was unavoidable without him here to embody the space.

She cried for the opportunities not taken and those that would never come again. But mostly, she cried because her mother's brother had been her only family. Now he was gone, and she was truly alone.

Pulling a tissue from her sundress pocket, Claire wiped her eyes, blew her nose, and took a deep breath. She opened the door to the studio and stopped. The lovely space of her memories was nothing like she remembered. The room was a mess.

Papers crinkled as Claire stepped into the room. Her foot slipped on a golf ball hidden under the debris. Beads, paste jewels, and antique keys littered the table and the floor. The jars had been dumped, and the contents were scattered on the shelves. Paint brushes were strewn throughout the room, and paint had been slung onto the floor, the walls, and the ceiling, as if someone had been in a raging frenzy. The sink was littered with sand and shells. The only intact item was a jar of turpentine that was turned on its side but unopened.

Claire's pulse rate soared. This was totally unlike Uncle Marty. What had he been doing? This was much more than disorganization. It looked like the studio had been ransacked. But she couldn't be sure since she didn't know what it looked like when Uncle Marty died. She'd look foolish if she called the police because when they asked questions, "I don't know" was the only answer she'd have.

She—spent all afternoon sorting through the trinkets, baubles, and various items, trying to clean the area until her stomach rumbled, signaling it was time to eat. Descending the steps, she walked into the well-appointed kitchen, straight to the refrigerator.

When she opened the paneled door, the bright light revealed a jar of grape jelly already turned to sugar, a shriveled apple, half a stick of butter, and three cans of Diet Coke. She'd used all the eggs for breakfast, but surely there was some cheese left. Nope. Last night's grilled cheese sandwich utilized the last of the bread and cheese.

"Looks like a trip to Maude's Market before dinner," she mumbled.

Claire checked her backpack for keys and headed out the kitchen door to the detached garage. Muffled angry words followed by a crash caused her to stop and look toward the neighbor's house. Vic Harrington was standing on his back porch with a shattered planter at his feet. He looked up, dark eyes piercing hers. She lifted her hand in a feeble wave that was preempted by the malevolence in his gaze. Surely, she was overreacting. What reason would Vic have to look at her in such a way? He must have had a bad day.

The garage was another luxury Claire was thankful for. Spacious and clean, it was roomy enough to house her apple-red BMW convertible with vanity plates. Not the most practical car, but it gave her a sense of stability and worth even when she lived as a nomad. Sliding behind the wheel, she clicked her seatbelt in place and turned the key to hear the low purr of the car engine. Top down, she opened the garage door and wheeled out into the sunny street.

* * *

Claire parked in front of the porch steps. She slid out of the car, leaving the top down, and stepped into the shade of the front porch.

"What time warp have I stepped into?" She took off her sunglasses and gaped.

"I don't know about a time warp, but welcome to Maude's!" chuckled a bald older man sitting on a porch rocker.

"Best lemonade in three states." A whiskered ZZ Top lookalike lifted his condensation-covered plastic Solo Cup. "Want some?"

"Maybe later," Claire smiled as she nodded hello.

The third gentleman wore a vintage T-shirt commemorating the 1992 Iron Bowl. He tipped his git-'er-done ball cap and winked. "We can set you up with a good fishing guide if you're interested. I know all the good spots."

This set off a round of fish tales and other lies. Claire took the opportunity to take it all in.

Maude's Market was the go-to place on the island. It had the look of a fish camp that had weathered all the storms in the past century, plus a bit of technology. The porch had signs hanging on the wall advertising live bait, and pool noodles stood in the large crock in the corner. A large television hung beside the door advertising the weekly sales, lunch special offerings, and daily flavor of beautiful homemade cookies in a turquoise pastry box.

Opening the door, Claire was blasted by cold air, which caused her to shiver after the heat of the day. The inside of the market was a study in contrasts that delighted her artistic heart. The fishy smell of shrimp on ice battled with the scents of fresh-baked bread, deli cheeses and meats, and flowers. Classic country music played overhead.

A lively conversation between two businessman types about the Kiwanis Club pancake breakfast while a group of teenagers debated the probability of the Fourth of July fireworks on the beach.

The outside of the store looked right out of the 1940s Florida swamp, but the inside had fresh neutral paint, bright lights, and colorful fruits and vegetables, as well as canned goods and pantry items. Fish camp meets bougie. Something for everyone.

"Hey! I've been waiting for you to come in."

Chapter Four

Claire looked behind her and to the sides. Who was the checker with a beehive hairdo talking to?

"Lady with the fancy car, I want to meet you."

She was the "lady" being singled out by the checker. Claire wheeled her buggy a little closer to the register so she didn't have to yell. "Are you speaking to me?"

"I surely am," the bottled blonde crone said. "Name's Maude, and I own this place. I know everybody around here, but I don't know you, so I'm going to assume you're Marty's girl. Am I right?" She grinned, showing a full set of bright white dentures, and a road map to her life in the Florida sun all over her face. She must have opened the store before time began.

"I guess you could call me that. My name is Claire Anderson. Marty was my uncle."

"I figured it was you. Nice to meet-cha." Maude chuckled and clapped her arthritic hands together, seemingly delighted with her deductive prowess. She yelled to the middle-aged stockboy, "Hey, Dover! I was right. This is Marty's girl, Claire." Dover grunted and gave a thumbs-up.

Claire glanced around in embarrassment. Yep. She was the center of attention.

"Umm, it's nice to meet you, Maude. I need to get my groceries and get back, so I'll just ..." Claire nodded and stepped back to her cart.

"You just do what you need to, and we'll talk when you check out. Go along and buy lots of good stuff."

Claire went over to the produce, conscious of being on display. She smiled at the young mom in the sundress, who smiled back as her two-year-old whined for apples. A lady about her age introduced herself and invited Claire to yoga class at the community church on Tuesdays and Thursdays. In the bakery section, she selected a baguette, and the woman behind the counter offered her a delicious cookie as a welcome gift. On every aisle, someone smiled or nodded a welcome. The folks in the store were making her feel like she could become part of the community.

Claire wheeled her cart toward the flower display, still with a strange awareness of being observed. She had spoken to almost everyone in the market. Glancing around, no one seemed to be paying her any particular attention. Then, her eyes landed on two men standing by the mangos. Both were dressed casually, yet somehow out of place. They were wearing the obligatory sunglasses on their heads, tropical-tailored shirts, and shorts. She couldn't tell whether or not they were actually looking at her, but their heads were angled toward her.

Weird.

If what she saw on TV was accurate in real life, their appearance screamed upscale Miami tourists, not panhandle solar shirt vacationers. If so, how did they take a left turn to Trinity Sands, of all places?

Finished with her shopping and ready to go home and make something to eat, she got into Maude's checkout lane, mentally preparing for the verbal onslaught. She wasn't disappointed.

"Well, honey, I'm glad you're here. I was so sad to hear that Marty had keeled over. He was a good man, and a real looker. If I'd been in the market, I might've landed that one. He came in here almost every day and got a pastrami sandwich. He hadn't been in to see me in quite a few days, which wasn't like Marty. So when I heard, I thought he'd gotten sick and croaked. Come to find out, he was just clumsy. I guess it's true—you gotta be ready to meet your Maker at any time."

Before Claire could respond, Maude took a breath and changed subjects.

"So, where ya from? People come in here for the news. I gotta have the answers."

"Umm, I don't think—"

"Aw, you don't have to think, honey. Just tell me about that fancy car ya got out there. Did you buy it with what Marty left ya? You're lookin' pretty good, toolin' around in that little red sports car."

"Thank you? But I'd rather just get to know people slowly."

Maude kept talking over her as she rang up her groceries, hands waving in the air. "People want to know about newcomers, and they come here for the answers. They can have facts from you or facts from me, but either way, they're gonna get the facts." She smiled, cutting her eyes toward Claire as if assessing her reaction to this brazen statement.

What could this woman possibly say about her? "You mean you, uh, you'd, um, lie about me?"

"Oh, no, honey! Never would I lie. But it's like this—I've got a keen eye, and I'm always watching." She squinted, making her point. "I know you didn't just buy that pretty little car and that it means a lot to you because those personalized plates take time to get."

She pointed to Claire's Beemer. "Also, the plate is from Kentucky, so you got it before you moved here. I know you're an artist like your uncle, or you want to be, 'cause your license plate says ARTZDR." She sounded it out phonetically to figure it out. "And you've got some spice in you, driving a red-hot sports car. So, how'd I do? Facts?" She grinned.

Claire's eyes widened as she acknowledged that Maude had correctly surmised many things about her. "I don't know about being spicy, but I do like the color red." She smiled and shook her head. "I think I'm going to leave while I can. Thanks, Maude. This has certainly been an experience." She gathered her bags of groceries to go to her car.

Maude leaned over, voice lowered. "Claire, no foolin' right now, ya hear. See those tourists?" She nodded toward the Miami types who were exiting the store. "They've been watching you like my son watches a Bama fourth down in the fourth quarter of a playoff game. Do you know 'em? You're a pretty little girl, and they're not from the island."

A "pretty little girl"? At her age? "No, I think they just heard you greet me when I came in and are curious," Claire whispered back. "I'm sure it's fine, Maude."

"You be careful, that's all."

Waving to Maude, Claire walked out the doors into the heat and humidity, stopping to put on her sunglasses and avoid the glare of the late afternoon sun. The old men were still shooting the breeze, wearing out the rocking chairs, so she nodded to them as she stepped off the porch and over to her car. Lifting her grocery bags into the back seat, she noticed from the corner of her eye that a black SUV with tinted windows was idling in the parking lot. She couldn't see in, but maybe someone had been watching her, like Maude said.

"Hey, Claire!" She raised her eyebrows and turned toward git-'er-done. He shrugged. "Heard Maude call you

Claire. Name's Hank. My brothers are JT and Rich. We need to ask you something about your little red car. Come on over here."

She walked back onto the porch. JT or Rich leaned over and thumbed toward the SUV. "Missy, something strange is going on with the boys in that black wagon. Are they waiting on you?"

The old men seemed to have her best interest at heart, so she couldn't be annoyed. But was everyone going to stay in her business?

"I don't think so, but there's no sense speculating when I can go ask." She left the porch, walking deliberately toward the SUV. Direct action usually yielded better results than gossip and hypothesizing. Before she got into the parking lot the SUV backed into her fender, then peeled out, slinging gravel as it sped away. So much for waiting on her.

Turning west on Ferry Road, Ben swerved to the right as a big black SUV barreled down the middle of the road. Another coat of paint, and his not-quite-new truck would have taken a hit.

"Where's the fire? He'd clock at eighty, for sure." Flashing back to his time as Military Police, muscle memory had Ben pulling a U-turn and reaching for his nonexistent siren and lights—and mentally taking down the Florida license plate. It only took a hundred yards for the reality of retirement to kick in. He pulled over, took a couple of deep breaths to quiet the rush of adrenaline, and then turned the truck around to continue on his way.

"Tourists doing eighty in a thirty-five-mph zone. Somebody's gonna get killed." Still muttering, Ben turned toward Maude's Market, in need of a soft drink. The little red convertible parked by the porch steps caught his eye, but the silver-haired beauty beside the car kept it.

Claire was crouched by the rear side of her car, smoothing her hand over the fender.

"What's the problem?"

"How dare they! What a blatant disregard for someone else's property! I'm calling the police over this." She stood up, visibly shaking.

"What's going on? Who are you calling the police about?"

Hank lifted his gnarled hand and waved Ben over. "Hey-o, Ben! You know Claire?"

"Yeah, Hank, we're acquainted. Whatcha know?"

"Little Missy here, she attracted some attention from some tourist types." The porch sitters nodded their heads at Hank's assessment.

Claire snorted, glaring at the old man with her hands fisted on her hips. "Little Missy? My name's Claire Anderson. And I'll have you know, I'm a full-grown woman."

She turned her glare to Ben. "The problem isn't that they supposedly were watching and waiting for me. The problem is that they backed into my car, then spun out of the parking lot, throwing rocks as they went. They need to pay for any damages." As she talked her voice broke.

Hank snorted. "That's making a mountain out of a molehill."

Her glare crumbled.

TJ slapped his knee. "That car's gonna get dinged every time you park in Maude's parking lot."

Her eyes filled.

Oh, no. Not tears. He needed to fix this. A good body shop —wait. What did she say?

"What do you mean watching and waiting for you?" He looked at the old men for confirmation.

"Yep. Wondered if you'd pick up on that." Rheumy eyes twinkled under JT's bushy eyebrows.

"Acquainted, huh?" Hank elbowed his brother Rich, whose yellowed teeth could be seen beyond his snowy white facial hair.

"Claire? Explain, please." Ben crossed his arms across his chest, assuming his natural authoritative stance.

When she tried to make light of her unease and the observations of the three octogenarian brothers, Ben wasn't buying it. He'd learned long ago to trust his gut. The black SUV that ran him off the road was most likely the same men from Maude's Market.

Coincidence? Not in his experience.

Chapter Five

Claire poured her morning coffee, still grumbling about flying gravel, a dented bumper, and a certain high-handed security man who acted like she was overreacting. Having filled out a police report at the market and called her insurance company, she needed to find the best body shop to work on her Beemer. She frowned, thinking about the offending fender and the need to get her prized car to the shop before any rust or deterioration started.

Coffee in hand, she drug her dirty clothes into the laundry room off the kitchen. A large window over the folding table gave a clear view into Rene and Vic Harrington's backyard. As she loaded the washer, movement from the window caught her eye. Her neighbors had come out to their covered porch in what looked like an intense conversation.

Vic's head inclined toward Rene, and his hands whipped through the air. Even though Rene was a little louder, Claire couldn't distinguish their words. Rene's tight shoulders and black streaks running down her face suggested tears were involved. She tensed. Was Vic going to hit his wife? Claire was glad to see his hands didn't land.

The couple went back inside, leaving Claire's memories to lead her down a dark road into the past. Loud accusations, recriminations, tears, and wounded hearts. Especially hers. She shook her head as if to dislodge the picture show in her brain.

She climbed the stairs to the studio, determined to purge unwanted memories by delving into the notebooks and journals that had been hidden behind stacked canvases. It was the only area of the studio that hadn't been trashed. Since she had set the studio to rights, cleaned the mess, and sorted through the debris, she was anxious to go back upstairs and get inspired.

The first notebook she opened contained sketches of project ideas to put in the local art gallery, dating back thirty years when Marty came to live at the beach. Some of his sketches had photos taped to the next page with purchase information listed. Others were still in the idea phase. What Claire found most interesting was the list of mediums—paint, plaster, shells, trinkets, jewelry, keys, and so on.

"Uncle Marty,"—she gazed at the ceiling—"you amaze me with your creativity. And organization." She shook her head and smiled at her whimsy. Her long-ago beliefs convinced her Marty was too busy enjoying the delights of heaven to be listening to her mumbling down here.

Since his artwork was part of her inheritance, Claire decided she needed to put a complete compilation on a spreadsheet, but that could wait until she had gone through his notes. When she pulled out the rest of the notebooks and journals, she saw a little door to an inobtrusive wall safe. She tried the knob, and it was unlocked. Opening the door, she found a bowl with all manner of jumbled jewelry. Necklaces, rings, pendants, and loose gems. She poured them onto the work table and started to untangle the chains. These pieces were noticeably different from the jewelry in the jars on the shelf. Weightier. More natural looking. Real?

Knocking came from downstairs, and Ben's muffled voice followed. "Hey, Claire? You home?"

A little thrill went through her at the sound of his voice. Claire called back, "I'm in the studio. Be right there."

Rounding the corner from the stairwell, she smiled when she saw him in his pressed uniform, looking crisp and spit-shined. He certainly was dreamy, but she reminded herself that she'd had romance dreams turn dark with misplaced trust before. *Don't go there. Looking is fine, but don't attach.*

"Morning." Ben's smile reached his eyes. "I called the body shop, and they can get to your Beemer first thing Monday."

"What?" There went dreamy, and here comes nightmare. "I didn't ask you to do that."

"I know you didn't ask me to. I just thought—"

"No. You *didn't* think." The pitch of her voice rose with every word. "Do I look like I need help? Like I need to be controlled?"

"Whoa, lady." His warm eyes flash froze, and his voice hardened. "I don't know who raised your anchor this morning, or why you think being neighborly is controlling. But yes, I *did* think you needed help. That red car seems to mean a lot to you, so I decided to call the best body shop in the area with the best reputation to see if they could do the work for you. I didn't want you to end up at a local chop shop. Your call. I'm out." He turned to leave.

"Wait, Ben." She reached her hand toward him but stopped just short of touching him as he opened the door. "I overreacted, and I'm so sorry." She stepped forward. "You're right. I wouldn't have known where to take her, and I probably would have asked you later this afternoon anyhow."

He stepped back toward her, voice and eyes just a bit less

frosty. "Claire, you're hard to figure out. I'm trying to get to know you, and maybe make myself useful, but you aren't making it easy."

"I know, and I do appreciate you. And as for, what did you call it, raising my anchor? I may have some trust issues. It's the thought of having a man try to control me again."

"Again? What do you mean?"

Claire groaned. She hadn't meant to open up about her ex, but Ben deserved some sort of explanation. "Just unresolved emotional matters. A long time ago, I was engaged. His version of love was changing me more than spending life with me. Everything I did had to be sanctioned by him. He made all the decisions. I realized I couldn't live like that, so I called it off. He broke my trust and my faith in men." She shrugged and looked away, trying to convey to herself and Ben that she wasn't affected by it anymore. She wasn't convinced.

"Claire. Look at me. Please."

She turned to face him.

"I will never try to control you. Your independent spirit and your feistiness drew me to you. I like it. I like *you*. Your ex was a fool to want to change you. Hear me and mark it down. I. Am. No. Fool."

Oh, my! Her face flushed, and she just managed to keep her hand from going to her racing heart.

When he moved to take her in his arms for a hug, Claire sidestepped. Ben's words were like ointment on an abrasion, mending old wounds, but could she step out of the past and allow long-time hurts to heal? Could she choose to trust him? Maybe.

Overwhelmed and needing some space, she ignored his arched brow, slowly blew out her breath, and turned toward the staircase. "Could you come upstairs and look at something I found? It surprised me."

"Whatever you need, Claire." Ben's smirk was back.

Claire hurried upstairs into the studio with Ben behind her. She led him to the worktable and gestured for him to take a look.

He walked around the table, touching the chains, hefting the pendants for weight, and taking one ring in particular, buffing the large red stone on his uniform shirt. Finally, he looked at her with a question and whistled. "Wow. Where did you find all of this?"

"It was in a safe behind the personal books on the bookshelf. I wouldn't have even thought to look for it, but I found it when I moved the large canvases and saw the bookcase. Then I moved the notebooks to the side and took the journals down. It wasn't locked, so they can't be worth very much, right?"

"No, I think these are valuable. And old. Where'd Marty get this stuff? Did it belong to your family?"

"I was afraid you were going to say that. I can't imagine it being family heirlooms, or at least not my family. Besides, I've never seen these pieces before. But why wasn't the safe locked? And I should probably tell you ..." She hesitated.

"Uh-oh. Sounds like you probably should."

"When I came into the studio for the first time, it was a wreck. Like it had been ransacked."

"Definitely, something I want to know." His eyes narrowed as they scanned the room. "That puts a different spin on things. Only Marty could tell us where they came from and why he had them, but we can try to find out. Do you know the combination for the safe so you can lock it?"

"I have an idea, and I also have a little key that could go to it." She checked that the key fit, then closed the door, turned the dial, and tried her mother's birthday backward. It worked. "He always said that was the day his life changed, and everything was in reverse from then on." She chuckled at the memory, then used the reset function to change the combination.

Claire and Ben gathered up the jewelry, put it back in the bowl, and placed it in the safe, making sure to lock it and replace the books. She even replaced the canvasses. Everything looked the same as before.

"Why don't I make us some lunch?"

At the foot of the stairs, Ben took her hand and turned her toward him, giving her time to either consent or run. She looked into his face for any signs of deceit or deflection, and she saw none. With a deep breath, Claire raised her hand to his jaw. "I want to trust you. I have a feeling I'll regret it if I don't at least try."

She lifted her face to meet Ben's lips, but instead, he jerked his head back. "Ouch!" High-pitched barking and growling were coming from a small chihuahua at their feet.

"Where did the rat come from?" Ben kicked his feet to dislodge the animal as he pushed her behind him. "These mutts are death from the ankles down. Watch out."

"Henrietta! Henrietta! Come here, my darling. What are you doing in Mr. Marty's old house? He isn't here anymore, dear. You know that." A stout, balding man in a tropical shirt stuck his head around the open front door. "Hello, there. I'm Charlie Thomas from next door. I see Henrietta has made your acquaintance." Charlie smiled as he peeled the still growling Henrietta's teeth from Ben's pants leg. "She gets so excited meeting new people. Don't you, snookums?"

"Mr. Thomas." Claire nodded. "How did Henrietta get in my house?"

"You must have left the door open. And Henrietta still thinks of this as Mr. Marty's house." Charlie stroked his dog's head. "Marty, Henrietta, and I would beachcomb in the mornings, so she was over here quite a bit. She thinks of it as her home away from home. But we have somewhere to be now. Toodles." He swished out the door, picked up a five-gallon bucket from the porch, and sauntered back to his side of the fence.

"I remember Uncle Marty talking about a Henrietta, but I thought she was a particularly aggressive woman whom he tried to avoid." Claire made sure she closed the door firmly.

"I'd say that the little rat-mutt fits that description. She tore my pants leg. That's not even a dog. A retriever is a dog. Or a shepherd." Ben looked out the front window to make sure the chihuahua was back in its own yard with its owner. "It's an undersized but overrated nuisance.

"He also said something about a nosey neighbor. Could that be Charlie?" She called over her shoulder as she went to the refrigerator to get out the sandwich fixings.

"Not sure. And how could I not have met them before now? I have to check out him and his little mutt." Ben stared hard at the kitchen cabinets opposite the sink and fridge. "But first ..."

"What?" Claire turned around.

Spray-painted words, like bright red blood, dripped down the soft aqua cabinets.

WHERE IS IT?

Chapter Six

B en opened the front door to let in Sgt. Mike Spencer from the Trinity Sands Police Department.

"Hey, Mike. Come on in." He opened the door wide.

"Ben? I thought you retired from investigating?" Mike stepped into the foyer.

"Yep, I'm retired. That's why we called you." Ben rubbed the side of his nose. Not that he didn't want to investigate. Old habits died hard. "Claire Anderson's a friend of mine. I was here when she found the message."

Mike raised an eyebrow.

Claire came into the living room holding out her hand toward the policeman. "I'm Claire Anderson. Thanks for coming so quickly." She crossed her arms in front of her body in a defensive posture.

Ben stepped to her side and placed his hand on her back, aware of Mike's speculative glances between the two of them.

He heard Mike mumble, "Fast work." Ben hoped Claire hadn't heard, but it was good to know Mike understood he planned to be friends—and hopefully more—with Claire for the long haul.

Mike introduced himself to Claire and pulled out his badge. "You said something about a message and a break-in?"

She led the way into the kitchen and pointed to the red mess on the cabinets. "I guess you can call that a message. It might as well be Greek because I have no idea what *it* is. In fact, I've only been here a few days, so whatever the message is might not even be meant for me."

"I'm assuming you didn't touch or move anything?"

"Dude." Ben side-eyed him with a frown. "I haven't been retired that long."

"Ben wouldn't let me touch a thing. And he insisted we call the police." Claire held up her hands.

Mike took pictures and collected evidence. Ben tried not to look over his shoulder, but once an investigator, always an investigator. He had turned down a job on the police force when he moved to Trinity Sands because he knew he needed a break from regular law enforcement.

Being Head of Security might be "policing light," but it came with perks—great hours, a wonderful location, meeting new people, and still being invited to play on the LEO softball team. And now a budding friendship with a certain lovely, new resident.

Mike finished his report, stood, and started to leave. He hesitated, then turned toward Claire. "Can you think of anything that this might be referring to? Anything that 'it' could be?"

After a couple of heartbeats, she said, "You know, Sergeant, I told you—I have no idea. I really haven't even gotten my bearings in Trinity Sands yet." Her eyes shifted toward Ben, then slid away.

Ben knew she was holding back information, but he wasn't going to call her on it just yet. He trusted her reasons were valid. They would talk later.

"Okay, you have my number. Call if you think of anything I should know. It may just be kids, but lock your doors anyhow. I'm going to talk to the neighbors." Sergeant Mike Spencer left the house. "See you at the next softball practice, Ben."

Ben watched him leave from the doorway, then studied the nearby houses. Across the street, a curtain moved. A big grey fluff of a cat jumped into the window. Next door, Charlie was watering his porch plants with Henrietta in the crook of his arm. If he rubbernecked any farther, he'd turn into a giraffe.

Smoke curled from under the bougainvillea at the Harrington's house. Vic turned from watching Mike and took a long drag from his cigarette, eyes now turned toward Claire's house. With a flick of his fingers, Vic extinguished the coal, pocketed the butt, and disappeared around the side of his house.

Curious. Maybe Ben's investigating days weren't quite over. But for now, he had work to do.

* * *

Claire stretched her back, releasing the tension from hard work and concern. Scrubbing spray paint off cabinets was a tedious task. Too bad Ben couldn't be there to help. "Ursula, I am so thankful you were available this afternoon. There is no way I could have accomplished this without you. Let's sit and have some sweet tea for our efforts."

Ursula's grey corkscrew curls stuck out from under a bandanna, and the muscles on her skinny arms bulged as she poured the bucket of dirty red water down the drain.

"Whew, Miss Claire. I'll take you up on that tea. Whoever the pond scum is who defaced these cabinets sure did a fine mess of it. But we're getting it right again. Although I've got to admit, I'm feeling it." Her bright eyes were a bit dimmed by exhaustion, but the smile lines implied satisfaction with her work.

Claire got the tea pitcher from the refrigerator, put ice in the glasses, and set out her box of cookies from Maude's Market. She arranged everything on a tray and took it to the sunroom that overlooked the pool, calling for Ursula to join her.

"Mm. Long, tall, with a bit of sweat—that's how I like my tea and my men." She flashed a dimpled grin at Claire. "How 'bout you, Miss Claire? I hear that's how you like your men too." Tired eyes twinkled.

"Uh, well … I … um …" She scrambled for something to say. "Well …"

"I'm just pulling your leg. I know you've been seeing Ben, and we all know he's a firecracker. If you're gonna pass, I might even consider him for husband number five. Or is it six?" She laughed out loud and slapped her knees. "Oh, my lands, Miss Claire. You rise to the bait like a hungry catfish. Your face is the prettiest shade of pink with just a touch of green."

Claire resisted the impulse to put her hands to her face, knowing that Ursula was right. She was blushing but probably crimson instead of pink. And her outrageousness had provoked a touch of jealousy. Where had that come from? She didn't own Ben. They weren't even in a relationship.

"Ursula, Uncle Marty said you were a character, and now you've proven it. It feels good to laugh with you after this trying day." She nibbled on a cookie. "I haven't been here long enough to make any enemies. I've only met a few people."

"Well, let me see if I can help get you acquainted. I know most everything worth knowing that goes on around here."

Ursula proceeded to tell Claire more than she could retain about the people who lived at the Beach Club, even about a murder that had happened earlier in the summer.

"The day I moved in, I met my neighbors, Rene and Vic. Rene even invited me to dinner, but I didn't go."

"Well, you might want to take them up on dinner. Heard tell he's a fine chef, even if he is a little loco. And she makes a scrumptious chocolate cake." Ursula smacked her lips. "They travel a lot. Scuba diving, you know. He spearfishes and catches a lot of what he cooks—sort of ocean to table cooking is what he's known for."

"That sounds delicious. I'll be sure to accept if they invite me again."

"Have you met Charlie and Henrietta yet? Charlie was my third husband's brother. He never warmed up to me until dear Carl keeled over dead. He still might not like me, except Henrietta holds a lot of sway with him, and she likes me just fine."

Claire failed to imagine Henrietta liking anyone. "Are you talking about Henrietta the chihuahua? She almost took Ben's leg off."

"Poor Henny is just misunderstood. Ben needs to slip her a bit of cheese or some blueberries. She can be bribed." She grinned and winked. "Ask me how I know."

"I'll tell him that the next time she attacks." Claire didn't want to be nosey, but she wanted to know. "Why do you think Charlie doesn't like you? He seems like a live and let live kind of guy."

"Oh, he's a good sort, but Charlie thinks he and his little doggie are a bit above the ordinary. And me, my folks, we're just common. He thought his brother could do much better. Henrietta? She doesn't put on airs like Charlie. She hates everyone."

Claire smiled, imagining Henrietta with her snooty little nose in the air and her teeth bared. "Does Charlie still think Carl could have done better?"

Ursula's gaze drifted outdoors and far away. "Nope. He knows that I was the best thing that ever happened to that man."

Chapter Seven

Where was Ben? He left right after calling Ursula to help clean up the mess, and Claire hadn't heard from him since. This was not at all what she expected, especially since the look he gave her after she answered Mike's questions.

She'd fully expected a quick reckoning with him about not disclosing the safe and jewelry, but he'd pulled a disappearing act. And had they really almost kissed? She should have anticipated he would make her crazy. She'd never been very good at understanding men.

Intent on putting Ben from her mind, Claire showered and changed into a cool sundress in order to feel human again. She then climbed the stairs to the studio, thinking about all she had learned from Ursula. She would find it difficult to meet some of her neighbors and keep a straight face. A definite downside to listening to gossip. The woman was a wealth of information, even if only some of it was true.

Claire was tired. Physically, mentally, and emotionally.

She took one of the journals off the shelf and opened it to distract herself from spray-painted messages, new neighbors, and secret safes. It was dated the year before. Handwritten notes and websites were scribbled inside. Newspaper clippings were also stapled to the pages. They all seemed to deal with Florida shipwrecks and treasure.

The first was an account of salvage work going on in the Florida Keys by Castillo Salvage, a company out of Miami. A website detailing the work of Spanish university students using new technology to map shipwrecks in the Caribbean. The next was a historical account of a doomed fleet heading home to Spain from Havana with treasures from the Americas. The last one detailed contraband and a lavish cargo rescued from a Spanish galleon wrecked off Ecuador.

What, if anything, did all of this have to do with Uncle Marty, the jewelry, the hidden safe, and cryptic messages?

* * *

The sounds of soft jazz filled the air as Ben stood in front of Claire's bungalow. He breathed in deeply to settle himself. Had that little chihuahua demon-dog thrown a kink in the works, or saved him from making a big mistake? He remembered the blush on Claire's cheeks and how flustered she got when he tried to hug her. Along with her admission that some man had tried to control her and make her into someone she wasn't. He shook his head, unable to even imagine. He didn't want to change her. He was a big fan. But he did want to protect her, even though she might consider it controlling. He needed to tread carefully.

Determined to get to know her, Ben raised his fist to knock. Before his fist met wood, the door opened, and Claire came through it, plowing into his chest. He grabbed her shoulders to steady her, inhaling her crisp, feminine scent and delighting in the softness of her skin.

"Ben." She stepped back, out of his reach. "What are you doing here?"

"Did Ursula help you clean up? I wanted to see if there was anything else you needed." He smiled, appreciating the subtle smudge of eye makeup and the pink gloss on her lips. "And if you're not too tired, do you want to go to dinner? We can walk to the Club House Grille. Stay on site."

He imagined walking in the moonlight afterward, talking about the events of the day. They needed to compare notes and thoughts about the cabinet defacement. And maybe revisit the interrupted moment that wasn't.

"You startled me. I was coming out because I heard something and thought it might be the cabinet tagger coming back for more mischief." She blew out a long breath and then looked into Ben's eyes. "You weren't scratching at the door, were you?"

"Not hardly, but I have been standing here a minute trying to work up the nerve to knock."

Her mouth quirked. Did she think it was funny that he was nervous?

"It must have been you. I've just been a little on edge since this afternoon. But I rarely turn down dinner. Let me lock the doors and get my sandals."

"Make sure you can walk in them. I'll check the doors." This was also a good chance to check the windows as well, make sure there wasn't an easy point of entry while they were gone. He was glad she wasn't scared but using an abundance of caution.

"Do I look okay?" Claire smoothed her skirt and smiled.

He took her hand, looked her up and down, then twirled her slowly around like they were on a dance floor.

"Would it be terribly chauvinistic of me if I wolf whistled, beat my chest, and shouted, 'She's with me'?" He made a playful face at her.

"I don't think that would get you any brownie points. I'm sure you can do better."

"Then I need to think of a way to tell you you're gorgeous without getting myself into too much trouble while we walk." They headed toward the restaurant, holding hands. "It's really hard to be self-aware in these modern times."

"You can do this, caveman," she joked while acknowledging his effort.

"Nice to know you've got faith in me." He hoped it was true as they reached the beach restaurant and checked in at the reservation desk.

As the hostess led them to their table on the beachside porch, Ben scanned the other diners, greeting many of them by name. He may have been on the job for less than a year, but he had made it his business to meet all the year-round residents of Trinity Sands Beach Club as well as the snowbird owners who came down for the winter. Recognizing the vacation renters was more difficult because the turnover was so rapid.

"Thanks, Jaime. Looks like a good crowd tonight." He grinned at the pretty young woman who lived with her grandmother during college breaks. She was a beach girl, tanned and toned, working hard to get back to the University of Florida in the fall. She did a great job at the Grille and had been known to help Ben with names on occasion when his memory failed him. "Have you met Claire Anderson yet?"

"Hi, Claire. I'm Jaime. I'm so sorry for your loss. I loved Mr. Marty, and so did my Gran. He would come in every morning to have breakfast with the grey gang ... and most evenings too. We had some fun conversations. He would tell me he loved the beach and everything about it and then talk about how you couldn't get him in the water on a bet." She chuckled as she wiped her eyes.

"Thanks, Jaime. He was such a character. He loved living here, especially coming to the Grille for what he called family meals with friends." Claire sighed as she reminisced. "And you're right. I'd forgotten, but he had an overpowering fear of the ocean. That's why he splurged on the pool. He loved to swim, but you wouldn't catch him out on the pier over the Gulf."

"That's why he always wanted to fish from shore or go to DeFuniak Springs and fish for bass." Ben's eyes widened, and he nodded as he mentally connected the dots. "I never thought about him being afraid of the ocean, but it makes sense."

He scanned the room again, noting the unfamiliar faces. "Anyone I need to meet, Jaime? Anyone new?"

"Mostly the regulars, and vacay folks tonight. A few tables are off-property diners, but we aren't real busy yet. That's going to be this weekend for the fireworks. The Fourth of July is always a big deal around here."

Motioning the waiter over, Jaime returned to her hostess duties. Ben and Claire placed their order for the catch of the day, relaxed into their chairs, and watched the sun settle into the Gulf. The golden pathway over the water looked like the yellow brick road, but the call of the gulls, waves slapping the shore, and the scent of briny salt reminded Ben that he was already home. He had found his healing place.

* * *

Red snapper a la silver hair wasn't appetizing in the least so Claire clipped her mane into submission. Or she tried. The refreshing breeze coming off the Gulf was ramping up, causing napkins as well as anything not tied down to fly away.

"Do you want to find a table inside?"

"Absolutely not. Maybe when I've lived here a while I'll get tired of this, but being out here with the wind, the setting sun, the ocean ... it's glorious. Just what I need after today." She grinned and looked around at the other diners. "Everyone else seems to be enjoying it as well."

"This is one of my favorite things about living here. Sitting out in the elements. Look inside, and you will see the full-timers." Ben shrugged with a little smirk. "It probably stamps me as a newbie, but I hope to never get tired of living here or take it for granted."

Ben told anecdotes about some of the diners, helping Claire put personalities to faces and remember names. She tried to imagine herself interacting with the people, integrating with the community, feeling like she belonged. It wasn't as far-fetched as she previously thought.

Maybe ...

"Ben." She grabbed his arm and pointed to a corner table inside. "Look."

"What is it?"

"It's them. The guys who dented my Beemer. They're here. Eating at the Grille."

Chapter Eight

Claire threw her napkin on the table and stood, almost turning over her chair. "I'm going over there and giving them a piece of my mind."

"Hold on. Wait a second, Claire. Are you sure that's them? You told me the car had tinted windows. And you never saw who was in the truck. You can't just pop off and start accusing people." He stood up. "Let me go over there and talk to them."

"Oh, no, you don't. I know it was them, and you weren't there." She pointed her finger at his chest, pitch rising. "I really don't need you mansplaining what I know, and I don't need you—"

"Mansplaining? You're going to go there? It's one step forward with you then two steps back." He looked around, took a deep breath and slowly blew it out through his nose. "I'm not mansplaining. I'm trying to help you. But more than that, I have an obligation as the Director of Security. I know you don't need me. That is what you were going to say, isn't it? But I have a job to do, and I'm going to do it."

Ben growled his words through a clenched jaw. Claire could see the frustration pour off him like sweat. And maybe hurt as well. She hadn't known him long, but she knew he was working hard to maintain his cool. He was right. She had been about to say she didn't need him. Because she didn't. But she was beginning to think she *wanted* his help. And maybe she was beginning to trust him?

"All right, Ben. Do your job. Those tourists need to be held responsible for their reckless behavior and disregard for other people. But I'm going with you." She turned to go inside but stopped short. "They're gone."

Claire entered the restaurant with Ben right behind her. She cornered Jaime and asked her where the two men had disappeared, but Jaime didn't remember seating them. They weren't regulars, but townies or off-property diners. Claire circled around to the table where they'd been sitting and scanned the area to see if they were anywhere to be found. They weren't.

Ben bent over, looking at an item on the floor. He took his phone out and snapped a picture, then signaled Jaime and asked her for a clean napkin and a Ziploc bag, which she retrieved from the kitchen.

"What are you doing?" Claire looked under the table, puzzled.

"My job. Maybe more than my job, but that's who I am, and old habits die hard." Using the napkin, he picked up the item and placed it in the baggie, zipping the top. He stood and held the makeshift evidence bag toward her. "Could be nothing. Then again ... I'd rather have evidence I don't need than wish I'd gathered it because it meant something."

Claire leaned over to see what had caught his attention and launched him into super-sleuth mode. It was a pen. With a design. Maybe a logo. It looked like a castle with intertwined letters, C and S. She raised her brows, impressed with his skills, even if it turned out to be nothing.

* * *

A brisk breeze was blowing off the water, and the moonlight cast a silver path out into the Gulf. It was a beautiful evening, full of potential, but Ben felt like kicking sand as he escorted Claire home by way of a walk on the beach.

He bit down on his back molars in frustration. What happened to the romantic evening he'd imagined? The evening was going so well, and then *bam*! They were at a goat rodeo, and he was the goat. Again.

"Are you going to tell me why you are grinding your teeth?"

"Nope." He tried to loosen his jaw.

"You're really tense."

"Yep." Observant, wasn't she? *Breathe in through the nose, out through the mouth. Again. Relax the shoulders. Not so tense now.*

"Was it something I said?"

Ben nearly gave himself whiplash when he looked at her. At least he managed to keep his mouth from dropping open. She wanted to dive head-first into a potentially antagonistic situation. But she didn't want his help or protection. How could she not know it was something she said? He looked straight ahead again, concentrating on continuing to breathe deeply and manage stress.

"Ben, you know that part of being friends is communicating."

Slow boil ... *Lord, don't let me lose my temper ...*

"I really wish you'd talk to me ..."

Oh, no, Jesus, help. Slow boil just started rolling ...

"... but if you're going to sulk—"

And there it is. "Sulk? Is that what you think I'm doing?" His eyes narrowed, and his voice lowered. "I'm not sulking. I am trying to keep from blowing up and destroying whatever we have going on." His neck tendons bulged until he consciously lowered his shoulders. "You say we're friends? Okay, let's go with that. Are we friends?" His voice carried the intensity of his frustration and hurt.

He heard the sniffle, then the quiet, "I hope so. I hope we're friends."

Ben's heart stopped. His temper fizzled from inferno to embers. The emotions that fueled it were bottled and corked when he turned and really looked at Claire for the first time since leaving the Grille.

Her face was pale even in the moonlight. Her mouth was skewed, trying to keep her tears from falling. Not a laugh line was visible. And she wouldn't look at him. When he reached out to tip her chin up, she closed her eyes rather than meet his gaze.

He breathed a desperate prayer. *Oh, Lord, how do I salvage this?*

Ben didn't know whether to touch her or back away and keep talking, but as her throat worked to contain her sobs, he opened his arms. Claire leaned against his chest as her first cries erupted. His arms closed around her as if to shield her from the force of her emotions, pulling her even closer to his heart. He could protect her. *Would* protect her.

But who was going to protect *him?*

* * *

This was not exactly how Claire had imagined being fully embraced in Ben's arms for the first time. With her forehead against his chest, she assessed the situation. Mascara? She couldn't be sure, but she undoubtably looked like a treed raccoon. Snot? Pooling on her upper lip and probably smeared all over his shirt. Hiccupping? The kind that jerked her whole body.

The next hiccup, her head bumped under Ben's chin. She pushed away from his body and took a step back, pretending fascination with his shoes. "Umm. I'm sorry, Ben." She peeked up at him, then back down. If she clicked her heels together, could she disappear? It was worth a try.

"Hey, Claire." His hands were still on her upper arms, rubbing up and down. "Can you look at me?"

"I'd rather not." Anything but.

His hands continued their soothing rhythm.

She took a deep breath, stiffened her spine, and lifted her head. Then she stared at his nose. He leaned down and met her eyes. She'd like to be a coward and close them, but she was made of sterner stuff. She lifted her lips in what she hoped was a smile, but the snot-mustache probably made it look more like a grimace.

Ben pulled a folded, old-fashioned white handkerchief out of his back pocket. "My daddy said I'd need one of these for a pretty woman one day." He handed it to her, and she wiped her nose, keeping the cloth when he indicated he didn't want it back. "I guess today is the day."

"Really. I'm so sorry for breaking down on you like that." Claire took another step back, out of his reach. She replaced his hands with hers, crossing her arms over her body as if to close herself off.

"So ... can you let me in on what happened?"

She took notice of her surroundings as she gathered her

thoughts. They were on the boardwalk in front of the Grille, heading toward the pier. The sky was the deep twilight grey before the night settled in, and the moon cast a glow over the waves rolling toward shore. The wind had died down, but the stiff Gulf breeze still had her hair flying in her face. It could have been a beautiful, romantic evening.

"Do you want to sit or walk while we talk?" She gestured to the bench, then to the pier, brows raised. Ben indicated the bench, so she walked over and sat. "I'm not sure where to start ..."

"Why were you so upset?"

"Because I ruined our evening. You were upset. Like, obviously angry." She cut her eyes toward him, expecting him to deny it.

"You're right. I was, but I'm not now." Elbows on knees, head hung between his shoulders, he nodded. "I started out just frustrated and was praying I wouldn't lose my temper. Lost it anyhow." He turned his head sideways and met her eyes. "I'm sorry. God's still got a lot of work to do on me."

His body, even more than his words, spoke remorse.

"I have an inkling, but why?" She put her hand on his forearm, reaching to make a connection.

"Claire." He shook his head and groaned. "You go barreling into situations that could get you hurt or in trouble. You stomped into the Grille ..."

She scoffed. "I did not stomp."

"... determined to make some men who you saw in a store pay for the paint job to your car." He stood up, facing the waves. "You have someone come into your house and write a threatening message in your kitchen, and you don't miss a beat. Just act like it never happened."

"It wasn't really threatening ..." She grimaced, recalling the red paint that looked like blood.

"You're making my point. You aren't taking this seriously." Hands in his pockets, he started pacing in front of her. "You found what looks like jewels in your house, with no explanation for where they came from. Before that, you suspected someone had ransacked the studio."

He stopped, faced her, and ran both hands through the sides of his hair. "What infuriates me most is you won't let me protect you. And I'm not sure if it's because you don't think it's necessary or if it's just me." He abruptly faced the waves again, shoulders hunched. "You don't want my help."

Claire blinked rapidly to keep the welling tears at bay. If Ben noticed, she hoped he would think it was just the wind. Was he right? Were all these incidents more serious than she wanted to admit?

"I don't want to believe someone is threatening me. Why would they? It makes no sense. But when you string all the strange incidents together and say it like that, it does feel more malevolent." She shivered in the heat. "But even then, I can take care of myself. I always have. I've learned not to depend on other people."

He pivoted and faced her, staring. What was he thinking? Fleeting emotions registered on his face faster than she could process. Finally, he spoke.

"That's an indictment of the people around you. I hate it for you. Who taught you not to trust or depend on anyone else?" His eyes pled for transparency.

"Everyone. I told you before, I'm independent. And capable." She lifted her chin in defiance. "I don't need you or anyone to protect me." When he sighed, her voice softened. "But one thing you got wrong. I choose to trust you. And I want you as my friend."

"Your friend?" His voice was rich with underlying meaning that she chose not to understand. His gaze searched hers but then shuttered. Jaw set, he nodded and held out his hand. "Okay then, friend. Let's walk home."

She should be happy. Her friendship with Ben hadn't been ruined. Why did it feel so lacking, like she had just whiffled the ball in the big game? This was how she wanted it—wasn't it? She gave Ben a small smile, then took his hand, comforted by his strong, protective grip.

Chapter Nine

The path from the Grille to the bungalows was a popular evening walk. Neighbors and passers-by were flashing encouraging grins and pointed looks at their linked hands. Ben unentwined their fingers, determined to douse speculation before Ursula and Maude caught wind of it. They would have them married before he even left the friend zone. Holding her hand had been a confusing mistake.

As they approached the lagoon bridge, Ben guided Claire to the rail. They leaned against it, listening to nature's choir. The insects sang the melody, with bullfrogs providing harmony. Small, scurrying animals added percussion to the night music.

"Look. There's Annie." Claire lifted her arm and pointed to the lagoon and glowing orbs.

He turned toward her, finding her shiny eyes much more fascinating than those of the amphibian. The delight on her face overrode caution and his decision to be satisfied with a friendly relationship.

He put his hands on her shoulders and gently pulled her to

him, watching her for any signs of resistance. Her eyes widened. She opened her mouth as if to say something but instead licked her top lip and closed her eyes. He bent his head to hers, almost lip to lip, and breathed deeply. When she leaned in, he met her mouth with his, kissing her first with caution, then confidence. He raised his head and settled hers in the crook of his neck.

"Friends?" He asked with a deep chuckle. "I want that and more."

"Uh-huh." She sighed. "I'm not very good at the more part, which is why I tried to friend-zone you. But maybe..." Her voice was muffled but he could hear the hesitation in her voice. And something else. Was that hope?

"Never been very good at this myself, but I want to give it a go. With you."

He felt her stiffen, then pull back. Oh, no. Too much too fast?

"Ben. Is that Vic and Rene? I think they're in trouble." She pointed across the bridge to the other side of the lagoon.

Ben turned, keeping Claire a bit behind him. There were four figures in the clearing beside the fence. He could see tears on Rene's face, and she was shrinking back behind Vic, whose jaw was clenched, and his hands were fisted at his sides. One of the other people was standing close, arms akimbo, while the other was pacing and pointing at Vic while he talked.

"Hey, Vic," Ben yelled at the same time Vic shoved the nearest man into the other, and chaos reigned. One of the strangers jumped up and landed a punch in Vic's face, then they both ran.

"Stay here." Ben pushed away from Claire and ran across the bridge to break up the fight, but when he got to the scene, Rene was on the ground, silent, with Vic in the grass beside her.

"Ben, help us. Please." Vic wiped his bloody nose with his

forearm. "When he punched me, I fell into Rene, and she hit her head on the fence post."

"I've got this. You go." Claire knelt beside Rene, pushing hair from Rene's forehead to reveal a fast-blooming goose egg. "Go. Catch them. But be careful."

Vic jumped up and ran with Ben in the direction the assailants took toward the bungalows. Ben ran along the most direct route, looking for vehicles that didn't belong or moving shadows until Vic called out that he saw them in the other direction—out toward the Wilds.

Ben pivoted and ran back to Vic, winded. "Are you sure?" Breathing hard. "They're going to be in trouble ... whew ... out there in the dark." *Breathe.* "Even harder to find." He had to take another deep breath, but his heart rate was coming down. "They wore all black. You know them, Vic?"

"I ... uh ... don't know ... give me a minute ..." Vic's breathing was labored. "I know ... I saw them ... go that way ..." He pointed into the dark.

"We've probably lost them. Let me call it in." Ben pulled out his cell phone and dialed.

* * *

Ben and Sgt Mike Spencer stood in the alley behind the Harrington's home, watching the ambulance pull away. The paramedics came and evaluated both Rene and Vic. Vic's blackeye was already beginning to shine, but his cramps had abated. They wanted to transport Rene due to the blow to the head and loss of consciousness, but she refused, more concerned with how to style her hair to disguise the multicolored knot on her forehead. Claire stayed inside to provide moral support.

"My mind wants in the game, but my body's complaining.

It's reminding me I retired from this business. What happened to my cushy job?" Ben rubbed his spasmed back muscles. His sprint through the resort was a good idea at the moment, but he was paying for it. "It's time to get back in the gym on the regular. Softball isn't keeping me in fighting shape."

"Glad you didn't have to slide into home tonight." Mike chuckled, then started talking shop. "You think the Harringtons are on the up and up? Bad guys came on the resort property to randomly mug somebody? And they drew the short straw?"

"I haven't had that kind of trouble since I've been here, so it's unlikely, but not impossible. Criminals are getting dumber by the day. But what bothers me most is why a mugging when they could have broken into the house?" Ben faced the house, brow wrinkled as he noted the points of entry. "Especially when you figure summer clothes, no purse, very little jewelry. All that stuff was at home."

"*Humph.* You have a point. Based on what you and Claire saw, Vic was the target, so it wasn't a sexually based assault." Mike pinched his bottom lip with his fingers, thinking. "Something feels off about this one, Ben. Better keep your eyes open. And keep me on speed dial."

Ben gestured between the Harrington backyard and Claire's garage. "Seems weird that side-by-side residents have both been targeted. Have you heard anything back about the paint?"

"Yeah. It's a marine spray paint. Could've been purchased at any hardware store or boat shop around here. Folks use it for outdoor projects too. Anything weather or water-related." Mike shrugged. "And fingerprints were inconclusive. There isn't much to go on."

Ben shook his head, focused on the proximity between the houses. "You know, Claire keeps saying they tagged the wrong house. I don't think so."

Chapter Ten

The smell of blueberry muffins filled the bungalow. Claire had used the baking time puzzling over the jewels. She processed best with a graphite pencil in her hand, so she got the jewels out of the safe and sketched as she wondered what to do with them. Her representations were good, managing to convey the heft and age of the pieces.

When the buzzer announced the muffins were finished baking, she put the jewels back in the safe, the journals in front of them, and went downstairs to go on with her day, leaving the drawings on the worktable.

She grabbed a mitt and pulled the pans out of the oven, setting them on the counter to cool. They looked and smelled delicious.

Baking was good therapy, especially when she had decisions to make. While she measured and mixed ingredients, her subconscious worked on bigger issues. Like being brave and moving forward with Ben. And calling someone about the jewels. Claire made some phone calls as the muffins cooled.

When she finished speaking to her professional contacts at

the local university, Claire adjusted the napkin covering the pastries. She resisted the urge to pinch a taste test. Some of the muffins were to take to Rene and Vic after their ordeal, and Charlie, just to be neighborly. Others were set aside for coffee with Ben if he came by this morning.

Balancing the basket of muffins on her arm, she locked her front door. Just a couple of days ago, it seemed silly to lock up to go next door, but she didn't want another lecture from Ben. She also didn't want any more surprises.

Walking down the porch steps and over to the Harringtons' house she delighted in the different birdsongs. The sun had already promised a hot day, but the breeze hinted at relief. It was a beautiful summer day, and it seemed like all was right with the world. Until Rene opened the door, and the reality of last night was evident on her face.

"Oh, Rene. How are you feeling today?" Claire tried not to gape. Rene had bruising that seeped from the knot on her forehead up into her hairline. Her eyes were black puddles. She looked like she had gone a few rounds with a world-class boxing kangaroo. And lost. "Do you need an icepack or a steak or something?"

"That would be a waste of a good steak." Rene scoffed and lifted the bag in her hands. "I'll stick to frozen mixed veggies to help with the swelling, thanks." She turned away from the door, gesturing for Claire to come in.

"They won't help with swelling, but blueberry muffins do a body good." Claire smiled as she handed the basket over, looking down and comparing her cut-off shorts and tank top with Rene's model-perfect look. How did she manage? Maybe she should ask for fashion tips over a muffin.

"Yum. The muffins smell great. And they're just in time for breakfast." She sat down and sighed. "I can't thank you and Ben enough for intervening last night. It was so scary,"

"Ben did the rescuing. But I'm glad we were there to help. I hope the police catch these guys."

"Me too. Before anyone really gets hurt."

"I'm glad you're feeling better. I need to get on with my day."

Claire crossed the lawn back to her house, humming that illusive tune Ben seemed to whistle all the time. Yep, looks like that man was getting under her skin. She smiled, amazed at how close they were last night.

She gathered the next basket of muffins to deliver when she felt a tickle of unease between her shoulder blades. Something felt off. Almost like a shift in the air. She looked around the kitchen. Nothing was amiss. It must be her imagination at work.

Locking her front door for the second time in an hour, she stilled. Did she unlock her door to go in? She thought so ... but she couldn't say for sure. Her mind had only been half engaged, if that. She'd been too busy thinking about Ben. She finished locking up after giving herself a mental shake.

Claire stepped up to Charlie's door and noticed his efforts to spruce up his porch. She gave the freshly painted red swing an approving nod and silently complimented the vibrant colors of the cushion. It was such an inviting space. Henrietta's shrill barking broke into her thoughts.

"Henrietta, darlin', who are you announcing?" Charlie could be heard from inside. He looked through the glass door and then opened it wide as he wiped his hands on a white handkerchief. "Oh, Miss Claire. I smell baked goods." He gushed as he smacked his lips together. "I'd invite you in, but I'm still cleaning up after some projects." Red stains smeared his fingers and the fabric that he pushed into his back pocket.

"No problem, Charlie. I just wanted to bring some muffins over for you and Henrietta. The porch looks lovely."

"I've been meaning to spruce things up for a while and finally got around to it. I spend a lot of time out here, you know. Me and Henrietta. Watching over the neighborhood." He gestured for her to join him on the porch swing. They sat side by side, the chihuahua between them.

"I'm sure with Henrietta's help, you don't miss much." She smiled to soften the insinuation that he and the dog were busybodies. Henrietta's ears perked up, so she rubbed one of them.

"Henny and I try not to let anything get by us." Maybe he took being a busybody as a compliment? "We saw the commotion at Rene and Vic's last night. Couldn't hear what was going on, though. You have anything to share?" He pushed up on the swing.

"They just ran into some trouble down by the lagoon bridge. Ben and Sgt Mike helped them out. Everything is fine, though." She pushed down on the swing. Henrietta dozed.

They were swinging in tandem, discussing raising flowers, the weather, and nothing at all, when Ben's whistle came across the yard. That same tune she couldn't get out of her head.

"Morning, Ben." Charlie waved him over. "Claire made muffins."

"Muffins?" He side-eyed her, sitting next to the older man, cuddling the dog. "How do you rate, man?"

Charlie laughed out loud. "Must be Henrietta that rates." He grinned and winked at Ben. "I think some other man caught Miss Claire's eye."

No, nothing got past those two.

Clair felt the color rise to her cheeks. "You, sir, talk too much. These might be the last muffins you get." She stood up, turned, and rubbed Henrietta under the chin. "Make him behave, Henny." Smiling, she returned to her own house.

Chapter Eleven

Ben looked from Charlie to Claire then back to Charlie. Did he miss something? "Man, what did you say? You've run off my girl. Gotta go." He nodded to the older man and ran after Claire, reaching the porch as she started walking up the steps.

"What was that about muffins? Did you save one for me?" He wiggled his eyebrows, hoping to ooze charm. Her laughter made him suspect he wasn't the oozing type, so he reached for her hand instead. "A cup of coffee and a muffin sounds really good."

"I have both, officer, but I'm thinking a donut might be more your style." She smirked as she opened the door and led him into the kitchen.

"You wound me with the stereotype, and remember, I'm retired. Matter of fact, I've always been a muffin man, especially the type with that sugary stuff on top." He licked his lips when he spied the sugar-topped confection on the plate she handed him. "I knew you were a keeper from the very first day. I just didn't know it was for your baked goods."

Her eyes flew to his and widened. Then she blinked. Twice. He saw her throat move convulsively until she could talk. Taking a deep breath and blowing it out through pursed lips, she said, "You'd better at least taste it before you go saying things like that. I might believe your nonsense."

He leaned over and gently kissed her, just a whisper of his lips on hers. As he raised his head, he took a big bite of his muffin. He chewed, swallowed, then winked. "Yep. Delicious."

Pink looked good on her. Especially the graduated pink of a blush that started on her neck and rose up to her cheeks. He enjoyed causing her flustered reactions, and thought about kissing her again, but noticed she seemed distracted.

"What's on your mind?"

"I'm expecting an acquaintance who is a history professor at the University to come by. He's also a gemologist and dabbles in old jewelry. I've asked him to try to authenticate the jewelry in the safe or at least point me in the right direction." She paced the kitchen as she talked. "I need to find out if they're valuable and maybe where they came from. I'm hoping David can help."

"David, huh? Do you think this guy is trustworthy?" Ben narrowed his eyes and clenched his jaw. "What do you know about him? And how do you know he isn't the person targeting you?"

"He's an academic acquaintance, and he didn't even know about the jewels until I told him this morning. I thought you'd be glad I know of someone to help us find answers." She searched his face. "Ben, I like your green eyes. A lot. But I don't like a green-eyed monster. Jealousy doesn't make me feel valued. It's a form of control."

"I'm not ..." He stopped, breathing hard. *Love is patient and kind. It's not jealous, boastful, proud, or rude. Love is truthful ... What? Love?* He took both of her hands and looked closely at her face, which was turned toward his. *Looks like that may be where I'm headed. Fast.*

"Okay. I hate to admit I might be a bit jealous, but I'll do my best to ditch the little monster. I can't promise he won't get out and come back, but I can promise not to feed him."

"Thank you." Her eyes were shining, but he was hesitant to define the emotion in them. "That's a good start on making a girl feel appreciated."

"Then I'll check that off my to-do list." He grinned. "So, you think this guy can help?"

The doorbell rang.

"Let's find out." She squeezed his hand before letting go and answering the door.

* * *

Claire lifted her face into the breeze and enjoyed the warmth of the midday sun on her face. It felt good to be outside again after spending a few hours in an obscure office of the history department at the University of Northwest Florida. She had forgotten a sweater and her strappy sundress wasn't enough in the air-conditioning.

David convinced her to bring the treasure to the University and put the jewels in their vault for safekeeping. Since her car was still in the shop, she rode with him and arranged to call Ben to pick her up when they finished.

All the papers were signed, i's dotted, and t's crossed, so everything in the safe could be authenticated, and a definite chain of possession could be traced from her to the university. She was relieved that the jewels were out of her home, secure at the university, and possibly about to have their story told.

Talking to herself, she rummaged around in her purse for

her phone. "Next order of business, call a handsome man to pick me up."

She called Ben but as it started to ring she was hit on her flank and went sprawling into the shade of a Southern magnolia. Landing on her back, the breath knocked out of her, she gasped for air. And gasped again. Finally catching a breath, the sweet, citrusy scent of fallen blooms assailed her as she tried to sit.

A crowd of students gathered around her. A young woman on her left and a young man on her right checked her over to make sure she was okay, then helped her into a sitting position. The murmurs of the crowd penetrated her brain.

"Guy came out of nowhere. Bam. Just hit her."

"Brutal to do that to an old lady." *Brutal, yeah. But what old lady?*

"Man, that's like hitting my grandma. Nobody messes with Grandma."

"Dude was gonna snatch her purse." *My purse? Oh, no, no, no ...*

She searched for her purse and found it under her hips.

"Claire. Claire. Claire, can you hear me? Talk to me ..." Ben's voice was coming from the pile of debris under the tree.

"Ma'am? I think your call connected." A blonde, tanned, girl in a sorority tank top held out her the phone.

Glad to be able to talk again, she took her phone.

"Hi, Ben ..."

* * *

An emotional straitjacket kept Ben from taking in enough air. He leaned forward, white-knuckling the steering wheel, castigating himself as he drove to the hospital. He knew better than to let her go onto the mainland with that university guy.

What was his name? David. He knew she wouldn't be safe. He knew ...

Are you trusting me, Ben? That still small voice. *Or are you leaning on what you understand?*

Ben slumped back into his truck seat, shoulders loosening. *Oh, Lord, forgive me.* He mentally bowed his head as he drove. *I'm not trusting you. I'm trying to protect Claire from things that I don't even understand. Per usual, Lord, I'm going it alone.*

Not alone, Ben. I am with you.

He breathed, relaxing his hands. *Thank you, Jesus. I should know this by now.*

The vise across his chest fell away as he started to whistle, mentally reciting the lyrics.

It is well

With my soul.

It is well, it is well with my soul.

* * *

A university faculty member had arrived on scene and called security. They took Claire's statement, the students' statements, and then called an ambulance per university policy. She didn't want to go to the hospital, but realized it was in the best interests of the university and a better place to wait for Ben than the parking lot.

She was sitting on the exam table in the ER when Ben appeared around the corner of the exam room like he was on the softball field, coming into home. She couldn't help but chuckle at his attempt to appear calm. He had stopped short after flinging the curtain aside, gave himself a little shake, readjusted the curtain for her privacy, and then walked to her side and took her hand. Sweet.

"How are you?" His eyes shifted from her to the medical

paraphernalia in the room, none of which was connected to her.

"I'm fine. Nothing hurt but my pride, right Doc?" She turned to the man in the white coat on the other side of the bed. He handed her a clipboard, and she signed the release papers.

"You're very lucky you didn't break a hip or some other bone. But no, you're just a bit banged up. Nothing that shouldn't heal. However, at your age ..."

"You heard him, right? I'm good. Let's go before my mental health takes a deep dive with all this talk about my advanced age." She swung her legs over the side of the bed, ready to go. "You're only as old as you feel, and I feel fine."

"But how are you going to feel tomorrow?" Ben gathered her purse and handed it to her. He pulled back the curtain, and they left the exam room.

"I'll deal with it then. Tylenol is my friend. Let's go." She made her way out of the exit, trying to conceal the tell-tale limp. "And we need to talk. Somewhere else."

"I'll go get the truck. It will be easier on you." He tried to steer her toward a bench outside the ER.

"No. I don't care if you think I'm clingy, but I'm not letting you leave me." She put on her sunglasses and startled when she heard a motor crank. Her head swiveled right and left, looking for any threat. She didn't want to be blindsided again. "I'll be okay once I'm not out in the open. I'm on edge enough to be a bit squirrely."

"Then let's get you where you feel safe the fastest way possible." He scooped her up and arrived at his truck in just a few long strides.

After he gently settled her into the passenger seat, she relaxed into the soft leather. Keenly aware of how quickly she was coming to depend upon him and struggling to fan any flame of independence, she was thankful for his presence.

In an atrocious Ricky Ricardo accent, she heard, "Lucy, you got some 'splainin' to do."

Chapter Twelve

Ben tried to keep the mood light by falling back on a 1960s sitcom shtick, but he got into the driver's side of his truck with his blood pressure up and his senses on alert. He knew she'd been mowed down, but had that made her vulnerable and disarmed? He might appreciate the change, but what had caused it?

"Okay. I got you in the truck. You ready to talk?" He cranked the engine to start the air-conditioner, then leaned his back against the door, one arm over the steering wheel, the other over the back of the seat, giving her his full attention. "What gives?"

"I know you don't think that I've been taking all the weird things that have happened seriously, but now you're going to think I'm being paranoid." She looked at him, eyes concealed behind her shades. "I am almost positive that my accident today was on purpose." She nodded, laced her fingers, and circled her thumbs around each other. He noticed she did that when she seemed nervous or out of sorts. "Actually, I'm positive it was no accident."

"How can you be so sure?"

"I didn't see who hit me, but I heard the students talking while I was on the ground. They were saying he tried to grab my purse, that he was aiming for me. Didn't even try to slow down. One girl said when I fell, he stopped, turned like he was going to help me up, and ran when he saw them coming to my aid."

Her brimming eyes turned toward his, troubled. "What if he wasn't going to help me, but to take my bag? I have the papers for the authentication of valuable jewels in there. *And* the paperwork necessary to get them back. That can't be coincidence, can it?"

Valuable? She was certain? The last he knew, they were speculating. But more important, she was scared. Her tense posture and restless fingers gave it away. He wanted her to be alert and on guard, seriously considering her safety, but he hated seeing her frightened.

"Let's look at this logically." He glanced at her to make sure she hadn't taken offense. "Do you have a copy of the police report? Did they get a description of the assailant?"

She pulled a yellow piece of paper from a folder in her bag and handed it to him. "He had a cloth over his face, and a hat on. He was dressed like every other male on campus. No one could give any better description."

"It says here, average height, average weight, average male. No idea of age. Hair color, ethnicity, and eye color are indeterminate. Clothing unremarkable." He flipped the page over and huffed. "Loads of information. Waste of paper." He handed the report back to her, and she returned it to the folder.

The flesh above her elbow was beginning to discolor. And her knee. Visible signs of what could have been. His jaw tensed, and his teeth ground together. He hadn't been there to—Stop. She hadn't been permanently injured. He consciously unclenched his jaw and ran his tongue through his teeth.

"Be real. Are you okay?"

"It's just bumps and bruises. I'll be fine in a few days. And a good swim will help work the soreness out." She grimaced as she rolled her shoulders. "Want to join me?"

"Of course. That's an invitation I can't turn down." He touched her arm with a small smile, then sobered. "The bruises are already beginning to shine. You could've been seriously hurt. I'm sorry I wasn't there to protect you, even if you don't want me to."

"How about a compromise? I'm a big girl, so I don't need a protector to put me in bubble wrap ..."

Was that what he was trying to do? Is that how she saw his concern?

"But I wouldn't mind a rescue when I need one." She reached out and squeezed his hand.

* * *

His granny said to always look for the silver lining. Claire's ER visit meant they missed the lunch rush. Ben held open the door of the local farm-to-table restaurant for her to hobble in. He caught the eye of the waitress and gestured to a sunny corner booth in the back by a wall of windows. When she nodded, he guided Claire in that direction.

"This okay? It seems like a good place to talk."

She smiled as she scooted into the booth. "Talk and eat. I was already hungry when I left David's office. Now I'm starving." He took a seat across the table.

The waitress brought water and fresh bread and then recommended the catch of the day, grouper. They both ordered it grilled with lemon butter and a salad on the side.

"If there is any key lime pie, I'd love a piece of that as well." The lady has a sweet tooth. Good to know. His knack for noticing the smallest details had often helped him crack hard cases. Maybe it would help his love life.

When they were alone, he put his elbows on the table and leaned toward her, in listening mode. "You said something about the gems being valuable. Care to expand on that?"

Claire buttered a piece of fresh bread, popped a piece of it in her mouth, and closed her eyes. She chewed slowly, swallowed, then opened her eyes and answered.

"David had a jeweler's loupe in his office and was able to tell me that we were right. They're real. Amethysts, rubies, emeralds, diamonds, and pearls. Also, some uncut gems along with the antique cuts. Precursory testing authenticated the gold as antique as well. He didn't see any obvious goldsmith marks on the chains." She took a deep breath and blew it out slowly, then grinned. "His preliminary guess at valuation is a small fortune. He didn't want to use hard numbers."

He let out a low, slow whistle through his teeth. "I'd say 'small fortune' is a pretty valuable estimate, hard numbers or not." He furrowed his brow, confused. "Where would Marty have gotten antique jewels?"

"David has some thoughts but wants to do more research before he shares them. I agreed." She buttered another piece of bread, ate it, and pushed the basket away.

"So, let's go back. Do you really think you being run down and the jewels are connected?" He reached over the table and took her hand, lightly kneading her knuckles. "Can you trust David, or did he tell someone about this 'small fortune' of yours?"

"I don't believe David orchestrated anything. He's excited about the research and the academics. I do trust him on a professional basis." She worried her lip with her teeth. "But since you put all the strange incidents together yesterday, I'm having a hard time unseeing a connection. It only makes sense for 'it' to be the jewels. The ransacked studio tells us someone is looking for them. And they know that I know about them. Could I have been followed?"

"It is a working theory." They both sat back as the waitress delivered their meals. The smell made him salivate. Claire had picked up her fork, ready to dive in. He hesitated but decided to be bold. "Do you mind if I pray?"

Claire slowly put down her fork and adjusted the napkin in her lap. "I don't mind. In fact, I think I'd like that." She bowed her head.

"Lord God, thank you for the food, the hands that prepared it, and the ability to pay for it. Thank you for protecting Claire today. Help us figure out what is going on. Amen."

Ben lifted his head to find Claire staring at him. He rubbed the back of his neck self-consciously and wrinkled his nose. She smiled, and her gaze softened. "Thank you, Ben. That was nice."

"You're welcome." He nodded his head and then looked out the window. His gaze shifted right back to her.

They ate in companionable silence, enjoying the meal. She leaned back from the table. "That was absolutely divine."

He put down his fork, wiped his hands and mouth with his napkin, and grinned at the satisfaction on her face. "Did you leave room for the key lime pie you ordered?"

"I always have room for pie." She smacked her lips as the waitress delivered a large piece of chartreuse confection covered with dollops of whipped cream and lime zest. The crust was made from coconut macaroon cookie dough. She groaned as she took her first bite. "I know why they called it famous."

He stared. She was relaxed. Radiant. And she had a little

bit of whipped cream in the corner of her mouth. He leaned over the table, and wiped his thumb along her mouth, then sucked the pie from his thumb.

He settled back in his chair, waiting for her reaction. Eyes wide, she ran her tongue across her bottom lip.

"You had whipped cream on your mouth."

"And you didn't think a napkin was sufficient?" She laughed.

"Not really. I needed a taste of that pie. You said it was delicious, and I agree."

"I would have given you a bite."

"Yeah. But my taste had an extra little something." He smirked.

"I guess it did." She blushed.

He looked out the window to give her time to compose herself. The trees provided shade to the parking area on this side of the building. The lot was filling with the early dinner crowd. He amused himself by reading the bumper stickers. So many people advertising where their kids hung out.

He wanted to shout the dangers, but most parents didn't listen. Then there were the folks who loved their dogs. But his favorite—the medieval crowd. "Do not meddle in the affairs of dragons, for you are crunchy and go well with ketchup." He didn't know any dragons, but the idea made him snort.

Claire pointed to a black SUV in the lot. "That looks like the vehicle belonging to the guys who ruined the bumper on my car."

Chapter Thirteen

"You know there are a lot of black SUVs out there, don't you?" Ben asked.

"I do. Wishful thinking that I could get them to pay the damages, I guess."

He looked closer at the vehicle. It had a bumper sticker on the back. No words, but maybe a logo? A castle with intertwined letters—a C and S? Where had he seen that logo before?

The logo needed a closer look, so he stood up and stretched. "I'll be back in a minute. Will you stay here?"

"If I need to. I can't go anywhere fast, you know."

He left the restaurant, heading to the side lot. As he rounded the corner of the building, the SUV in question started and backed out of the parking space. He walked toward the driver's side, one hand up, indicating he wanted to talk. The driver ignored him and peeled out. Because of the tinted windows, he couldn't be positive the driver saw him. But he would be willing to bet on it.

Not exactly evidence, but definitely curious.

This time, however, he got a license plate number.

* * *

Claire was dozing when Ben pulled up behind her bungalow. She felt the truck stop and Ben's hand on her knee.

"Hey. We're here, sleepyhead. Good meds must have kicked in."

"Uh-uh. Just the whole day." She stretched, grimaced, and groaned. "Besides, I wasn't asleep."

"You were giving a good impression of it."

"Funny." She stretched again. Oh, my. Her body ached all over. "You still want to swim?"

"I think I'm going to help you inside, then go on home so you can get in bed." He got out of the truck then, walked around, and opened the passenger door.

She took his hand and got out. Why had he lifted the cab so high? It felt like she was sliding down the side of a mountain. Thankfully, he was there to catch her. She was getting used to this.

"I'm still going to swim. If I don't move my body, I'll be forever getting the kinks out."

"If you insist on swimming, let me get my gear." He reached in the back seat and grabbed his bag with his workout gear and swim trunks in it. "In your condition I think it's wise to have someone else here. Just in case."

He held her elbow and guided her through the back gate and into the yard to the kitchen door, where he took her key from her and unlocked it.

"Come on in. Through that hall is the guest room and bath where you can change." She pointed to a small alcove off the living room. "Make yourself at home. I'm going to put this paperwork in the safe before I do anything else. Then I'll

179

change and be out in a minute." She went to the studio, opened the safe, and deposited the papers. Satisfied, she went back downstairs and disappeared into the master bedroom to change.

Entering the kitchen, she raised her brows in appreciation when she saw Ben. He wore an aqua sun shirt that complimented his coloring and emphasized his shoulders. Long, lean legs tapered down to bare feet. When he turned, and his gaze met hers, his smile made her breath hitch.

"You good? Ready to swim?" He held his hand out to hers and she took it.

"Let's go. I'd like to get some laps in and work out some of the soreness." She led him out to the deck chairs around the pool. They put down their towels, and she walked to the shallow end to get in. The water was blue, reflective of the sky. Water diamonds sparkled in the late afternoon sun. But there was something.

She caught movement out of the corner of her eye. Ben, looking into the depth of the pool, froze.

"Ben. Do you see something in the pool?"

* * *

Jellyfish.

Claire's voice broke into his thoughts, reminding him that she was about to get into the water.

"Claire. Don't get in. There are jellyfish in your pool." He shuddered.

"Jellyfish? But how?"

"Someone must have put them in. You can't swim while they are there." He thanked God he was already sweating, and Claire wouldn't notice it was fear coming off him.

"I wouldn't want to. Don't they sting?" She sounded more

curious than frightened. Good. He was terrified enough for both of them.

"They do. They burn like fire. And if you're allergic, they can kill you." He swallowed the bile rising in his throat.

Taking a deep breath, he looked around for the pool net. Maybe he could get them out before he went into full panic mode. It had to be jellyfish. And Claire was here to witness his melt down.

"Are you okay? You don't look so good." She walked over to where he was struggling to breathe normally and helped him sit. Her hand on his face brought him back to the present. "What's wrong?"

He wanted to be stoic, but he couldn't. Not in the face of jellyfish. "Please call someone else to get them out. I can't do it."

"Are you afraid of jellyfish?" Her incredulous eyes pierced him.

He hung his head. "Yeah. Deathly." He mumbled into his chest.

"Ben. It's fine. You don't have to be a hero all the time. Even Superman has his kryptonite." She put her hands on his shoulders and squeezed lightly. "Let me get the dipper."

He wanted to protest. To tell her to wait, let him do it. But he knew he wouldn't be able to. She would have to rely on herself or someone else. She'd been telling him all along.

Claire got a five-gallon bucket from the garage, filled it with the saline pool water, then used the pool net to dip eight jellyfish out of the pool and put them into the bucket. She then set the bucket on the decking, away from the pool. Ben couldn't watch but closed his eyes and mentally whistled the tune of his personal anthem while concentrating on rhythmic breathing.

"Do you want to talk about it?" Claire sat next to him.

"Seems like I asked you that once, and you said no."

"And if I remember correctly, we talked anyhow." She smiled wryly. "How about we just talk and get it over with? What's going on?"

"You've called me a hero, but you just got an up-close-and-personal view of my clay feet." He shrugged. "I have an unreasonable, deep-seated fear of jellyfish. Ever since I was a kid." His head dropped back, exposing his neck. Vulnerable. "I was with my dad when he stepped on one. He had a bad reaction." She touched his arm. "I can't get past seeing my dad writhing in pain, unable to catch his breath. His foot and leg swelled up to twice its size."

He lifted his head and looked at her face for the first time since panicking. "It hasn't stopped my love for the beach, but you might notice that I try to always wear sand shoes. It's because of jellyfish."

"You do know everyone is afraid of something, don't you?"

"Yeah. But why can't I be afraid of polar bears and volcanos? We don't have either of those in Florida." He still wouldn't meet her eyes. "I'm taken out by a spineless water animal. It's humiliating."

He waited a lifetime for her to respond.

"Only if you let it be, Superman." She got up and dove into the pool.

When she surfaced, she captured and held his gaze. "Occasionally, Lois Lane had to save Superman. And I happen to think Clark Kent is sexy."

Chapter Fourteen

Claire sipped her morning coffee as she looked out at the pool. She shuddered at the thought of diving into a pool filled with jellyfish. It was a good thing she had needed to focus on Ben's fear instead of her own. He seemed to think it was a fear tactic, but why? And did someone know about his jellyfish phobia, or was it a lucky hit? That made no sense.

This had the potential of a prank gone bad but somehow seemed more personal, even malicious. Add this to all the other things that had happened, and she was hard-pressed not to see a bogeymen around every corner. She shook her head, attempting to rid herself of the rising fear.

There was no one to hear her groan as she rose to freshen her coffee, so she didn't try to stifle it. She hurt. Every joint, every muscle. Stretching made her groan louder. The swim was supposed to help but only increased the tension in her back and neck—because of the jellyfish.

Ben had wanted to do away with the creatures because he felt that no jellyfish was a good jellyfish, but she had prevailed, and they had taken the bucket of sea creatures down to the Gulf and dumped them in.

Afterward, they walked on the beach in the moonlight. Given the romantic setting and Ben's previous willingness to kiss her, she was surprised when he hadn't even reached for her hand. He hadn't touched her except to be courteous. Only his comment about being humiliated kept her from thinking he was fickle, and her assessment of his character was wrong. But she knew he wasn't a player. Even after such a brief time, she trusted him.

He just didn't trust himself.

* * *

The security office overlooked the lush entrance to the Trinity Sands Beach Community. Colorful hibiscus and bromeliads, drought-resistant succulents, and the ever-present palms were planted throughout the community. The groundskeepers worked diligently to ensure the flowers looked natural and wild instead of carefully cultivated.

Ben saw none of it as he gazed out the window. His mind was recycling Claire's Clark Kent comment while he tapped his ring finger on the desk. And that crack about Lois Lane? He stopped tapping and furrowed his brow. She did save Superman a few times. They balanced each other. He was the brute force. She was the finesse. Could he and Claire find a similar balance? He grinned. There was hope because he identified more with Clark Kent than Superman, and she called the ordinary guy sexy.

He pulled his cell phone from his breast pocket to call her when it suddenly rang. Mike.

"Hey, Mike. You run those plates for me?" Ben reached

into a drawer and got out a yellow legal pad and pen. "What did you come up with?"

"Plates are out of Key West. The SUV is registered to a company called Castillo Salvage." A rustling noise came over the phone. "They mainly do marine salvage of swamped boats, cars that have gone into the drink, stuff like that. It's a surprisingly lucrative business."

"What are they doing in the Panhandle? It's a long way to go for business, especially when there are locals doing the job." He wrote the information on his pad.

Mike scoffed. "Maybe they're vacationing or just checking out how other companies are doing things. Collaborating."

"Yeah. Maybe. Seems a little hinky, if you ask me." Ben doodled as he talked.

"Everything seems hinky to you, man. It's in your DNA." Mike laughed. "Call me if you need me."

"You know I will."

Ben studied his pad and the doodles he'd made. It was mostly chicken scratch, but he also had a familiar design. He opened his desk drawer and drew out a plastic baggie with a pen inside. A castle. With intertwined C and S.

Castillo Salvage.

Castle.

It was worth looking into.

* * *

The hanging flower baskets on Claire's porch required daily drenching in the July heat. She was about three days late. The drooping foliage was getting water, but not her attention, because her thoughts were wandering from question to more questions.

Who knew about the gems in the safe? Would Uncle

Marty have told anyone? And what had David found out about their origination? It all made her head hurt.

A blur among the bushes caught her eye. Henrietta was stalking a gecko. Claire chuckled at the little dog being the brave hunter. In her peripheral vision, she saw movement. Vic was pointing his finger in Charlie's face, getting into his personal space. She couldn't hear what was going on, but it looked intense. Charlie didn't look fearful, but curiously, Vic did.

Something felt off. She itched between her shoulder blades again. Stepping into the shade of her porch, she sat on the porch swing, hoping to be camouflaged. If she craned her neck, she could still see the men. Charlie shrugged, went into his garage, then came out with an elongated can and gave it to Vic. Vic huffed and turned toward Claire's house.

"Hey, Claire. How are you?" Burrowing into the cushions and trying not to be noticed, Claire slumped when she heard Vic's greeting.

"Hi, Vic. I'm good. Just um,"—she looked around and spied an outdated magazine on the side table—"gonna read. How are you and Rene after your excitement the other night?"

"Doing well. No problems." He stepped up onto the porch.

"That's good." She rose from the swing and moved back into the sunshine, in view of the street. Vic's proximity made her feel like she had consumed four espressos in a short amount of time. She could feel the pressure mounting in her chest.

"You okay after your accident?" He stepped closer, peering at her without blinking.

"Accident? What do you mean?" She looked toward Charlie's to see if he was still in the yard. No sign of him.

"The one on campus. Didn't you go to the ER from there?"

She wrinkled her forehead, wondering how he knew. "Yeah, I did. Were you there?"

"No. Just the gossip mill churning. You can't do anything around here without everybody knowing." He backed down the steps and turned toward his house. "Take care now." He waved and walked home.

Claire went into the house and reached for her phone to call Ben. She wanted to process what had just happened, and she needed Ben to know she wanted his help with some things. He answered on the first ring.

"Hey. I was just about to call you." He sounded glad to talk to her. Encouraging.

"Hey." She felt the tension leave her shoulders just knowing he was on the other end of the connection. "Have you told anyone about what happened yesterday? About my ER visit?"

"Just Mike when I called to get him to run the plates of the SUV. Why?" She could hear him morphing into hero mode.

"Something weird just happened. Vic asked me about my accident." She wrinkled her nose. "He said the community gossips told him."

"You don't believe him?" She imagined him leaning forward, listening to every nuance of what she said.

"Why would they know if neither one of us said anything?" She sat on the couch and leaned her head back on the cushions. "Something doesn't ring true, and besides, he sort of makes my skin crawl. Probably because of how I've heard him interacting with Rene."

"Let me check him out a little more. In the meantime, if he makes you uncomfortable, don't engage with him."

"That's the plan." She worried her top lip with her teeth. Now to see if he was back to normal. "Do you want to come over for dinner tonight? I'm cooking."

"Are you sure? Aren't you still sore?" There was concern in his voice, but did she hear a little embarrassment as well?

"A girl's got to eat. And I'd like to eat with you." She laid it out. Would he choose her over his pride?

She heard him inhale, then breathe out. He cleared his throat. "Can you cook? Or is it takeout?" He chuckled. "I know you can bake. And a man might be able to live off your muffins."

"You'll find out when you get here. I hope you like pork tenderloin." She grinned and raised her hands in delight. He was coming. "And muffins are a given."

"I'll be there."

He chose her.

Chapter Fifteen

Ben stared at his computer screen. Castillo Salvage seemed to be a thriving business in Key West. They offered eco-friendly boat disposal and recovery services as well as automobile water recovery services. Their reputation was good, and they had stellar reviews online. So, what was bugging him about this operation? And why were they in Trinity Sands?

He called the number listed on their website. Just to shake the tree.

"Castillo Salvage. Can I help you?" The voice on the other end sounded young and female. Maybe he could use that to his advantage.

"Hi. I think so." He hoped he sounded charming. "I need some salvage work done off the coast of Trinity Sands Island. Could I get a quote from your company?"

"Sir ..." Giggle. "We are in Key West. We don't do work in the Panhandle."

Check. "But I saw one of your trucks advertising your services yesterday. Are they up here on vacation?" He crossed his fingers.

"No, sir. Nobody takes the trucks unless they're on a job. But we don't have any jobs in your area."

"It was a big black SUV, so not quite a truck. But I'm certain it had Castillo Salvage on it. Do you have a logo for your company? Maybe I was mistaken." He needed to use a little more charm. "It's a mystery that will bug me if I don't figure it out." He tried to put a smile in his voice that she could hear over the airwaves.

"I understand that. I think about things like that too." He could hear her gush, so the charm must be working. "We do have a logo. It's a castle, because Castillo means castle, and the owner of the company is Sebastion Castillo. And his initials are SC so they are linked in the middle. It's red on black. Is that what you saw on the truck?"

Most of his questions had been answered, so it was time to let her down gently. "Oh, man. I was so mistaken. The logo that I saw had a seahorse on it." He was talking off the top of his head, and a twinge of guilt twisted his gut at the blatant lie. "Maybe the company name wasn't Castillo, but *Caballo* for horse. I'm so sorry for wasting your time." After a few more pleasantries, they hung up.

The phone rang as soon as he put it down. Mike again.

"Yeah, Mike. What have you got?"

"I did some more digging on that salvage company. Seems they've been in some trouble with salvage diving where they weren't permitted. The company CEO—"

"Sebastion Castillo?"

"Looks like you've been doing some digging too."

"Yeah. I'll share when you finish."

"As I was saying, the company CEO, Sebastion Castillo, bills himself as a descendant of the Spanish conquistadores and a treasure hunter looking for the lost family fortunes from the Spanish Treasure Fleet. Seems like hundreds of Spanish vessels sank on this transatlantic trade route over the years. Most of them had a pretty hefty haul of gold and gems when they went down."

"Whoa. That might provide a few answers." Ben's eyes were wide as he processed this information.

"And here I thought it brought up more questions." Mike paused as if waiting for Ben to tell him something. Big sigh. "Anyhow, Castillo has found himself in some deep trouble over trying to find and salvage these ships. He claims he has a right to them as a descendant of Spain, but Spain doesn't recognize his claim, and neither does the United States. Even under international law, the rights to the bounty are murky at best. This guy, though, he's ruthless. I don't know if it's a money thing or a heritage and pride thing, but he's determined to get his hands on whatever the sea will give up that was on those ships."

"Mike, this is good information. It might clear up why these folks are here."

"Care to share?"

"You aren't gonna like it, but in my defense, I hadn't made the connection." Ben proceeded to tell Mike about the jewels and gems, the ransacked studio, Claire's accident, where they were now, and the jellyfish in the pool. As he talked, Ben processed and tried to put the puzzle pieces together. There were still some missing, but things were taking shape.

"You've been holding out, buddy. That's a lot." Mike whistled through his teeth. "Anything else you want to add?"

"Only that we need to find out what David has learned."

* * *

The tenderloin was seasoned and ready to go on the grill. Potato salad, green beans, fresh tomatoes from the farmer's market, and muffins. It was a meal fit for a hero—or an ordinary man. Claire smiled to herself as she went out to the pool deck to set the sun tea to steep. There was no reason a man couldn't be both.

She recognized her growth over the past few days. Her friendship with Ben had opened her eyes to how closed off to other people she had been. Even her best friends were only colleagues. Since her engagement so many years ago, she hadn't welcomed relationships. She had cheated herself out of the joy of knowing and being known. She could mourn the loss, or she could embrace a new way of being.

Setting the table for dinner with pretty fiesta ware she found in the china cabinet, she hummed the familiar tune Ben always whistled. She remembered it from her early years, going to church with Gran and Uncle Marty. Something about peace like a river and sea billows rolling. Embracing the melody, her heart turned to the God she'd known but walked away from. Her thoughts quieted, her shoulders dropped, and her countenance lifted as perfect peace enveloped her mind and body.

The doorbell rang. Ben must be early, and she smiled. She hadn't had time to put on music, and she was still wearing her shorts and tank top, but none of that mattered. The extra time in his company was a bonus.

"Ben ... oh. I'm sorry. Hi, Rene. I was expecting someone else." Claire opened the door wide to allow Rene to enter. "How are you?"

Rene stood at the door, dark shades in place to hide her bruised, black eyes, her hair pulled back into a ball cap. She looked tired—features drawn and her makeup not as pristine as usual. Her body language depicted a rubber band at its breaking point.

"I hate to ask you, Claire, but could you come to the house for a minute? I need your help."

"Um, sure. I have just a couple of minutes. I'm expecting someone, and I have something baking. What do you need?" She untied her apron and put it on the foyer bench beside the door as she left the house.

"Thank you, Claire. You're a lifesaver. Literally." Rene looked all around as they crossed Claire's front yard to hers. As they went up the porch steps, Rene continued to apologize. "I am so sorry to take you away. I know you're busy, and you don't deserve this, but it just can't be helped. Thank you for coming with me."

"Really it isn't any problem, but I don't even know what you need or if I can do anything useful." She entered the front door after Rene. "How exactly can I help—"

The door shut forcefully behind her, interrupting her question. She was halted from turning around by a hand on her upper arm. When she looked to see who had hold of her, she gasped to see one of the tourists from Maude's Market who'd scratched her car.

"You! I've been looking for you. You damaged my car and need to pay for the repairs." She pulled away and put her hands on her hips, glaring up at the dark-haired man.

"Hey, T. She's been looking for you, man." The other man from the SUV laughed at his companion while backing Claire into the corner. "We should've let her find you. We'd be on our way home already."

When her back hit the wall, Claire stiffened and turned accusing eyes to Rene, who was huddled on the living room couch. She hadn't removed her sunglasses, so Claire couldn't knowingly make eye contact, but tears tracking from under the shades caused Claire's stomach to clench. Rene had led her into a trap.

T lifted his chin at her and narrowed his eyes. "Give us the treasure. We'll be gone."

"Treasure? I don't understand." Claire stalled, trying to process the situation. The short and stocky man was closest to her and lifted a hand. She flinched involuntarily, mentally kicking herself for showing fear.

"Manny. Control yourself." T spoke to his companion while staring at her. "I'm sure violence won't be necessary to come to an understanding." He lifted one brow. "Can you think of anything, Dr. Anderson, that might be in your possession and be considered treasure?"

Uh-oh. They knew her name and title. And they weren't shy about using their own names. She guessed it was safe to assume they weren't tourists and wouldn't be paying for her Beemer.

"I can't be certain. Treasure means different things to different people. Could you be more specific?" Ben should be arriving soon. If she could stall, he would come looking for her.

Manny took another intimidating step toward her, forestalled by T's lifted hand and a soft spoken, "Not yet," which was more frightening than the hints of brutality.

"You are so right. The things we care so much about differ from person to person. Some people care about a car and its bumper." He smiled, amused. "Other people value things a bit more permanent. Like gold and gems. Or things more fragile like reputations and relationships. Then there is health and education. Should I continue, Dr. Anderson? Or could you hazard a guess as to what I may be seeking?"

Claire suppressed a shudder. The old-world vibe of his clarification made her think of all the gangster movies she had ever seen. None of them had a happy ending. T seemed to be the brains and Manny the brawn. She was thankful that the brawn was leashed, but T seemed more lethal.

"Now that you explain it, seems like I found something you might consider treasure." She tried to gain Rene's attention, but she had turned away from them. No help there. "But I think you're aware it isn't in my possession."

"What do you mean it isn't in your possession?" He rounded, striding toward the couch. "Are you holding out on me? Double-crossing me?"

Rene shrank back, arms up, shielding her head. "No. No. I mean, we knew she took them to the University, but we thought she brought them back."

He stalked back to Claire, coming close enough she could smell the mint on his breath. "Enough of the wordplay. Where are the jewels?" His eyes glittered, hard and focused.

"They're at the University in a safe. In the history department."

"Then let's go, Professor." He grabbed her hand and pulled her into the kitchen toward the back door. She struggled, pulling back, countering his weight with hers. He abruptly turned, causing her to fall into him. He grabbed her by the upper arms and squeezed. "Manny, get the other woman."

She stifled a scream as Manny's fist met Rene's head. He lifted her unconscious body and carried her through the back door.

"Will you come with me, or should I have Manny take you?"

Trembling, she swallowed hard. "I'll come with you."

The glare of the sun made her eyes water when T propelled her into the backyard and around the garage. She stumbled in the alley, almost falling to her knees, but catching herself with her hands on the pavement. While she was down, she thought she saw movement in the bushes between her house and the Harringtons' garage. T pulled her up before she could be sure.

"Get in." He opened the back passenger door to the SUV. She pulled back and took a deep breath to scream, knowing that if she went with them she might never return. The air left her lungs when he reached behind his back and withdrew a gun. She got in.

As the SUV drove out of the alley, she prayed at least one of her nosey neighbors was watching.

Chapter Sixteen

Ben parked his golf cart in front of Claire's bungalow and took the steps two at a time to get to the front door, his gut fluttering in anticipation. A home-cooked meal and interesting conversation with his favorite silver-haired lady sounded a lot like heaven on earth.

His smile faded when he knocked and there was no answer. Wasn't she expecting him? She must not be as excited to see him as he was to see her. He jumped down from the porch and walked around to the back.

"Claire? Are you out here?" Nothing.

Brow furrowed, he looked around to make sure he hadn't missed her. His gaze landed on a piece of cardboard leaning against Charlie's garage, inside his fence, next to a sandy five-gallon bucket. It had the outline of something spray painted on it. In red.

Ben stepped to the gate going into Charlie's backyard and heard a tiny growl, then yapping. He looked down to a snarling, teeth-baring micro-dog.

"Henrietta. Good dog. Don't bite me." He reached down to

pet her and jerked his hand back as she lunged, making enough racket to wake the dead. Charlie came out his back door and around the corner to save him.

"Ben? What's wrong? Henrietta. Leave Ben alone and stop your chatter. He's a friend." He squatted, and Henrietta jumped into the man's arms, snuggling close yet still growling at Ben as Charlie stood.

"Thanks for the rescue, Charlie." Ben assumed the hands-up position. He chuckled and reached for the gate. "Have you seen Claire? She knew I was coming over but doesn't seem to be around. I thought she might've borrowed a cup of sugar or something."

"Last I saw of her, she'd come back from the farmer's market and was going to cook dinner for some lucky fellow." Charlie wiggled his eyebrows suggestively. Then, what Ben said seemed to register. He frowned. "You say she isn't there?"

"She's not answering her door. And her phone goes to voicemail." Ben looked pointedly at the cardboard. "What have you been painting?"

Charlie started at the change of subject. "Uh ... my wooden swing. It was part of my summer project to freshen up my porch. Why?"

"Why red?" Ben squinted at him, mining his words for truth. "And what do you use that bucket for?"

"Are you interrogating me? I happen to like the color red, and I use the bucket for beachcombing. For certain, you've seen it on the back of my golf cart." Charlie almost dropped Henrietta when he flung his arms out in exasperation. Henrietta yelped. "Now look what you've done. No wonder she doesn't like you."

"Charlie, I'm just going to ask you. Did you paint Claire's cabinets red earlier this week? Or put jellyfish,"—he flinched—"in her pool?"

"Of course, I didn't! How dare you accuse me of—" He broke off as Vic ran across the front yard and then out of sight. "It wasn't even my paint. I borrowed it from Vic." He gestured toward the front of the house. "Where is he going, like a bull for the gate?"

Ben turned to see what Charlie was talking about when he heard Vic's voice yelling. He took off, coming to a stop when Vic ran into him.

"Ben, you gotta help me, man." He was gasping. "I was just … trying to scare her … away from the house." He grabbed Ben's arm. "I didn't mean for anyone to get hurt, but those guys … they mean business …"

"What are you saying?" Ben shook Vic off him, grabbed his T-shirt neck, and pulled him up to look him in the face. "Scare Claire? And who is hurt?"

"It was me. I was trying to get the jewels to give them back. Marty came in and caught me in his house. I pushed him, and he fell. It was an accident, man. I'm sorry." Vic was blubbering, writhing to get away from Ben.

"What about Claire? Where is she?" He shook Vic to make him focus.

"They've got her. Her and Rene. If they don't get the jewels back they're gonna kill them." He jerked away from Ben, then grabbed him, pleading. "You've got to help me. They have my wife."

Ben's heart sank. Sometimes he hated being right. "Who has the girls?"

"Sabastion Castillo."

* * *

Claire strained to hear T's side of the conversation. Too bad he wasn't like half the population and used his phone on speaker.

Just her luck to be kidnapped by someone with good hearing and a mumble.

Hoping neither T nor Manny would notice, she turned in her seat to check on Rene and was relieved to see her chest moving up and down. A dead body would raise the already high stakes to heights she didn't want to contemplate. Things were already precarious enough.

"Rene." Breathing her name, she hoped Rene could respond, but quietly. Her sunglasses fell off when Manny hit her, so her bruises and black eyes were noticeable. Her beautiful face would recover, but she had taken some significant blows. Right now, Claire needed her to open her eyes. She tried again. "Rene."

Lids fluttering, Rene seemed to be coming around. She was lying on the bench seat and starting to wriggle. She jumped when Claire reached around her captain's chair to touch her on the leg.

"Shh. Don't let them know you're awake," she whispered.

Rene grabbed her hand and squeezed.

T put his phone on the console with an unholy outburst. He turned around and glared at Claire, muttering in Spanish. Seeming to come to a conclusion, he directed Manny to cross the bridge into Destin to the Emerald Waters Marina.

Claire looked out the windows to try to see how they were traveling and what they were passing, but it all looked the same, like Florida on a beautiful day. When they pulled into a parking lot near the water, she hoped to gain the attention of someone passing by. T anticipated her move and warned her of the consequences, showing her the gun.

Manny got out of the SUV, opened the back passenger door, and lifted the captain's chair for access to the third row. He reached in and grabbed Rene to pull her out. She yelped and pulled back.

"Good to know I didn't kill ya back there. Get on out here. And nothing funny." Manny stepped back to give her room to get out. She stumbled out, fidgeting and looking side to side. Manny grabbed her bicep and shoved her against the vehicle, getting his gun from behind him to show her his options. She settled against him and stopped resisting.

Claire watched, wondering if Rene would help them get out of this situation or if she would be a hindrance. She wasn't even sure she had the ability to help herself. But she was going to get away, or die ... Nope, not going to give that mental real estate.

T came to her door and opened it, gesturing for her to climb out. When she stood beside him, he put his arm around her waist like they were intimate, leaned over and whispered in her ear, "Act as if you like me, and no one will know about the gun." She swallowed against rising bile and allowed him to pull her closer. Any casual observer would see two couples enjoying a walk along the dock to their vessel.

The dock was well-maintained and fairly new. Sea birds perched on posts, and pelicans floated in the water, looking for an easy snack. The smell of fish and the sea permeated everything.

Halfway down the dock, T turned her into a slip that held a sailboat. He helped her onboard, and Manny helped Rene. They took them to the cabin and shoved them inside, closing the door and locking them in. There was no air conditioning, so the cabin was stuffy and hot.

Claire pushed up from the floor into a sitting position. "Are you okay?"

"I think so." Rene crouched, looking ready to jump if necessary. "I am so sorry for dragging you into this mess." She started to cry.

"We don't have time for that. Stop crying and tell me what

is going on. Exactly what mess did you drag me into?" Claire huffed in exasperation, pushing her hair from her eyes and twisting it in back. "I hope you're going to help get me out of it."

She stopped talking and looked at the door with wide eyes as T entered the cabin. He motioned for her to get up. "How do we get the jewels from the University?"

"I'm the only one who can do it, and I need the paperwork in the safe at my house to verify my identity." She tried to hide her excitement. If they took her back to her house, Ben would be there, and he could rescue her. Her excitement faded when T shook his head.

"You aren't going. Manny will go get the papers. Then you will make the call, and we will get the jewels." T pushed a pad of paper on the table toward her. "Write down the combo. Make sure it is right, or your friend will pay."

She wrote down the combination and location of the safe. T took the information topside and stayed up there, out of the cabin's stuffiness.

Rene started speaking when it was obvious T wasn't coming back into the cabin. She closed her eyes and shook her head. "I hid the jewels in Marty's house about a year ago, and when I went back for them, I couldn't find them."

"A year ago! Where did you get them, and why did you hide them at Uncle Marty's?" Claire worked hard to keep her voice to a whisper. Her pitch was rising with each word. "And, by the way, I found them in the studio."

"You did?" Rene looked at her in surprise. Her eyes held a spark of hope. "That's great. We can bargain our way out of here with them."

"Didn't you hear us talking?" Rene looked confused as Claire spoke. "I don't have access to them anymore. They're in the University's vault. I didn't know what they were, so I needed them researched."

"Oh, no. It's all been for nothing. I am so sorry." She started to sob.

"You never answered my questions. Why my house?"

Rene's eyes held remorse and sorrow. She took a deep breath and told her story. "We were diving in Key West and overheard some guys in a bar talk about salvaging treasure from one of the sunken Spanish Treasure Fleet's ships. Vic and I thought it would be a lark to try to find some. We went out with lights before sunrise and found a treasure trove in about eight feet of water. It was exactly where that guy said it might be. We brought it home and tried to find a way to sell it. Come to find out, it isn't legal, and we had to do some dark web-type stuff. I guess that's how the Castillos found us. When things started getting weird, we decided to hide it at Marty's because he lived alone next door, and we knew where the extra key was. It just seemed easy."

She started crying. "When we thought we had a buyer, I went back to retrieve the treasure, but it was gone. I had hidden it in one of the jars with junk jewelry, but Marty must have gotten it down to use it and realized those pieces were real. Anyhow, Vic went back to search the house, and Marty returned. He confronted Vic, and Vic shoved him. Marty fell and hit his head."

Claire gasped. She had been quiet up until this point but could hold her tongue no longer. "Vic killed him? Over stolen stuff? He would have told him where it was if he'd just asked." Her sobs welled up and overflowed.

"I know that. Vic knows it too. It was an accident, I promise." Rene resumed her story through her tears. "The Castillos had found us and wanted the gems. We tried scaring you away so we could search, but you don't scare easy."

"I'm scared now." Claire rolled her eyes and huffed.

"Today, they came to the door and told me they were going to kill me if I didn't get you to come over. They just wanted the jewels. If you had them, we wouldn't be in this mess now."

"Don't turn this on me, sister. I was an innocent bystander who inherited stolen jewels. Let's get to safety, and then we can assign blame." Claire put her head on her arms and thought about their options. What was in her control? How could she get them out of this? Nothing came to mind.

She could only think of one thing to do. Pray.

Chapter Seventeen

Ben took the burned muffins out of Claire's oven and threw them in the trash. The shame of failure threatened to overpower him. He had failed to keep her safe.

When he called Mike and told him that the Castillos had Claire and Rene, Mike instructed him to wait at Claire's. He paced the floor, making and discarding plans, and waiting for his friend to arrive.

Vic was in the living room. Ben wouldn't let him leave, but neither did he want to be in the same room with him. To think that the man had been instrumental in Marty's death. If he had gotten help, Marty might still be alive. He was afraid that he would get violent despite his training and new nature in Christ.

He was leaning on the doorframe of Claire's bedroom, thinking of all his hopes and dreams, when he saw movement through the window looking out back. He shifted where he could see but not be seen, trying to identify what spooked him. As he watched, a short and stocky man lifted the gate latch and entered the pool area. He walked confidently to the back door, stooped down to move a planter and get a key, then used the key to come into the house.

Vic lifted his head and yelled. "Manny! Where's my wife?"

Ben ran into the kitchen and blocked the back door so the man couldn't get away. "Vic, let's get him." The intruder turned and rushed Vic, who grappled him around the waist. They fell to the ground with the intruder on top. Ben grabbed him before he could unentangle himself and run off. The man scrambled, trying to get away, but Ben held tight.

"Vic, go get some zip ties out of my golf cart." Ben struggled to keep hold of the guy who was protesting in Spanish. "You aren't going anywhere. Where's Claire? Where've you taken her?"

Vic ran in with the zip ties and helped Ben restrain him. "You called this guy Manny. You know him?"

"Yeah. He's one of Castillo's men. Manny Vargus."

"Did I miss all the action?" Mike entered the house, zeroing in on the man in the zip ties. "Looks like you did all the work, Hastings. Are you sure you're retired?" He motioned over a patrolman who had come as backup.

"Not today. I'm just about to start the inquisition." Ben's eyes were fierce with the light of battle as he growled his question again. "Where's Claire?" He shook Manny for emphasis as the patrolman took him into custody.

Mike listened to the radio in his ear. "Ben, I think we've got her. I put an APB out on the plates you gave me and the vehicle's been spotted at the marina. Let's go get your girl."

They raced out to Mike's patrol car, told the patrolman to call for another vehicle, and got in, putting Vic in back. Blue lights flashing, they sped out of the community and onto the highway, across the bridge, and to the marina.

Ben's thoughts raced to Claire. Was she hurt? Would they get to her in time? He bowed his head, acknowledging his powerlessness in the outcome of this situation. He had tried to protect her, but ultimately, protecting Claire wasn't up to him. She was the Lord's to protect. He was just a warrior in service to the King. He prayed to arrive in time to serve.

* * *

Claire and Rene were sitting on opposite sides of the small cabin, Rene still crying and Claire gazing at nothing, lost in her memories of Marty. So many questions answered, but so many left to ask.

The whine of a siren filled the air, getting louder and coming closer, then stopping its progression close by. Claire's pulse increased. She felt it beating in her neck. Was someone coming?

T ran into the cabin. "Get up. Come with me." He grabbed for her hand, but ignored Rene, choosing to leave her.

"No." Claire snatched her hand back and scampered behind the table, putting it between her and T. "I'm not going with you."

"Don't make me hurt you, Dr. Anderson." He shook his head, reminding her he had a gun.

The door to the cabin burst open, and Ben filled the doorway. His eyes searched and found Claire. "You good?"

She nodded, eyes shining.

T turned around, jerking the gun from his waistband. Before he could retrieve it, Claire rounded the table and shoved him hard. He fell with little room to maneuver.

Ben joined the melee, and put a knee in T's back, subduing him. Face down, hands behind his back, Ben zip-tied him.

Mike entered the cabin, looked around, and grinned. "Hastings, I like working with you. I don't even get sweaty." He took hold of T by the upper arm and led him out of the cabin to read him his rights.

Turning to Claire, Ben opened his arms, and she rushed in.

"I prayed you'd get to us in time." Tears trickled down her cheeks.

"So did I." He kissed the top of her head.

She snuggled close, pulled back and looked up at him. "Can we get out of here?"

"Of course. Let's get some air." He smiled down at her.

Climbing the steps onto the deck, she was conscious of his hand at her back. The breeze cooled her skin and ruffled her hair as she watched the police lead T and Rene away. She was thankful the police would deal with the fallout.

Claire turned into his arms, hands on his chest. She looked up into his eyes, wanting him to see into hers. "Thank you for rescuing me."

She felt Ben's breath hitch and saw his eyes dilate. His head came toward hers in slow motion, giving her time to consent and control. She stood on tiptoes to meet his lips halfway, ready to trust him. Sliding down his muscular chest, she leaned against him, breathing hard.

Ben rested his cheek against the top of her head and closed his eyes for just a moment. He lifted his head, pushed her to arms' length, and smirked. "That's what Superman does."

THE END

About Sharon Carpenter

Sharon Carpenter has lived an incredible adventure through all the transitions of life. She grew up on Air force bases around the globe, and then married her very own Army officer, Jesse. She has three adult children who gifted her with three other amazing kids, and then leveled up to "Sassy" to eight grands.

Journaling and doodling have always been how Sharon processes the events of life. Notebooks and journals litter the bookshelves of her home, chronicling the details, moods, and emotions of marriage, motherhood, education, teaching, navigating becoming a mother-in-law, grandparenting, retirement, caregiving, and loss. All the transitions of life and so much story fodder can be found throughout these pages.

The habit of writing for herself soon became writing for

others in *Chicken Soup for the Soul* and other publications, and then writing for story. Whenever pen scratches on paper or fingers pound the keys, Sharon's greatest desire is for the words that she writes to touch lives, count for eternity, and point her readers to Jesus.

Sharon's philosophy of life is when the foundation is firm (Jesus), then you can dance any dance to any rhythm and pivot when you need to.

You can connect with Sharon on her website www.SharonHCarpenter.com, Facebook https://www.facebook.com/sharon.h.carpenter.5/, or Instagram https://www.instagram.com/sharon.carpenter.writes/

Searching for Serenity

Deborah Sprinkle

Quench your thirst for story.
www.ScriveningsPress.com

Chapter One

Harp music penetrated Grace Caldwell's dreams. She flung her left arm over to wake her husband. "Go see what that is." Her hand hit the cold mattress, and pain arrowed through her heart. He'd been gone three years. She lay her arm across her forehead and let the tears flow down her cheeks onto the pillow. Would she ever get used to being alone?

The harp music changed to violins. She glanced at the clock before swinging her feet out of bed and pulling on her robe. The baseball bat she kept by the bed wouldn't be much use against an intruder with a gun, but then, what burglar would be watching the Music Channel at four in the morning? And the bat would have to do. She'd vowed never to touch a gun again. Not after ...

Grace padded down the hall with the bat cocked on her shoulder. At the door to the family room, she paused. What if there really was someone in there? Her nightgown clung to her where she'd begun to sweat. She'd worried about something like this happening since John died. Maybe she should retreat to the bedroom and call nine-one-one.

But if the house was empty, she'd feel like a fool. However, she could at least be prepared to call if need be.

Back at the doorway to the family room, Grace took a deep breath. "Whoever's in there, I'm coming in. This is your chance to leave the way you came." She pressed nine-one-one, held her thumb over the green button, and stepped through.

Everything looked the way she'd left it the night before. Including the urn on the mantle that cradled her husband's ashes. Her courage bolstered, she continued her search of the house, flipping on lights and checking in closets in every room. Everything appeared just as she'd left it. All the windows and doors securely locked.

Returning to the family room, Grace canceled the call and eased into her recliner. She peered at the big screen across the room. Why did her television suddenly turn on in the middle of the night? Could it have been an oops on the cable company's end? She gazed around the familiar room.

The soft music washed over her, and she closed her eyes. How many times had she and her husband sat like this together? Too many to count. She needed a break.

In this house, the memories of their life together pressed in on her from all sides. Even though they had a wonderful marriage, she likely still had many years to fill without his loving presence by her side, and she wasn't sure how to do that.

She curled into her chair and sobbed. "Oh, Lord, I miss him so much. Show me how to move forward." Spent, she gave in to the avoidance of reality that sleep held for her since John died.

Chiming and a vibration against her thigh drew Grace from the depths of a black place into the light of day. She pulled her phone from her robe pocket.

"Mom?" The worried voice of her daughter Liz sounded in her ear. "You're not still sleeping, are you?"

"No." Grace straightened in her chair and tried to put some force into her words. "I just sat down for a breather. I've been up for hours."

"Uh-huh." Doubt replaced worry.

"Did you call just to give your mom a hard time, or is there another reason I get to hear from my favorite daughter?"

"I'm your only daughter." Liz chuckled at the old family joke. "I wanted to invite you over for dinner tonight."

"I'd love to." Grace levered the recliner to its upright position. "What time?"

"How about five?"

"I'll be there." She stood. "Will the boys be joining us?"

"Yep," Liz said. "And you know what that means."

"A rousing game of Phase Ten. My favorite card game." Grace smiled to herself. "I'll try not to trounce them this time."

"Hey, I don't mind. It's the boys who get frustrated, and that's their problem." Liz laughed again. "See you tonight. Love you."

"Love you more." Another zing to her heart. John used to say that to her.

Grace pushed to her feet and stretched. Another empty day spread before her. She'd shower, eat breakfast, and climb the stairs to her office, where she'd pretend to write. At least she wouldn't have to make the decision between a frozen pot pie or running out for a hamburger and fries for dinner.

What a rut she'd gotten into. How had she let that happen? But more importantly, did she have the energy to break it? "Not today." She combed a hand through her hair and shuffled back to her bedroom with her baseball bat propped on her shoulder.

Clean and dressed, Grace entered her state-of-the-art kitchen and made coffee and toast. The sun shone out of a cloudless blue sky.

"Another perfect day in paradise." The sarcasm in her tone plucked a nerve of guilt in her. "Sorry, Lord. I am truly grateful for all Your blessings." But some days, it was hard, and she knew He understood.

As Grace deposited her plate in the dishwasher, her phone sprang to life. The face of her best friend, and publisher, appeared on the screen. She groaned before sliding her finger across the screen to answer the call. "Hello, Olga. How are you this morning?"

"The bigger question is, how are you? Are you writing?" A trace of her Scandinavian accent came through in her voice when she was worried.

"It's slow, but yes." Grace grabbed her coffee and headed for the stairs. "Hang on. I need both hands for a minute." She tucked her phone into her pocket and took hold of the banister. At the top, she caught her breath and pulled her phone out. "I'm back."

"Are you okay?"

"Yes. Either I'm out of shape, or those stairs are multiplying." Grace plopped into her chair in the office.

"Do you exercise? You have that beautiful pool. You should be out there doing laps every day. It's good cardio."

"Says the woman who once told me that exercise is a four-letter word." Grace chuckled.

"We haven't gotten together lately." Her voice turned cool. "I have type two diabetes, and I've been watching what I eat and exercising regularly."

"Olga, I'm sorry." Grace straightened. "I ..."

"No worries." Her usual friendly tone returned. "But I've dropped ten pounds already."

"That's great." She glanced down at her own midriff and sighed.

"Anyway, I didn't call to brag. I want to know how you're doing with your book."

Another quiet sigh as Grace put on her reading glasses and squinted at her computer screen. The word count glared at her from the left corner of the document. Not good. She was faced with a choice. Pretend as if everything was moving along great, or tell the truth. She closed her eyes.

"Grace, are you there?" The worry in Olga's voice notched up a level.

"I'm here." She cleared her throat. "I'm having some trouble."

"What kind of trouble?"

"I can't seem to write anymore." Tears choked her words. She removed her glasses and pressed her fingers to her eyes.

"Oh, sweetie." Olga-publisher turned into Olga-best friend. "Grieving is a process. It can't be rushed. You thought you were ready, but you just aren't. It's okay."

"It's not okay." Anger surged in her. "I want to move on with my life. Will somebody tell me how to do that? Please?"

"Nobody has the answers, but ..."

"But what? Say it." Grace gripped her phone tighter.

"I was just going to say it might help if you had a change of scenery. Went someplace for a while." Olga paused. "I could take some time off if you wanted to take a trip together?"

Time away. A break. Something stirred in Grace. "Let me think about it for a couple of days. Thanks, my friend." She hung up and let her eyes roam around the small room they'd once used as a nursery.

Her gaze snagged on the photo of her and John in front of their beach house on Trinity Sands Island. That would be a change of scenery, but she hadn't been there since he'd passed away. It too held so many memories.

But she'd always loved it there. And her good friend,

Serenity James, still lived at Trinity Sands Beach Club. In fact, she'd received a letter from her yesterday. Grace hadn't opened it yet. She hadn't been in the mood to read all the gossip Serenity had heard from Ursula, the housekeeper, or all the problems she was having with the renters next door. Maybe when she got back from dinner, she'd feel up to it.

Chapter Two

Grace stifled a laugh when Liz brought out a homemade pot pie for dinner. At least it wasn't the frozen variety she'd been eating. The aroma of roasted chicken, potatoes, and carrots baked in a pie crust made her mouth water. She'd never be able to settle for the frozen kind again.

"Grandma, can we come swim tomorrow?" her oldest grandson, Quinn, asked.

"Who's we?"

"Vic and me." He pointed to his younger brother. "And a couple of friends."

"One friend each." Grace eyed the boys sternly. "No more, or I'll send you all home."

"We got it, Grams." They rolled their eyes.

Liz waited for her sons to leave the room. "Do you want me to come over too?"

"They'll be fine." Grace patted her daughter's hand. "But there is something I want to talk to you and Chase about."

A look of concern passed across Liz's face.

"It's nothing serious." Grace withdrew her hand. "I'm thinking about taking a trip."

"Where to?" Chase asked.

"I'm not sure, but Olga suggested it might be a good idea, and she offered to go on a sort of girls' trip with me." She folded her hands on the table in front of her. "What do you think?"

"I think it's a great idea." Chase scooted his chair back and stood. "You could use a change of scenery."

"That's what Olga said." Grace chuckled.

"I don't know, Mom." Liz picked at a cuticle on her right hand. "Two old ladies alone on a trip?"

"Hey." Grace bristled. "We're not that old, and we're not helpless."

"I know, but ..."

"Well, I'm just thinking about it." Grace settled her glasses on her nose. "Let's get this game of Phase Ten started. I need to get home. Us old people need our rest, you know."

"Mother." Liz wailed.

Grace patted her hand again. "Don't worry. It was just a thought. I understand what you're saying." But inside, a cloud settled over her heart.

Was she too old? Past the time when she could feel confident about taking care of herself? Her next birthday, she would be sixty-eight. Her parents both lived into their nineties. She could have lots of years left.

Grace shuffled the cards, her mind on her earlier conversation with Olga. Exercise was the key. Tomorrow, before the boys got there, she would get in the pool. She gazed around the table. "Are you boys prepared to be stomped on?"

"Grandma, you cheat."

"I do not." She grinned and dealt ten cards to each of them.

* * *

On her drive home, Grace chuckled to herself as she recalled all the moaning and groaning from her grandsons. Phase Ten was a game of chance that depended entirely on how the cards were dealt. She wasn't winning through any skill of her own, but for some reason, she'd been on a winning streak.

They thought she had some secret method. The boys hated to lose, but they couldn't wait to play another game, each hoping to be the one to triumph over Grandma. Liz told her they spent hours trying to figure out what she was doing.

As she turned onto her driveway, her headlights swept across her neighbor's drive. Spotlights shone on several pickups she hadn't seen before, a few four-wheelers, and a large green enclosed trailer took up every square inch of space. Why such bright lights? Had they had trouble? She'd call in the morning.

Grace pulled into her garage, closed the door, and got out of the car. She never used to worry about such things, but living alone required learning new survival techniques.

Some of her single friends assumed there might be a predator around every corner. What a depressing way to live. She chose a more moderate approach. To know her limitations, not get herself into dangerous situations, be vigilant, and adopt practices that seemed reasonable to her.

And to approach life with as much joy as she could muster each day. Harder some days than others. She hung her purse on a kitchen chair and pulled a bottled water from the fridge. "Let's see what news Serenity has from the beach."

Grace retrieved the letter from her friend and settled into her recliner. Just two pages this time. Shorter than most. She turned on the lamp beside her and picked up a pair of readers she kept next to her chair.

Dear Grace,

I'm sorry it's been so long since my last letter. I've been sick and ended up in the hospital for a while, but I'm fine now. Things here have been hot and humid, as usual. And interesting!

First, let me give you the update on my sister and her bunch.

Grace skimmed through the next few paragraphs, barely taking in facts about illnesses, skinned knees, and family drama. Until her gaze snagged on the word murder. She backed up a paragraph.

... couple in the house on the left? They got a divorce, and she got the house. Well, she opened a business specializing in beach décor. She is amazing! I'm thinking of having her do my kitchen and family room. Anyway, she had a stalker! The guy turned up dead! Murdered! And she and her ex were suspects. It was so exciting! They didn't do it, of course, but boy, did it get things stirred up around here.

Then, last month, we had another wild thing happen! Remember Marty? He passed away a couple of months ago, and his niece showed up because she inherited the cottage. What a mess! That man collected so many odds and ends for his art! But it seems there was something in there that was worth something because somebody tried to break in and steal it. They caught them, but again, life was interesting. You've been missing all the fun, my friend.

The tone of her friend's letter changed, and Grace gripped the pages tighter as she read.

Seriously, I want you to come down. Something strange is going on in the wilds late at night. I'm either hallucinating, or I'm seeing something I shouldn't.

I need to figure this out, and I need you to help me. But one way or the other, I'm going to find out what's going on.

Get here as soon as you can.

Love, Serenity

Grace shuffled the pages of Serenity's letter. This wasn't

the kind of trip she had in mind, but—She jumped at the sudden saxophone blaring from her phone. "Hello?"

"Grace, Walt your neighbor next door here. Wanted to warn you about leaving your car outside."

"Did something happen? I saw you have new lights on your house."

"Yeah. Some moron was messing around last night. I ran him off."

Chapter Three

Grace gave a sharp intake of breath. Had the man been inside her house? Had she scared him away? But she'd checked all the doors and windows. They'd been securely locked.

"Are you there?"

"Sorry. I thought I heard something last night in my house."

"This guy was outside. He had some kind of remote that opens trucks and cars, but the fool thing turned on my TV. That's how I almost caught him. He came close to getting a load of buckshot in the … rear end."

"Was this about four in the morning?"

"Yeah."

"My television came on too. That's why I thought I had an intruder."

"If that ever happens again, you call me. I'll be right over with my gun. Yessir."

"I appreciate that, Walt." A shiver ran down her spine, and she prayed she'd never have to call him.

"Glad to do it. If it were my widowed mother or aunt, I'd want someone looking out for her."

"Thank you." Why did the term widowed mother or aunt sound so old? She wasn't *that* old. Was she?

"Well, just glad I can help. You take care now."

"You too." Grace pressed End, stood, and strode to the mantle. "John Caldwell, sometimes I could just kill you for dying on me."

Hot tears ran down her face and dripped off her chin. She swiped them away. At least she now knew why the music channel woke her early ... was it just this morning? Time for a cup of lavender tea.

Grace changed into her nightgown and robe before heading for the kitchen. She paused at the stairs leading to the second floor. No writing again today. Self-recriminations threatened to pull her down the path that spiraled into depression, but she refused to follow.

Tomorrow was another day. She filled her favorite mug with water and put it in the microwave. The aroma of the steeping lavender-chamomile tea soon filled the kitchen, and the upsets of the day seemed to drift away.

Grace carried her mug into the family room and angled back in her recliner once more. Everyone believed it would be good for her to take a trip—except Liz. She loved her daughter, but she'd gotten protective since her father died. It was like a role reversal.

If she did go away, where would she go? Should she take Olga up on her offer of a girls' trip? Or go somewhere on her own? The idea of traveling alone scared her a little, even though she'd done it many times when John was alive. Somehow, this was different.

What about driving down to the beach house? Did she feel

confident enough to do that by herself? It was a seven-hour drive. She'd done those back and forth to her parents a lot.

She picked up Serenity's letter from the table where she'd left it. Her friend needed her at the beach club. A flutter of excitement passed through her.

Trinity Sands Beach Club, I'm coming back.

* * *

Another clear, sunny day greeted Grace. This time, she made no sarcastic remarks that required repentance. She sat at the kitchen table with her toast and coffee, and a pad and pencil. It had been a long time since she'd traveled, and a list of things to do was a must. Things like call Serenity, stop mail, remember meds, and let the beach club know to have the bungalow opened and cleaned. And the hardest one of all. Call Liz.

The boys were coming over in the afternoon, but they wouldn't need Grace out there with them. She should be able to get everything together today and leave in the morning. That way, she'd arrive before dark.

The pool. She'd forgotten about the pool. Maybe the boys could keep an eye on it for her. All it needed other than the usual weekly maintenance was someone to make sure the water level didn't drop too low.

The more she prepared, the more excited she became. Why hadn't she done this a year ago? She stilled, her hands wrapped around her mug. A year ago, she wasn't ready. She could barely get to church some Sundays.

The Pink Panther theme interrupted her thoughts before they could take her to a dark place. "Hi, Olga."

"You sound better today."

"I've decided to take your advice. I'm going on a trip. I leave tomorrow." Tomorrow? What was she thinking? She looked down at her list.

"Really?" Olga's sing-song voice sang an octave higher. "Where?"

"To our beach house on Trinity Sands Island."

"Is that near Destin?"

"Yes, just off the coast there. Why?"

"I have a sister in Destin who's been begging me to visit. Would you like company on your drive down? I can always catch a flight back."

"That would be great." The reprieve Grace felt in her spirit caught her by surprise. She hadn't realized how nervous she was about driving down alone. "I'd like to get an early start. Can you do that?"

"Of course. I'm up at five to exercise. What time did you have in mind?"

"Pick you up at eight?"

"I'll be ready. Now I must go and pack. See you tomorrow, my friend."

While she had the phone in her hand, she might as well get the hardest thing on her list over with. Grace punched the buttons for Liz's number.

"Mom. Are you okay?"

"I'm fine. Looking forward to the boys coming over today." She knew she was stalling, but she only had so much courage.

"They are too." Liz coughed. "Sorry. Are you sure you don't want me to come too?"

"We'll be fine." Grace let the silence hang a moment. "I've decided to drive down to the beach house tomorrow. Olga is riding with me as far as Destin."

The dead air on the line had a different feel than the quiet a minute ago.

"You know how I feel about you taking a trip alone." Liz's

voice sounded thick, as if she were speaking through a throat clogged with tears.

"Honey, I'll be fine. And I won't be alone." Grace worked to put as much comfort into her words as she could. "Trust me. I'll be careful, and once I'm at the beach house, I'm inside a gated community surrounded by friends."

"How long do you plan to stay?"

"I'm thinking three weeks this time."

"This time?" Liz cried.

"If this works out, I'm hoping you and Chase and the boys might come down." Memories of the family at the house when John was alive streamed through her mind.

"I guess. We did have some good times."

Her daughter's soft sobs broke Grace's heart. John's death hurt Liz too, but this was something Grace had to do. For her own healing. "I need to go, but I'll keep in touch with you on the way down and let you know when I get there. I love you, sweetheart."

"I love you more."

The last thing on her list of things to do before the boys arrived was call Serenity. The phone rang four times before the answering machine picked up. She furrowed her brow at the clock. Where was she? Grace left a message and decided to send a text too.

A little lunch, and she was ready for the teenage invasion. When the boys arrived, she went over the rules of the pool—which resulted in eye rolling from her grandsons and several "Yes, ma'ams" from their friends—and left the boys to their fun. Her next chore was laundry. Not her favorite thing, but she hated to leave dirty clothes for three weeks.

After folding the last set of sheets, she was ready to take a swim. Except her pool was filled with four teenage boys.

Her phone rang. Serenity. "Hi. I tried to—"

"H-lp. I—be—k—d. C—ll—lic—"

Chapter Four

Grace stared at her cellphone. The call ended. She punched the buttons to restore the connection. A recorded voice informed her the mailbox for this number was full, and the call disconnected. She sat at the table and scribbled as much as she could make out of what Serenity said.

Help. Then "I" and "be," followed by "cad"? Next "kawl"? And then "lease"? Help. I be cad. Kawl lease. As much as Grace loved playing word games, this one had her stumped.

The back door burst open, and she lurched to her feet. Four tall, skinny teenage boys tumbled inside beach towels draped around their shoulders.

"Grams, we're hungry. Got something to eat and some Cokes?" Quinn grinned at her.

She grinned back and walked to the pantry. "I've got potato chips and cheese crackers. Let me get you a couple of bowls." She tipped her head toward the refrigerator. "Soft drinks are in there."

Victor, her youngest grandson, stood by the table reading her notes. "What's this, Grandma?"

"It's nothing. Just a word game." She filled the bowls with snacks and crossed to where Vic stood.

"Cool." He sat down. "Let me try."

Grace reached for the paper. "You should be outside with your friend."

"He won't mind." Vic slid it away from her. "You got the word help. I can't make out the middle two words, but I think "kawl" is call. If there was more to "lease," I'd say it was police."

The door opened. "Come on, goofball, we want to play more water volleyball," Quinn said.

"Hope that helps." Vic kissed her on the cheek and hurried outside.

Grace gave him a distracted wave and glanced at the words again. Call police? Had it just been a bad connection? Or was Serenity in trouble? She stared at her phone.

Should she call and have an officer go by her friend's house? What reason could she give for her concern? A letter and a garbled phone call? If she was fine, Grace would feel like an idiot.

She raised her gaze to the pool outside, where four boisterous teenagers laughed without a care in the world. Living alone was making her paranoid. Yesterday morning, she was sure someone was in the house, and that turned out to be nothing. Besides, she'd be down at the beach tomorrow. Plenty of time to—

A loud chime cut into her thoughts. Liz again. Her daughter worried the boys would be too much trouble for their grandmother. "Everything's fine. Don't worry." Grace spoke the words aloud as she keyed them into her phone and pressed send.

She watched once more as her grandsons and their friends splashed and dove under the water. Having them around reminded her of when her husband was alive, and Elizabeth and her brother, Douglas, were young.

Another item to add to her list of to-dos. Call her son and let him know about her trip. Would she be ready? She'd managed to stop the mail, call the beach club, and call Liz. But she still had to pack.

Which meant she had to find the suitcases. She glanced outside. The boys were drying off. Perfect timing.

"Grams, we're going now." Quinn stuck his head through the back door.

"Come in for a moment. I need your help." She smiled at him. "All of you."

"My grandma needs us." Quinn motioned to the boys behind him, and they stepped inside.

"I'm leaving tomorrow for the beach house."

"Cool," Vic said.

"But I have no idea where your grandfather kept the suitcases." She gazed from one to the other of the boys. "Would you mind helping me find them? They're in a closet, the attic, or the garage. I thought Quinn, you and your friend could search the garage and the first floor, and Victor and his friend could look on the second floor and attic. If you have time." She waved her hands in a dismissive gesture. "If not, that's fine. I can do it myself. Not a problem."

Quinn and Victor shared looks with their friends, and the boys shrugged like no big deal. They tossed their towels on the kitchen table and took off. Quinn and his buddy headed for the garage first. "Wait till you see all the cool stuff my gramps has in there."

Vic and his friend tromped up the stairs. "Want to start in the attic? It's not scary or nothing like in the movies."

Kid power. Nothing like it. Grace went into her bedroom and opened her closet. A rainbow of T-shirts hung arranged by color. She picked six or seven of her favorites and threw them on the bed, along with a few capris and two pairs of jeans. That should do.

She'd left a few clothes at the beach. Although—she eyed herself in the full-length mirror—whether they still fit was yet to be determined. Best to take some that she was sure of.

"They're not in the garage, Grams." Quinn slammed the door into the kitchen.

She poked her head out into the hall. "Try the closet under the stairs next."

"Okay."

She chuckled before returning to her task. Why did teenage boys sound like a herd of stampeding buffaloes wherever they went? Underwear, sleepwear, two swimsuits, and a couple pairs of shorts were added to the pile. As she entered the master bath for her travel kit, a peculiar banging sounded above her head.

"We found them, Grandma," Victor called from the head of the stairs. "Two big ones, two medium, and one small. You want them all?"

She hurried out of her room and looked up at him. "No, thanks, Vic. One big one and one of the medium ones will do."

He ducked out of sight.

"Wait."

His face reappeared.

"Bring the small one down too." She grinned at him.

He rolled his eyes at her. "You sure now? You don't want any more?"

"I'm sure." She nodded.

Murmuring was followed by the clatter and thump of suitcases being dragged down the stairs to the hall. "Man, these are dirty."

"Put them in the kitchen." She tossed her travel kit on the

bed and joined Vic, Quinn, and their friends. "Thanks, guys." She handed them each a five-dollar bill.

"No, Grams, we don't want this." Quinn pushed it back at her. "We were helping you."

Vic tried to hand his back as well. Their friends held onto theirs.

"Take it. I have another favor to ask." She glanced out at the pool. "I've got a pool service that comes every week to make sure the chemicals are good, but I'd like you and your brother to drop by occasionally to check the water level. Can you do that for me?"

"Sure." Quinn shrugged. "No problem."

She gave them a stern look. "But no swimming unless one of your parents is here. Got that?"

Another eye roll. "Yes, ma'am."

"Now go on, and thanks for finding my suitcases." She waved them out the door.

After the boys left, Grace decided to try calling Serenity one more time before turning her attention to the suitcases. It went straight to a canned voice informing her that the number she called could not be reached. She thrust a wave of unease away. "Don't borrow trouble." Grace admonished herself aloud and jammed her phone into her pocket.

The suitcases weren't dusty—they were filthy. She thought about putting them in the shower, but she was afraid they wouldn't dry in time for her to leave. Instead, she pulled a fist full of paper towels from the rack, dampened a few, and set to work wiping down the outside.

The large one was the worst. It had a nest of spiders between the wheels. Grace hated spiders. But she got the job done and rolled them into the bedroom. She lifted the big suitcase onto the bed and unzipped it. The inside was clean and empty. Except for one thing. There was an envelope in a side zippered pouch, and it had her name on it.

Grace pulled what proved to be an anniversary card from the envelope. John must have bought it early and stashed it in the suitcase. The printed sentiment was beautiful, but it was what he'd written that made her legs give way and ripped the bandage off her heart once more.

"If, for some reason, I had to give you up right now, I would still be thankful for all the wonderful years we've had. Life with you has been a blessing."

Did he know he'd be gone before they could celebrate that anniversary? Or was Grace being given a good-bye from John and his blessing to move on with her life? She stood and placed the card on her dresser. "Life with you was a blessing, too, my love."

Chapter Five

Grace chose one of the stronger coffee blends from her rack of pods and inserted it into her machine. She'd spent most of the night going over what she'd packed for the trip. Had she forgotten anything? She drummed her fingers on the counter, impatient for the stream of rich brown liquid to fill her mug.

The aroma began the work of stimulating her brain cells, but she needed that first jolt of caffeine to clear her mind completely. As soon as the last drip left the nozzle, Grace lifted the mug to her lips and blew on it before taking a sip. Hot, but so good.

She pulled out a chair at the kitchen table and placed her mug to one side. "Let's take one more look at the list." Thinking aloud had become a habit since John's death. It helped to hear a human voice—even if it was her own. She ran a finger down the items she'd written on the paper, each neatly checked off. For a moment, she glanced around and tried to think if there was anything she was forgetting. She shook her head. "Don't think so." But it had been so long since she'd traveled away from home.

The paper with the words written from Serenity's strange call caught her eye. "I wonder ..." Maybe her grandson was wrong. It could be her friend said something like "Call somebody or someplace please," instead of "Call the police." Grace lifted her gaze to the window. A sudden urgency filled her, and she pushed away from the table.

She loaded her luggage and computer in the car. After one more check to make sure all the lights were off and all was in order, Grace paused. "Take care of my house, Lord, while I'm gone. And please be with me on this trip." She set the alarm and locked the door.

* * *

"I can't believe I'm actually doing this." Grace cut her eyes to Olga. "Thanks, my friend."

"I planted the seed only, you ran with it." Olga grinned at her.

Grace laughed. Her Scandinavian friend was a great editor, but in her speech, she tended to mix metaphors. Especially when she was excited.

"Oops." Olga giggled. "Did I do it again?"

"Yes, but don't worry about it. It's charming, and it's part of who you are."

"That's why we're such good friends." Olga patted Grace's arm. "You are so kind. You accept people the way they are."

"I guess." The rude woman in the grocery store last week popped into Grace's mind. She wasn't too kind to her. In fact, she called her a bad word. To her face. Ouch. That one pinched her conscience until she finally asked the Lord for forgiveness—even if the woman did deserve it.

"So, did you bring your computer?"

"I wondered how long before my friend would turn into my publisher." Grace chuckled. "Yes, I brought my computer and all my notes, yada, yada."

"Good. Maybe you will get some inspiration at this beach village of yours."

"I may." Serenity's strange call flashed into her mind once more. "I just hope ..."

"Hope what?"

"Well, I received a letter from a friend, Serenity James, who lives in Trinity Sands Beach Club, and she told me that some strange things have been going on there."

"Like what strange things?"

"In the last few months, there's been an attempted robbery and a murder. And now she's been seeing something weird going on in the wilds, a nature preserve next to the Club."

"Ooh, sounds like you may have much to stimulate your brain." Olga's voice had a joyous lilt to it.

No doubt she envisioned a three-novel series about a small beach community soon.

"I tried to call her before we left but got her voicemail." Grace furrowed her brow. "When she called back, it was garbled."

"Do you think she's in trouble?"

"I'm not sure. I hope not."

"We will pray for her safety." Olga-publisher switched to Olga-friend once more.

"Thank you." Another thing they had in common—their faith.

"And now, if you will forgive me, I will get some work done."

The two friends rode in companionable silence for several hours. Grace had forgotten how much she liked driving. The scenery seemed new and fresh to her. She smiled to herself. Probably much of it was new. It had been three years since she'd been on this road.

Around Montgomery, Alabama, Grace's stomach growled for the first time. "Are you ready for some lunch?"

Olga looked up. "I can eat anytime."

They pulled into an Arby's, visited the restroom, and ordered two roast beef sandwiches with curly fries and sweet teas.

"How far are we?" Olga asked.

"About halfway. It should be another three to four hours."

"Would you like me to drive for a while?"

A tempting offer. Grace loved to sleep in the car when John drove. "No, that's okay. But would you mind if I listen to a book?"

"No, I'd love it. What book?"

"I have the latest John Grisham on my phone. Is that okay?"

"Perfect." Olga clapped her hands. "I haven't had a chance to read that one."

The remaining hours flew by as Grace and Olga listened to the adventures of a publisher and a novelist on an island. A tingling crept up Grace's spine. Could this be an omen of what was to come for her?

As they neared Destin, Grace turned off the book.

"I want to hear the ending." Olga punched her lightly in the arm.

"I need directions to your sister's house." Grace cut her eyes to her friend.

"Of course." Olga shrugged. "Sorry." She peered at the road signs. "Where are we? Ah, yes. Make a right at the next street."

"Good thing I got your attention when I did."

"But now I will have to buy the book to see how it ends."

"Too bad, my friend. Where to next?" Grace slowed. They

were in a neighborhood of beautiful homes on half-acre lots. The high-rent district as John would have called it.

"Left here. It's the third house on the right."

Grace steered her car onto a double driveway before a sprawling ranch home with several palm trees in the front. A tall, slim woman with white hair hurried out the front door.

"Olga." She flung her arms wide. "I can't believe you're here."

"Your sister?"

"Yah." Olga's face split into a big grin. "We are close."

"I can tell." A pang of jealousy zipped through Grace.

"Come, you must meet her." Olga jumped from the car.

Grace got out of the car. Every muscle in her body protested the change in position. How had Olga leaped out like that? She straightened and tried to walk with some semblance of a normal human being over to the sisters.

"This is my dear friend, Grace Caldwell." Olga swept her hand in Grace's direction. "Grace, this is my wonderful sister, Ana."

"Glad to meet you, Ana." She almost said, "Wonderful sister, Ana," but checked herself in time. She was tired, and she still had about forty-five minutes until she reached the island.

"Come inside." Ana's smile was broad and inviting.

"Thank you, but I really need to get to my beach house." She returned her smile. "Another time."

Olga grabbed her in a hug. "I'll be here for two weeks. If you need me, call."

"Thanks. Enjoy your visit. I'll see you back in Memphis." Grace folded herself into the driver's seat once more and started her car. Only forty-five minutes. Then she could collapse.

The two sisters strolled back to the house arm-in-arm, heads together, already deep in conversation. Grace gazed after them and sighed. She set the GPS for Trinity Sands Island and backed out of the driveway.

As she pulled onto the main street, she pressed play. No reason she couldn't listen to the end of the book. A woman's soft voice interrupted when she needed to make a turn, and soon, she was crossing the bridge to the island. As she pulled up to the guard shack, the Grisham novel came to an end.

A broad-shouldered man with graying dark hair stepped out. "Welcome to Trinity Sands Beach Club."

Grace handed him her driver's license and her membership card. "We have a house in the beach club, but my husband died, and I haven't been back for three years."

"Mrs. Caldwell, I'm so sorry for your loss." He perused her identification and card. "Let me get you a hang tag for your car." He stepped back into the booth.

Things had changed. Now they had hang tags. And who was this guy? What happened to the other man? Her stomach soured with unease. Had she made a big mistake coming here?

"Let me introduce myself. I'm the new Chief of Security, Ben Hastings." He handed her license and membership card back, along with a tag for her car. "If you'll hang that from your mirror, you won't have to stop every time you come into the club." He handed her a piece of paper. "We have a new set of rules since you've been here last. Please read these, and if you have any questions, my number is at the bottom." He touched the brim of his hat. "Glad to have you back with us, Mrs. Caldwell."

"Thank you. It's good to be back." Or was it? Grace drove slowly through the winding streets, not so anxious to see her house now that she was here. She turned the final corner. Its familiar gray clapboard with white trim came into view, and her heart beat a little faster.

What was that strange panel van doing in her driveway?

Chapter Six

Grace pulled up next to the van and stared up the driveway. This was her house, wasn't it? She double-checked the address on her membership card. Yes, she was at the right place. Grabbing her pepper spray and her keys, she climbed out of her car and ignored her stiff muscles.

The front door stood ajar behind the screen door. Pressing her lips together, she stepped into the foyer. She heard rustling in the kitchen to her right. "Hello. Who's there?" She fought to keep the waiver from her voice.

"Ms. Grace. You got here earlier than you should've. I mean, than I thought." The face of Ursula, the housecleaner, popped around the corner. "Welcome back." She smiled, showing new gaps in her toothy grin. "I'm almost done."

"It didn't take me as long as I thought it would. Take your time." Grace wandered toward the memory-filled rooms facing the ocean, touching photos and treasures from the beach. Her eyes welled with tears, and her chest ached where her heart pushed against old scars. She dropped into a chair.

"Oh, Ms. G. You want me to make you a cup of tea?"

Ursula appeared at Grace's side, her face lined with compassion.

"Do we have some?"

"Yep. There are some bags in the drawer. I'll heat up some water and brew us a cuppa."

The clinks of mugs and ring of a metal pot being set on a gas ring brought memories of hot chocolate in the fall.

"I can keep your mind off your ... I can keep you entertained with all the latest gossip while we drink our tea." She skittered out of the kitchen carrying two brimming mugs of hot tea. "Here you go."

Ursula always reminded Grace of one of those little sea birds that raced along the sand at the edge of the waves with her skinny legs and her quick movements.

"Thank you." Judging from the steam, Grace wasn't about to take a drink for a while.

After Ursula settled in a chair, she noisily sipped from her mug.

"How can you ...?" Grace stared in amazement.

"What?" The woman noticed her stare. "Oh, honey, I burnt out my tastebuds long ago. Hot, cold, don't mean much to me anymore." She gave Grace a sly grin. "But let me tell you what's been going on since you been away. Now that'll curl your hair."

"Serenity told me there's been a murder and a theft in the past couple of months." Grace brought the mug close to her face and inhaled.

"Oh." Ursula pinched her lips together.

"But she didn't tell me any of the details."

The woman's eyes brightened. "Well, she probably didn't know them, but I do."

After thirty minutes of more information than Grace ever wanted to know about her neighbors, she found the opportunity she'd been waiting for. "Ursula, did Serenity ever talk to you about something strange going on in the Wilds late at night?"

The woman narrowed her eyes in thought. "One time, she mentioned seeing lights moving around in the marshy area. I told her it was probably just kids being kids. You know."

"With the snakes and alligators?" Grace couldn't imagine any kid thinking that would be fun.

"Maybe hunters?" She stood and reached for Grace's mug. "I'll just wash these up. Got to be getting on."

Grace followed her into the kitchen. "Have you talked to Serenity lately? How is she?"

"Come to think of it." She wrinkled her brow. "The last time I went in to do for her, she wasn't there. But there was food on the table, and her purse hung on the hook."

A hard fist of unease grew in Grace's stomach. "Have you seen her since?"

"No, but I usually don't. I'm due to go back at the end of the week."

Grace walked the house cleaner to the door. "Thanks, Ursula. I appreciate you getting the house ready for me." She slipped a five-dollar bill into her hand.

"Thanks, Ms. G." The woman gave her a gap-toothed smile. "Always a pleasure."

Murder, robbery, and now a possible disappearance? In Trinity Sands Beach Club of all places. Grace gazed out at the houses on her street in the early evening glow. Palms waved gently. Lights were beginning to appear in the houses. Did one of them contain a criminal? Was there no place free from a possible monster?

A gust of warm, humid air blew in through the screen door, snapping her out of her reverie, and she shut the door. Her complaining stomach led her back to the kitchen and the refrigerator. God bless Ursula. She should have given her a twenty-dollar tip. The woman had stocked it with all the staples. Milk, cheese, butter, and eggs. A loaf of bread lay on the counter.

Grace pulled her hair back and got busy making a cheese omelet and toast. She took her meal into the dining area, where windows overlooked the beach and ocean beyond. The moon was full. Its reflection trailed away in the waves and turned the white sand into tiny diamonds. Her heart surged within her. How she'd missed this view.

Serenity's house was on the curve farther east. Her view out back was mostly of the Wilds, with only a sliver of the beach to the right. Grace opened the water bottle she'd brought in from the car and took a swig. She picked up her phone and punched in Serenity's number once more. A message came on that the number she'd dialed could not be reached at this time. Did that mean her phone was turned off? Or dead?

She took her plate to the kitchen and retrieved her suitcases from the car. There was nothing she could do now. But she needed to be ready in the morning. She unpacked and prepared for bed.

Her phone rang.

"Mom? Are you all right? Where are you?" Elizabeth's frantic voice sounded in her ear.

"I'm good." Grace put a lightness into her voice. "I'm at the beach house. Sorry I didn't call right away, but Ursula, the housecleaner, was here, and she insisted on telling me everything that's happened since I've been away. We had a great talk. I feel all caught up." She paused for a breath. "It's as beautiful as I remember. I hope you and Chase and the boys can come down sometime."

"I just wish you'd called. That's all." Her voice changed to one of hurt feelings. "You know I'm back here worried about you."

"I know. I'm sorry. Please forgive me."

"Well, call me every day. Okay?"

"I ... I'll try." Grace shook her head.

"Mom. I need to know you're okay."

"I have a life, Elizabeth. And I have friends here."

An uneasy silence filled the line.

"I love you, Elizabeth."

"Love you too, Mom. Please try."

"I will. Good night, sweetheart."

"Chase sends his love too. And the boys."

"Love to them too."

Grace put the phone next to her and laid her head back on the sofa cushion. "John, see what you're missing? What if I'd gone first?"

She lifted her head. But then, who'd search for Serenity?

Chapter Seven

Grace woke with a start. Where was she? Her heart raced as she took in the room around her. The beach house. She closed her eyes and waited for her muscles to relax. Tears dampened her lashes.

"No, I'm not going to start the day that way." Grace threw back the covers and swung her legs out of bed. "I've got work to do."

Showered and dressed in lightweight slacks and a loose cotton top, she headed for the kitchen and coffee. The back deck called her name. She opened the slider and stepped out.

The rhythmic sound of the waves, the call of the gulls, the sun sparkling off the white sand, and the breeze that danced over the dunes and tousled her hair all combined to lift her spirits and bring her a joy she hadn't felt in a long time. Why had she stayed away so long?

Grace went inside and returned with her Bible and a fresh cup of coffee.

After feeding her spirit, it was time to feed her body. She

scrambled the last of the eggs and put them on toast with a slice of cheese. A trip to Maude's was definitely on the agenda for today. But first on the list was a visit to Serenity's house. She needed to go through it before Ursula cleaned again.

Her broad-brimmed straw hat hung where she'd left it in the hall three years ago, and under it, the key to Serenity's bungalow. She slung her purse over her shoulder and grabbed both on her way out the door.

Serenity's bungalow was tucked in between newer two-story homes. All the houses on this end were elevated because they backed up to the Wilds, a part of the island left in its natural state. Grace climbed the stairs to the front door. Should she knock just in case?

Serenity's car wasn't parked beneath the house. Odd. Ursula had told her it was there last week. She slipped the key into the lock. It had been a long time. What if her friend had changed the locks? But she hadn't. The knob turned easily in her hand, and she paused in the entryway before closing the door behind her. "Serenity?" She listened intently, but other than the whirr of the refrigerator, heard nothing.

The house was set up much like hers except that the two bedroom doors were on the left with the bathroom between them. She slipped the key into her pocket and walked into the kitchen. The food was gone too. Grace opened the dishwasher slotted under the counter next to the sink. There was the plate, utensils, and cup Ursula mentioned. Had she done that? Or had Serenity been back home?

Grace turned on a lamp in the family room. It was as if she'd last visited yesterday, not three years ago. Everything looked the same to her. She opened the sliding door onto the deck and stepped out. The view was so different from hers that if it weren't for the steady sound of the ocean rushing in and receding, it would be hard to believe she was just down the street from her own home.

Instead of waves of water, rippling waves of green—every shade imaginable—filled the scene before her. The Wilds was a mixture of freshwater furnished by several springs blended with sea water flowing in at high tide to the low-lying area, and sometimes, the water level overflowed into the yards along the edge. The resulting brackish water supported duckweed, sand cord grass, and maiden cane, among other interesting vegetation.

And then there was the wildlife. Serenity told stories of finding everything from alligators to rabbits in her backyard, but mostly deer. She couldn't keep any flowers except in pots on the upper deck, and they needed watering.

Grace returned to the house, closing and locking the slider. She headed for the front bedroom—Serenity's room. The bed was made, and everything seemed undisturbed. When she entered, her friend's favorite scent lingered in the air and triggered so many good memories. *Where are you, Serenity?*

After searching through the closet, she moved on to the other bedroom. Serenity used this room as her office. Grace stared at her desk. Where was her computer? Maybe her friend had been back. Was she in hiding for some reason? But why?

Grace took a deep breath and forced her concentration back to the room. She thumbed through the papers on her desk. Only bills. An exploration of the file cabinet and the desk drawers yielded nothing of interest.

As she was leaving, she noticed a collection of whimsical key chains sitting on a shelf. They were in the shapes of animals. It didn't seem like the Serenity she remembered. The alligator one looked like it was broken. She picked it up. It wasn't broken, it came apart, and inside was a flash drive. A wave of excitement broke inside her, and her hands began to tremble.

Grace heard a key in the door, and her excitement turned to fear. She scooped all the key chains into her purse and zipped it close before tiptoeing to the bedroom door.

"Mrs. Caldwell, I know you're in here." A stern male voice sounded a few feet away from her. "You need to come out. You're trespassing."

She peeked out. Ben, the security guard, stood inside the door with his hands on his hips. She licked her lips and stepped from the room. "Hello, Officer."

"You shouldn't be here."

"I'm worried about my friend, Serenity." She put her hand in her pocket to pull out her key but stopped. Serenity's house key lay on the kitchen counter. With a penguin keychain. "I have a key." She grabbed Serenity's key. "I'm not really trespassing."

"Why are you concerned about Ms. James?" He crossed his arms in front of him.

"Maybe we could sit a minute?" Grace motioned toward the family room. "It's a rather long story."

He waved a hand for her to go ahead of him.

Was he being a gentleman? Or was he afraid she'd hit him on the head with her handbag and make a run for it?

Once settled, she told him about Serenity's letter and the strange phone call. "I decided I needed to come down and see for myself. When I got here, Ursula, was at my house. You know Ursula, don't you?"

"I know Ursula." He managed to do an eye roll with his tone of voice.

"She told me that there was food on the table, and Serenity's purse and car were both here." Grace waved toward the front door. "None of that is here now. Her car and purse are gone. And her computer." She narrowed her eyes. "But all her clothes are still in the house. Along with her toothbrush and favorite perfume."

"So, you think someone is trying to make it look like Ms. James has taken off when she's really been what? Kidnapped?"

A chill ran through Grace. "I guess I am."

Chapter Eight

Kidnapped. Grace was stunned into silence. That was the only explanation that made any sense. If Serenity left of her own accord, she'd have taken a change of clothes at least. Probably her toothbrush. She was always so particular about her teeth.

"Mrs. Caldwell." Ben tapped her knee.

"Sorry. I ..."

"I'll need to inform the authorities, and I'll need your key to Ms. James's house." He stood and held out his hand.

She removed Serenity's key from her purse. "Can I keep my keychain?"

"Certainly."

She extracted the key from the penguin keychain and placed it in Ben's hand.

"I imagine someone from the sheriff's office will be contacting you to take your statement." He ushered her to the front door. "Beyond that, please do not attempt to investigate on your own any further. Is there anything else you want to tell me?"

"No. I'll leave it to you." Grace kept her gaze on the floor, the other key burning a hole in her pocket and her lies burning a hole in her soul. But what could she do? She'd promised herself she'd help Serenity, and that's what she was going to do.

Back at her home, she dumped the contents of her purse on the table and sorted out the keychain animals. There was a gorilla, alligator, dog, penguin, and hippo. She shoveled the rest of the contents back into her purse and went in search of her computer.

She arranged them alphabetically according to name and inserted the alligator first. Serenity didn't use any security on the flash drive, God bless her, or Grace would have been out of luck. She chuckled. Unless she brought in her secret weapon— her grandson, Victor.

Alligator contained just that. Photos of alligators. Grace zipped through a few and closed the drive. Would the cat be photos of cats? She opened it and found photos of the family that rented the house to the right. And their dog. Again, she looked at a few and ejected the drive.

Three more to go. Her stomach growled. She closed her computer and pushed up from the table. There wasn't much left of the food Ursula had bought for her. She opened the cupboard. Did she remember seeing some peanut butter crackers?

The doorbell rang. A man in khakis and a blue golf shirt stood on her porch.

"I'm Detective Peter Young from the Trinity Island Sheriff's Department." He flashed a shield. "May I come in?"

A detective? So soon? And from our tiny department? "May I see your badge again?" She opened the screen door just enough to reach out and snatch the ID from his hand. Then she pulled it shut, locked it, and slammed the front door.

* * *

Peter Young stepped back. She slammed the door in his face. Never in all his years as a detective in Chicago had this happened to him. His first instinct was to pound on the offending door and demand entry. Or at least get his badge back.

He ran a hand over his bald head and looked around. What did he know about Grace Caldwell? She was a widow. Both she and her husband were long-time members in good standing. This was her first time back to the beach club in three years.

So, detective, what do you make of that? She was anxious. Fearful. Cautious. He glanced down at his casual dress and decided he'd have reacted the same way in her situation.

The door opened, and Grace ushered him inside without an apology. *And she's not ashamed of who she is.* He liked that in a woman.

"Would you care for something to drink? Until I get to the market, all I can offer is bottled water, coffee, or hot tea." Grace paused at the door to the kitchen.

"Water's good."

"I'm going to fix myself a cup of tea."

He moved through the hallway into the family room. Family photos took up space on walls and shelves. The pictures depicted a much younger Grace with a handsome man and two young children playing on the beach. Several others were of a growing family around the table and grandsons unwrapping presents while doting grandparents watched.

There were books behind the photos on the shelves that covered one wall. He homed in on a section of interesting titles. "Whoa." He turned his gaze toward the kitchen. Grace Caldwell was an author. A prolific one.

Grace entered the room and handed him a bottled water

with a napkin wrapped around it. "Please, have a seat." She lowered herself gracefully into an armchair and balanced her tea on her knee.

Peter took a seat on the sofa and opened his notebook. "I spoke with Ben, and he told me what you said, but I'd like to hear it from you."

"Of course." She placed her mug on the side table. "In fact, let me get the letter and my transcript of Serenity's phone message."

She handed them to him, and he got a whiff of sage. "Thanks. I'll take pictures, and you can have these back for now."

"My husband passed away three years ago, and I haven't been to our house at the beach club until now. But Serenity James and I have kept in touch, as you can see from her letter." Grace settled into the armchair and related the story once more. When she'd finished, she leveled her gaze at him. "I promised Serenity I'd help, and I never go back on a promise."

He considered her. "Meaning you're going to continue looking into her disappearance no matter what I say."

She gave a slight nod.

"In that case—" He slapped his notebook shut. "—I'm left with a choice. Either send you back to Memphis—which I can't do—or let you work *with* me." For an instant, her smile took his breath away. "In a limited capacity. And I'm the boss. You don't make a move without my approval."

Her eyes slipped away from his before returning. "Of course."

Why did he not believe her? She was definitely the most attractive partner he'd ever had. He forced his attention back to the papers she'd given him. "Any idea what Ms. James was trying to say?" He tapped the one with the phone message on it.

She rose and came to look over his shoulder. The pleasant scent of sage reached him once more, and his pulse sped up.

"My youngest grandson believes this last part—" She leaned over and pointed to a spot on the page. "—is 'call the police,' but I'm not convinced."

"What do you ..." He stopped and cleared his throat. "What do you think it says?"

"I think it might be 'call somebody please.'" She straightened and walked back to her chair.

He stared at the paper until his heart rate slowed, and he could focus again. This would never do. It had been a very long time since a woman had affected him this way. Not since ... He jumped up and strode over to the kitchen counter. "I'll get photos of these and go back to the station to open a missing persons file on Ms. James."

Grace rose and brought his water over to him. "Don't forget this."

That smile again. All he could do was nod. He needed to get out of there pronto. Two shots with his phone, and he turned to go.

She held out a hand and said something he didn't catch. He took it in his. It was soft and warm, and he struggled to keep from raising it to his lips.

"Thank you, Detective." She gave a small laugh. "Now may I have one of your cards?"

The heat rose from his neck. "Of course." He let go of her hand and fumbled in his wallet. "Let me write my cell number on it."

"Do you need mine?"

"Yes." He withdrew his notebook again. By now, the heat at his neck had reached his cheeks, and all he could think about was making a hasty exit. He jotted her number down and rushed out the door.

As he hurried to his car, he mumbled to himself. "You've really done it now, Young, you idiot." Why did he ever agree to include her in his investigation? She was a civilian. And an author. He'd probably end up as a character in her next novel. He groaned.

The closer he got to the police station, the more insane the whole scheme seemed to him, and the more he resolved to rectify his mistake. No working together to find Serenity James. He was the detective. Mrs. Caldwell would have to be content doing whatever she did—shop, enjoy the beach, work on her novel—and leave the investigating to him.

Chapter Nine

Grace read the card in her hand. Detective Peter Young. A tingle ran through her, followed closely by a wave of guilt. After three years, she still felt like a married woman, not a widow.

Her friend, Olga, would tell her it was about time she started living again. Her daughter, Elizabeth, on the other hand ... She tossed the card on the counter and sighed. Maybe it wasn't such a good idea to work with Detective Young. But, she'd made a promise to Serenity.

Grace grabbed some peanut butter crackers and her mug and went out on the deck. The day had gotten hot. Even the breeze was warm. August at the beach. She positioned her chair out of the direct sun and opened her snack.

The question was, could she keep her promise without getting in trouble with Detective Young? She narrowed her eyes. Maybe. She'd have to be very careful. She rose and brushed crumbs off her lap. Tomorrow she'd call and tell him that she'd decided to leave the investigation in his capable hands.

Now, she needed food, and that meant a trip to the market. And a chat with Maude. Grace went back inside and locked the slider. She rinsed her cup and grabbed her purse. From what she'd seen so far, things hadn't changed much. Which meant Maude would know all there was to know about the island—and Serenity James.

Maude's Market was situated in the small town of Trinity Sands, along with the post office, a café, a gas station, and the police department. Grace waved at Ben as she drove past the guard shack.

The town looked a lot like it had three years ago, and that brought a sense of comfort to her. Except the post office had a new sign, and the café sported a new coat of paint and landscaping. All signs the island was prospering, and that made her feel good.

Maude's was the same—down to the three old men on the porch. Grace smiled to herself and exited her car.

"Mrs. Caldwell." One of the men squinted at her. "Sorry about John. He was a good man."

The three removed their hats and nodded in unison.

"Thank you, gentlemen." She forced the words past the constriction of her throat. "He enjoyed talking fishing with you." She fought back tears and pushed the door open.

"Mrs. C, I heard you was back." The woman at the cash register rang up a can of peas and motioned for the young woman bagging to take over checking out the customer. "I need to chat with my friend here." Maude removed her apron and patted her beehive hairdo back into place before grabbing Grace in a bear hug.

"It's good to see you too." She gently disengaged.

Maude took a step back and ran a critical eye over her. "You are skin and bones, girl. Not good. Shows every wrinkle. You need to eat more." She touched Grace's hair with a gnarled finger. "At least you're still colorin' your hair. Goin' gray adds ten years to a girl's age."

"I've missed you, Maude." Grace couldn't contain her grin. "And I do need to eat more. That's why I'm here." Mostly.

"Well, let's get movin'." She yanked one of the carts from the line and pushed it over to Grace. "While you shop, I'll tell you what's been goin' on here."

"Ursula told me some of it."

"Pfft. Ursula." Maude waved a hand in the air. "She don't know half the story. I know what's *really* happening around here."

Grace selected a head of lettuce. "And that's the other reason I came."

"What did Ursula tell you?"

"There's been a murder and an attempted theft in the last two months." She picked up a tomato to check its freshness.

"Did she tell you Annie, the alligator, is missing? Or that UFOs have been seen over the Wilds?" Maude gave her a little shove. "Or that we have a detective on our police force now? Detective Peter Young, and he's a hunk."

Grace pressed her thumb into the tomato, and juice squirted everywhere. "I guess I'm buying this one." She placed it in her basket and looked around for something to clean her hand.

"Here ya go." Maude handed her a paper towel from her pocket. "You don't need to push so hard."

"Sorry." Grace chose two more tomatoes and moved on to the apples.

"As I was sayin', this new detective is mighty fine. I don't know what it is about him. He's bald, and I don't usually go for the hairless types."

Grace stopped moving. The image of Peter Young in her family room flashed before her.

"He's got this kind of scruffy beard-mustache thing goin'." Maude gestured around her mouth and chin. "But that's not it either."

"I think it's his eyes," Grace said. "They change color with his mood. Light when he's talking about things he's interested in, and dark when he's more serious."

"Well, well, well." Maude planted her hands on her hips. "You've met the dishy detective."

Uh-oh. Grace licked her lips. "Yes, I have." She turned to Maude. "I'm worried about Serenity James. She's missing. Maude, do you know anything about what's happened to her?"

"I'm so glad you asked." Maude moved closer and checked to see if anyone was around. "Serenity is the one who told me about the UFOs." She stared directly into Grace's eyes.

"And you think?" Did she really want Maude's look translated into words?

"They took her."

"Who took her?"

"The things in the UFOs." The disappointment in Maude's eyes was palpable. "You don't believe me either."

"No, Maude, but I do think she's been kidnapped." Grace looked away. "I just never thought of abduction by aliens."

"It's the only thing that makes sense."

Maude's urgent tone made Grace turn back to her. "Serenity told you she saw UFOs in the Wilds? What exactly did she say?"

"She said she saw lights in the sky over the Wilds. They were pointed down into the marsh. Then tendrils dropped down from the sky like the arms of a jellyfish. Only they had knobby things at the ends. After a while, they pulled back up, and the lights went out."

"She didn't hear anything? Like an engine or a motor?"

"No."

"How often did she see the UFOs?"

"Three or four times. I think they started about May."

"Why didn't she report it to the police?"

"She knew they wouldn't believe her." Maude waved a hand in the air. "The only reason she said anything to me is because one night I was at her house, and we'd had a few drinks on her back deck. She pointed to the Wilds and told me what she'd seen. Spooked me, I can tell you."

What had Serenity seen behind her house? There had to be a rational explanation. Grace didn't believe in UFOs.

"Honey, you need to quit doing your brow like that. Those wrinkles will set up, and you won't be able to get rid of them."

This coming from the woman whose face was a road map to her life in the Florida sun.

Grace relaxed her brow. "Better?"

"Much."

"Did Serenity tell you anything else?"

"She said something crazy. I figured it was the wine talkin'." Maude passed Grace three cans of green beans. "You need these."

"What did she say?"

"She said the penguin knows all about it." Maude lifted her shoulders.

Grace's mouth went dry. "That's goofy." She forced a laugh and glanced at her watch. "It's getting late, and I haven't eaten much all day." She needed to get back to the house.

"Well, we better get your food, girl." Maude hustled over to the meat section.

Chapter Ten

The penguin held the key. Grace knew exactly what that meant. Her heart beat against her ribs. But by the time she unloaded her groceries and put them away, she felt like she'd stepped into a sauna with her clothes on. She needed another shower and some real food before trying to make sense of what Serenity left for her to find on the flash drive.

After clearing the table, she brought her computer and the animal keychains into the dining area so she could work while watching the evening sky over the ocean. Clad in shorts and a tank top with her hair in a ponytail, she finally felt like she was at the beach.

Excitement coursed through her as she inserted the penguin into the USB port. After a few keystrokes, images popped up on her screen. She squinted through her reading glasses at each photo in turn. They were nighttime photos with spots of light.

She enlarged them as much as possible and could tell they were taken off Serenity's back deck. In one, she could make out the tendrils Maude talked about. There were several sets of photos taken at different times from as far back as May. She jotted down the dates.

When Grace compared her notes to a calendar, her hands began to tremble. She double-checked her information. The conclusion was the same: The lights were due to show again tomorrow night. Should she call Detective Young? What if she was wrong?

Color faded from the sky ahead of the relentless march of time. No moon lit up the night to replace the sun. Only the stars cast a soft glow on the waves as they continued their endless motion.

Grace opened the slider but pulled the screen door shut so she could hear the ocean without fighting off bugs. The air was cooler but still humid. If she was going to wait on Serenity's deck tomorrow night, she'd need a few things. Like bug spray. Or maybe mosquito netting. And a fan. She yawned and closed the glass door. That was enough fresh air for one day.

As she closed the curtains a portrait on the wall caught her eye. Her family had come to the beach for Thanksgiving one year. The weather was perfect and so was their time together. She pressed her palm to her forehead. She promised to call her daughter. Actually, she promised to *try to remember* to call her daughter. Best do it now.

"Mom, you remembered." Liz sounded almost cheerful.

"I did." Grace pulled her legs under her on the sofa. "How was your day?"

"Good. The boys and I went clothes shopping for school."

"Really? And they're alive and unharmed?"

Liz chuckled. "I bribed them with a new video game each."

"Ah."

"How was your day?"

Should she tell her daughter she got caught snooping in Serenity's house? No, probably not. "I met some new people."

Not a lie. She'd met Detective Young. "And I went grocery shopping."

"Is Maude's still the go-to market down there?" Liz laughed.

"Yes, and she's still a bottle-blonde who knows all about everything happening on the island." Grace joined Liz in her laughter. "And she still likes to hand out advice. She told me I need to eat more—that my wrinkles are showing."

There was a brief pause.

"She's right about that," Liz said. "The eating part I mean."

"Not you too. Believe me, I bought enough food to feed an army, and I intend to eat like a pig."

"Good."

"Seriously, it's beautiful here. Peaceful. I don't know why I've stayed away so long."

"Well, don't even think about moving down there permanently. I don't know what I'd do without you."

"I'm not, but you may have to come visit because I intend to spend more time here in the future. I love you, Elizabeth. And tell Chase and the boys I love them too."

"Love you too, Mom. I will. Call me tomorrow."

Grace scooched down on the sofa and closed her eyes. A sudden fatigue overtook her. Maybe she'd just lay there for a moment.

* * *

Grace pushed herself up, arched her back, and groaned. Sunlight filtered through the curtains. She was going to pay for this. The sofa was swell for napping but not so much for sleeping overnight. She ran her tongue over her teeth. Yuck.

She rose and stepped around the sofa headed for the kitchen. The doorbell chimed. "Who could that be?" She changed direction and peeked through the peephole. Detective Peter Young stood on her porch. This time, he was in a suit. Ribbons of excitement twirled inside her. She did like a man in a suit.

"Give me a minute." Grace called through the closed door. "I'm not ready for visitors."

She hurried toward her bedroom but detoured to the dining room where her computer, the animal keychains, and her notes covered the table. After stuffing the incriminating items under her bed, she ran a brush through her hair and cleaned her teeth. A new pair of shorts and tank top, and she was prepared to deal with Detective Young.

"Come in." Grace held the door open wide. "I was about to make some coffee. Would you like some?"

Detective Young stepped in and ran a hand down his tie. "Yes, I'd love a cup."

"Have a seat." She indicated the family room. "I'll bring it out. How do you like it?"

"Black." He hesitated as if he had more to add but turned and walked away.

What did she see in those dark, intense eyes? Whatever it was, it got her heart pumping a little faster. Was it hot in here? She checked the air conditioner setting.

Grace brewed the coffee and selected two of her favorite mugs. She added a dash of creamer to hers and shot a little prayer for help heavenward before joining Peter in the family room. "Here you are."

"Thanks." He gave her a quick smile before lowering his eyes.

Maybe she'd misread his look before. Could he be here to deliver bad news? She set her mug on the side table with shaky hands. Did they find Serenity? Had she been hurt? Or worse?

Best to get it over with. "Detective, is Serenity dead?"

"No." He jerked his gaze up to hers. "What made you think that?"

"You come here." Grace waved a hand around. "In a suit. Looking grim." She stared at him. "The only other time a policeman paid me a visit like this is when my ... my husband was killed." She bit her lip to keep them from trembling.

"Oh, Grace." Peter sat his mug down and squatted by her chair. "I'm sorry." He touched her hand. "I didn't mean to bring back bad memories."

She lifted her hand to his and their fingers intertwined. For a long moment, she forgot about everything else except the feel of his skin against hers. Neither of them spoke. After a while, she inhaled and gently withdrew her hand. Peter stood and went back to his chair.

"I came because I wanted to tell you in person I can't let you work with me on this case. It's too dangerous." He held his hands up palms out. "I know you made a promise, but this is one promise you'll have to agree to pass to me. I'll keep it for you."

So that was it. He anticipated an argument. Tension fell from Grace like a heavy weight she'd been carrying. "I understand."

"You do?" His eyes lightened.

"Yes. I came to the same conclusion." Grace picked up her mug and looked at him over the rim. "You're the detective."

"I am." He narrowed his eyes at her. "And I detect that was way too easy." He mimicked her with his coffee mug.

Oh, those eyes of his. Grace took a sip and looked away. Maybe that wasn't the only reason he came by to see her.

Chapter Eleven

Peter stood and smoothed his tie. "I need to go." He picked up his mug. "Thanks for the coffee. I'll take this back to the kitchen."

Grace rose and smiled at him. "I'll take care of it."

He walked to the door, head down. Was this the last time he'd see her? "How long do you plan on staying?"

"I'm not sure." Her gaze wandered over the photos on the walls. "I thought I was coming to help Serenity. But now that she's missing, I don't know."

"It must be tough. Being here for the first time after …" He studied her.

"It's okay." She gave him a soft smile. "I've done my grieving, and this place is so peaceful."

"Yeah." He ran a hand over his scalp and hesitated. "Especially on the beach. You know … the clubhouse has a nice restaurant right on Trinity Sands beach. You want to have dinner together some time?" Slick, Young. He hazarded a glance at her from under lowered eyelids.

"How about lunch?"

"Lunch is good." He grinned and caught himself before leaning over to kiss her. "I'll call you."

"Perfect." She opened the door and threw him another dazzling smile.

As he drove away, he broke into song. What a great day. Now, he'd interview Serenity James' neighbors and find the one clue he needed to solve the case.

He maintained his buoyant mood until he got to the first house. The family renting the two-story to the right of Serenity's bungalow didn't answer, and their van wasn't in the driveway.

As Peter walked back to his car, a little deflated, a woman came up to him. She wore white running shoes, lime green shorts, and a tank top made of a stretchy fabric. Her tanned skin glistened with sweat.

"I saw them loading up for a day out with the kids this morning." She took a swig of water. "They probably won't be back until this evening."

"Thanks." Peter took out his notebook. "And you are?"

She gave him her name. "I live over there. I'm permanent."

"Do you know Serenity James?"

"Oh, yeah. Me and her been buddies for a long time."

"Have you noticed anything or anyone suspicious around her bungalow lately?"

"There was this car there the other day. I called Ben, our security guard, and he came right away." She nodded several times. "He took care of the woman."

So, she's the one who called Ben about Grace. "Anything else?"

She pulled her brows together. "Not unless you count the nutcases in the house over there." She inclined her head toward the house to the left of Serenity's bungalow. "But they're always acting weird."

"How so?"

"Coming and going at odd hours. Bringing in strange-looking packages. That sort of thing."

"Have they had any run-ins with Ms. James?"

"Nah. They keep to themselves." She took another swig of water. "I need to get inside. I've been out for a run, and I really need a shower." She looked him up and down. "How do I get in touch if something else happens?"

Peter handed her a card. "Thanks for your time." He wiped the sweat from his brow, climbed into his car, and fired up the air conditioner. August on the island.

He hit the jackpot with the runner. She was that neighborhood woman who knew everyone's comings and goings. Not too cool for the neighbors, but a real boon for the police. He moved his car fifty feet farther along the street and peered at the two-story house where the "nutcases" lived.

A silver SUV was parked under the house in the shade. He climbed the stairs to the door and rang the bell. A loud thumping sounded from inside the house. He pressed his ear to the door, eased his jacket back, and put his hand on his gun.

The door flung open, and Peter straightened before falling inside. A short woman as broad as she was tall gasped and started to slam the door. This time, he was ready and stuck his foot over the threshold. What was it with women on the island shutting doors in his face?

"What do you want?" She glared at him.

"I'm Detective Peter Young of the Trinity Sands Police Department." He held out his ID. "I'd like to ask you a few questions about your neighbor, Serenity James."

"We don't know her."

"This won't take long." He held her stare.

She sighed. "Come in." A strong, fishy odor hung in the air.

Peter studied her as she led him into a sparsely furnished

family room. Her tight T-shirt revealed a back rippled with well-defined muscles. A body builder? Or a woman wrestler? He ran a hand down his tie and decided on a low-key approach. Or he could get hurt.

She sat in what was clearly her chair and motioned him onto the loveseat opposite. "Ask your questions, but I probably don't have any answers."

"Mrs. Hopper, correct?" Peter gave her his best smile to no avail.

She blinked.

He took that as a yes and flipped through his notebook to a blank page. "Have you noticed anything strange around here in the past month?"

"You mean like lights in the sky at night?" She waggled her fingers in the air.

"Yes." Had Wanda Hopper seen them too? Now he was getting somewhere.

"No." The woman rolled her eyes. "But my nutty neighbor has. You should be talking to her. She caught me outside one day and told me all about them. Asked if I'd noticed them. Like I stay up all night staring at that bog behind us."

"So, you do know Serenity James."

"Is that who she is?"

"You never introduced yourself?"

"I just wanted to get away from that crazy woman."

Interesting. The runner called Wanda Hopper a nutcase, and now Hopper was calling Serenity a crazy woman. Was there something about this section of the club? Did it have something to do with its proximity to the Wilds?

"You didn't believe her." He made it a statement rather than a question.

"Are you kidding?" The woman stood. "If that's all, I've got work—"

A loud noise sounded from upstairs. Peter jumped to his feet and turned toward the staircase.

"That's my husband, Frank. We've got some plumbing problems." The woman gave him a stiff smile.

"Does he need help?" Peter slipped his notebook into his coat pocket.

"No."

A look of panic skipped across her face so fast Peter wasn't sure he'd seen it. Except her ruddy cheeks had paled. He couldn't force the issue without a warrant, but Frank and Wanda Hopper were now persons of interest as far as he was concerned. "I'll be back to talk with your husband later. How long are you planning on staying at the beach club?"

"We've got the house through Labor Day."

Two weeks from today. "Good." Peter wrinkled his nose. "What's the smell?"

"Frank fell in the pond when he was fishing, and I can't wash his clothes until he gets the pipes fixed upstairs." Wanda opened the front door. "I better go see how he's doing."

"If you need help, call Ben. He can get the maintenance crew over."

"We will."

The door slammed on his heels, and he drew a breath of cleansing hot air into his nostrils. He sauntered across the scruffy lawn to his vehicle. The noise might have been from a plumbing issue, but his well-honed detective nose smelled more than dead fish.

He paused before getting into his car and looked back. Something was definitely going on in that house, but he wasn't sure it had anything to do with his case.

Chapter Twelve

Grace twisted her wedding ring around and around. Lunch with Detective Young? What had she done? She needed to speak to Olga. After the phone rang three times without an answer, she brought her finger up to press End.

"Grace?" Olga huffed into the phone. "I'm here. I left my phone in the kitchen and had to run for it."

"I'm sorry. I didn't mean to bother you."

"It's no bother. What's going on? Are you okay?"

"I'm fine." Grace dropped into her favorite chair. "In fact, something's happened I never expected. Something good, I think. That's the problem."

"I don't understand."

"I met a man." A bubble of pleasure rose in her throat and burst from her mouth as a giggle.

"How perfectly wonderful." Olga's voice lilted through the phone.

"Yes. And no." Grace let her agony fill her tone. "He asked me to dinner, and I suggested lunch, and now I feel like I'm cheating on John."

"That's a run-on sentence, my dear, and also makes no sense. John, God rest his soul, has been dead for three years. He lived to make you happy. Don't you think he would want that for you now?"

"You're right." Grace blinked back tears. "It's not easy."

"I know, but I trust your judgment. If you feel this man is good, he probably is worth a chance."

"He is."

"Besides, it's only lunch."

Grace smiled to herself. Olga always helped her put things in perspective.

"What's this lucky man's name?"

"Peter Young. Detective Peter Young."

"That's perfect. You will have a built-in reference for your books."

"Olga," She said, her tone one of light scolding. "He doesn't even know I'm an author."

"You must tell him and find out all about him. When is this lunch?"

"I haven't decided yet." Grace's stomach churned.

"Make it soon before you lose your nerve."

Her friend knew her too well. "Yes, *Mother*."

"And call me after."

"I will. Thanks for talking to me."

"What are friends for?"

"Love you."

"You as well."

After Grace hung up, she realized she hadn't asked how Olga's visit was going with her sister. Plus, she hadn't told her anything about Serenity and her investigation. Maybe it was for the best. Olga would probably have tried to talk her out of going to Serenity's bungalow tonight.

The later the hour, the more nervous she felt. Was it too late to call Peter and ask him to come with her? But she knew what he'd say. He'd tell her to stay home and leave the investigating to the police.

Grace changed into a pair of jeans and a long-sleeve cotton shirt before stepping onto her deck with a can of bug spray. The smell brought back memories of fishing trips with her husband. After dousing herself liberally, she finished getting together what she'd need for her nighttime vigil. A battery-operated fan, a small cooler, and a gear bag filled with anything else she thought might come in handy. She'd gotten her golf cart ready earlier and packed everything into it.

The light morning breeze had developed into an erratic wind from the south. Clouds scuttled across the darkening sky. The fine hairs on Grace's arms stood up as she walked outside the garage. She hadn't checked the weather, but the air smelled like rain. Maybe this wasn't such a good idea.

But if she didn't go tonight, she'd have to wait a whole month. And something inside told her that would be too late. She climbed onto the bench seat of her golf cart and pressed the pedal. It lurched forward, almost slamming into a support beam. She squealed and hit the brake.

Finding reverse, she tried again. She made it down the drive and onto the street without incident. Once on the road, the electric hum of the cart calmed her nerves. No curtains twitched in windows. No lights went on or doors opened. She moved silently through the warm night, and it gave her a little thrill.

At Serenity's bungalow, she slowed to a snail's pace and pulled into the deep shadows under the house. Grace waited to see if anyone had noticed her. When her surroundings seemed clear, she gathered her gear, tiptoed up the stairs to Serenity's back deck, and settled in to wait and watch for the mysterious lights.

She'd planned her timing to arrive an hour or so earlier than the previous sitings. Two chairs sat against the outside wall with a table between them. She put her fan on the table and made herself comfortable in the chair to the left with the cooler at her feet.

So far, the bugs hadn't bothered her. Grace didn't want to turn on her fan unless she absolutely had to, but she would if it meant keeping mosquitoes away. She checked her phone. Fifteen minutes had passed. It was going to be a long night.

A door opened in the house to her right. Grace pressed her back against the chair and sat still. Her heartbeat pounded in her ears.

A little dog raced into the yard and started barking furiously in her direction. She closed her eyes and prayed.

"Get over here, you stupid mutt," a man growled. "The nosey biddy isn't there anymore."

Grace slitted her eyes at him. Anger slowly made its way to the surface like a bubble in a pot of hot tar. Who was this guy with his yappy little dog? She started to get up but remembered she wasn't supposed to be there.

The sound of a car door had her on alert again. A man's voice sounded close by. Was that Peter?

"Mr. Williams? I'm Detective Peter Young. I'd like a word with you and your wife."

"Sure. No problem." The man's tone changed to jovial. "Come on, Sparky. Come on, boy."

No more stupid mutt. Grace couldn't make out what was said after that as they moved inside. She sighed. Knowing Peter was close helped her anxiety. It shouldn't, because if he found out she was there, he'd be furious. But it did all the same. She glanced at her phone and groaned. It was going to be a *very* long night.

Grace must have fallen asleep because she started at the sound of men's voices close by. Peter was leaving the house next door. Her phone vibrated with a text. It was from him. He wanted to know if she was still up. She decided to ignore it.

The time for the lights to show was close. Grace focused on the Wilds beyond Serenity's backyard. The tall grasses swayed in the wind like some invisible creature meandered through the vegetation, and the stars played peek-a-boo with the clouds. She grabbed her phone, ready to record anything suspicious.

"Mrs. Caldwell."

Grace yelped and dropped her phone on the deck. "Detective, what are you doing here?"

"I was about to ask you the same thing." Peter shined his flashlight on her cooler and her gear bag. "Camping out?"

She couldn't see his face, but the tone of his voice told her all she needed to know. Detective Peter Young was not happy to see her. "Not exactly." Grace retrieved her phone and stood. "But you're just in time. The mysterious lights are due to appear any moment."

"You mean the lights Ms. James claims to have seen."

"Not claims to have seen. *Did* see." Maybe she wasn't so happy to see him either. "You're here now. Let's see if Serenity was right."

"Afterward you can tell me why you thought the mysterious lights would show up tonight." Peter eased himself into the chair on the other side of the table. "And what part of 'you need to leave the investigating to me' don't you understand?"

Maybe she'd tell him, and maybe she wouldn't. She plopped into her chair, crossed her legs, and swung her foot back and forth to the angry beat of her heart. Maybe she'd misread Peter Young, and he wasn't such a wonderful man after all.

How did he know she was at Serenity's bungalow? Was he stalking her? Had he put some sort of bug on her vehicles? Maybe she didn't want to go to lunch with this guy. In fact—

Peter gave a low whistle and pushed to his feet.

Chapter Thirteen

Grace gasped and jumped up.

Bright lights hovered over the Wilds. Beams lit up an area of about an acre. After about five minutes, tendrils unrolled from the darkness into the grasses below. A moment later, they furled up out of sight, and the lights disappeared.

"You got video, right?" Excitement filled Peter's voice.

"No." Hot tears of frustration filled her eyes. "I froze." She'd been a fool on so many levels.

"No matter." Peter's tone was soothing. "We both saw it. That's what counts." He used his flashlight to locate her gear bag and cooler. "I'll help you get this stuff home. It's late."

"I brought my golf cart." She didn't relish the idea of the slow ride back to her house in the dark.

"I'll give you a ride. We can pick up your cart tomorrow." Peter tucked her fan under one arm. "You did come prepared."

"I doused myself in bug spray before I came too."

"I know. That's how I knew you were on the deck when I came around back. I smelled the repellant."

"Wait a minute." She stopped at his car. "You didn't see the golf cart?"

"Nope."

"And you hadn't been looking for me?"

"I'm not a stalker, Mrs. Caldwell." He chuckled.

"Then why did you—?"

"I was doing a routine check on Ms. James's house. When I got around back, I smelled the bug repellant—mixed with sage—and knew it had to be you on the back deck. I am a detective, after all."

Grace was thankful for the dark because her cheeks warmed with embarrassment after all the terrible thoughts she'd had. It seemed her first assessment had been correct. Peter was a good man. And a good detective.

But what did that tell her about herself? Why had she been so quick to think the worst of Peter? So quick to pull away from a relationship that had barely got started? She thought she was ready to move on with her life, but was she?

"You're quiet. I thought you'd be pleased."

Grace flashed him a look.

"You were right. The lights appeared just like you said they would." He pulled to a stop in her driveway and turned to her. "That was no lucky guess."

"No." She unbuckled her seatbelt. "You'd better come in. I have something to show you."

"I'll bring your gear." Peter got out and opened the trunk.

* * *

Peter placed the fan and gear bag against the wall inside the front door and took the cooler into the kitchen. Grace was nowhere to be seen, but the sound of running water from down the hall, clued him in to what she was doing.

He flipped open the top of the cooler and lifted the waters out of the ice. After wiping each with a paper towel, he put them back in the refrigerator. She'd been to the market. Lunchmeat and cheeses filled the meat drawer, and fresh produce was visible in the vegetable bin. Her drink selection had improved too. He plucked a can of Diet Coke from the door and popped it open as he walked into the family room.

How had she known about tonight? Peter strolled around the room. What had she seen or figured out that he hadn't? He pulled one of her books from the shelf and sat down his soft drink. Thumbing through the book, his eyes snagged on a romantic scene between the female and male protagonists. "Whew," he muttered. "She's good."

Peter closed the book and slipped it back onto the shelf. "Mr. Campbell, you were one lucky guy." He slipped his jacket off and rolled his sleeves up to his elbows. Was it hot in there? He retrieved his soda.

"I was going to say make yourself at home, but I see you already have." Grace placed her computer on the dining room table.

"I ... sorry. I was thirsty." He pointed to his can.

"I'll be back in a minute." When she returned, she deposited what looked like six or seven little animal toys onto the table.

"What are these?" He picked one up. "Keychains?"

"Very special keychains." Grace pulled the alligator apart, revealing the flash drive inside.

Peter whistled. "Where did you find these? Wait." He lifted his hand. "I don't think I want to know."

She sighed. "Am I in trouble?"

"That depends." He placed his hands on his hips. "Did you acquire them before or after I opened my formal investigation?"

A frown line appeared between her eyes for a moment. "Let me think."

He studied her. Was she in serious thought or deciding whether to lie to him?

Her face cleared. "Before."

"Are you certain?"

"Yes."

He saw it in her eyes. She was telling the truth. "But once I opened the case, you still should have come forward with these."

"I wasn't sure if there was anything of value on them. It wasn't until Maude told me about the penguin that I guessed that's where the evidence would be."

"Maude? How'd she know?"

"She didn't. Not really."

What had he gotten himself into?

Grace sat in front of her computer and inserted the flash drive from the penguin. "Sit." She patted the chair next to her. Within minutes, photos Serenity had taken of the hovering lights displayed on the computer screen. "I noted the dates of all her sightings and realized that tonight was when they would be due to show up again." She gave him a quick hug. "And they did."

He stared straight ahead. Heat climbed from his neck to his cheeks. His muscles tightened as he fought an overwhelming urge to take her in his arms and kiss her.

"I'm sorry," she said in a quiet voice. "I got excited."

"It's fine. No problem." He shifted the screen to get a better look. "Good work."

Grace pushed away from the table. "I need something to drink. Would you like another Diet Coke?"

"No, thanks." He took a couple of deep breaths in an

attempt to get his heart rate back to normal. "What's on the other drives?"

"Nothing much that I could see." She returned with a bottled water. "I haven't opened all of them. The alligator has photos of alligators."

She gave a low-throated laugh that sent sparks along his nerves. He stood. Time to go home. "I'll need to take these with me."

"Could I keep them till tomorrow?" She reached toward him and drew back. "I'd like to look at the ones I haven't seen yet."

He rubbed the bridge of his nose. Did it really matter? What was another few hours? "I'll be back in the morning. About ten."

"Thanks, Peter." She stood and followed him to the door.

He paused with his hand on the knob, his heart hammered against his ribs. He turned to face her.

Her cell phone sounded in her pocket. At first, she acted as if she was going to ignore it. But then she pulled it out. "It's my daughter. I'd better take this."

"Yeah. See you in the morning." He pulled the door firmly shut behind him and walked to his car. As he drove home, he focused on the case and tried to leave his reaction to the look and smell and feel of Grace behind. Especially her hug.

At home, he snatched a Diet Coke from the fridge and went out on his screened back porch. A gentle rain whispered in the air, and every now and then, he'd feel a cool spray when the breeze blew a certain way. All that he'd seen and learned tonight bounced around in his mind like pool balls careening off each other.

He needed to make some notes, but where was his jacket? Did he leave it in the car? No. His jacket, containing his notebook and cell phone, was lying across a chair in Grace's dining room. Moron. He'd need to go back.

Chapter Fourteen

Grace leaned against the kitchen counter, holding her phone in her hand. She hated to lie to her daughter, but what choice did she have? When Elizabeth asked what she was doing, why she hadn't called, Grace said she had a friend from the neighborhood over. Not a lie, so far. Peter did live in Trinity Sands Beach Club.

But when asked who it was, Grace muttered something about someone she just met—again, not a lie—followed by Elizabeth wouldn't know 'her.' And there was the lie. If she'd said 'him,' Grace would still be on the phone answering questions about Peter, and she wasn't up to it. At least not yet.

Her stomach did that flutter thing when she thought about Peter. She was convinced he was about to kiss her at the door. And what surprised her most was she wanted him to. But no sense crying over what could have happened.

Grace strode to her desk in the bedroom and rifled through the top drawer. "I know they're in here somewhere." She pulled a baggie filled with flash drives out from under some papers. "Aha."

At the dining room table, she inserted a plain flash drive from the baggie into her computer and copied the information from the penguin. She did the same with all the animal key chains before returning the bag of flash drives to the drawer in her desk.

Guilt washed over her, but she'd made a promise to Serenity. And the information on these drives was key to her keeping her promise—and to finding her friend. She would deal with her guilt after she'd finished what she started.

A phone rang, and Grace picked hers up. Her screen was dark. She rose and listened. The sound came from the family room. As she rounded the table, something draped on the chair caught her eye. Peter had left his jacket. With his phone. She moved it to a chair close to her. A flicker of hope flamed inside her. He'd come back for it, and maybe she'd get a second chance at that kiss.

The doorbell rang. Grace danced over to the door and flung it open. "You just missed a call."

A figure in black pushed her against the wall and slammed the door shut. "Where are they?" He asked in a hoarse whisper.

"What?" The arm pressing on her chest constricted her lungs, and she had a hard time breathing. Pain mixed with fear clouded her brain.

"The keychains."

She inclined her head toward the dining room.

"Show me." He gripped her upper arm and yanked her in that direction.

At the table, he produced a bag. "Put them in here. The computer too."

His hot breath prickled the skin on her neck, and something hard pushed against her rib cage. "Don't try anything."

With trembling hands, she scooped the keychains into the

bag. Was he going to kill her? How could she buy time? "My computer's about out of power. You'll need the cord. It's in the office."

"Never mind. I'll—"

The doorbell rang again. Grace gathered all the courage she could muster. "Peter. Help." The echo of her voice was the last thing she remembered.

* * *

At the sound of Grace's voice, adrenaline stormed through Peter's body. He yanked his gun out of the holster, shot the lock on the door, and shouldered it open. Grace lay crumpled on the dining room floor. Blood seeped from her head.

"No. No. No." He dropped to the floor beside her. Iron bands of dread tightened around his heart. His jacket hung on a chair in front of his face. He dug in the pocket for his cell phone.

"Nine-one-one. What's your emergency?"

"This is Detective Peter Young. A woman's been hurt and is bleeding from a head wound."

"Does she have a pulse?"

Peter bent close to Grace and placed his fingers on her neck. "Yes. She's alive." *Thank You, Jesus.*

"An ambulance is on its way."

The operator went on to give Peter more instructions as he sat next to Grace waiting for help to arrive. He should be examining the crime scene, but no way would he leave her. Not until he was certain she was going to be all right. Maybe not ever again.

The welcome sound of sirens split the night air. A man and a woman in cargo pants and short-sleeve polos with the county EMS insignia on the pocket rushed through the door.

Peter got to his feet. "Over here." The ache in his chest diminished, especially when they moved Grace, and she moaned.

Two police officers came up to him. "The Chief sent us to help you with the scene."

He tore his focus from Grace and forced himself to view the scene as he had so many others. "Do you have any evidence bags?"

"Yessir." One officer hurried away.

There was blood on Peter's jacket. "When the officer gets back, bag this for evidence." He scanned the dining room table.

The keychains were gone, and Grace's computer had been knocked to the floor and lay against the wall. He called the policemen over and had them bag the computer. That's when he noticed the open sliding door to the deck. "We need fingerprints on the computer and the back door."

"Got it."

Peter crouched and ran a light over the floor. No shoe prints. He slipped through the open door onto the deck and shone his flashlight over the sandy surface. Nothing. It was impossible to tell which way he went, and too dark to see very far.

The EMTs rolled Grace out on a stretcher to the waiting ambulance.

Peter pushed past the officers and hurried to catch up to them. "Where are you taking her?" He wanted to be there when she opened her eyes.

"HCA Fort Walton Destin."

"Do you need anything?"

"No. We got her information from her wallet."

"Good." Peter rubbed a hand over his scalp. "I'll be right behind you." He jogged back to the house. "Stay here with the forensics team, and don't let anyone else in. I'm going to the hospital." He gave them his cell number and hurried back to his car.

It was a frustrating thirty-minute drive to the hospital. The traffic in Destin reminded Peter why he avoided leaving the island. Some of the bars had just closed, and the people who'd been drinking all evening were making their way back to hotels.

There were more than a few he would have liked to pull over and held until the local police could get there, but he didn't have time. And his part-time status with the police department made him reluctant to use his siren and lights on the mainland.

Once there, he flashed his badge at the emergency room nurse and demanded to see Grace. She let him back with an arched eyebrow over a big deal look and told him the room number. When Peter got to the door, he heard Grace's voice lifted in outrage. He paused outside and listened.

"I'm sorry, doctor, but I do not intend to spend one more minute in your lovely hospital than is necessary."

There was a pause in which some nice doc tried to reason with her. Good luck.

"You've treated and stitched my wound. I have pain medicine. You've done an excellent job, and I'm ready to go."

Peter cracked the door.

"But you may have a concussion."

"I understand that." Grace caught sight of Peter. "Detective Young. Please come in."

"It sounds like I'm interrupting something." He couldn't contain his grin.

"I've been telling this good doctor that I want to go home." She inclined her head toward the doctor and winced. "I've called my friend, Olga, who happens to be here in Destin, and she's going to pick me up and take me home. She'll stay with me for a night or two to make sure I'm not concussed."

"I prefer you stay here so we can monitor your medicine." The young doctor turned to Peter obviously hoping the detective would back him up.

"Your home is a crime scene at the moment."

Grace furrowed her brow at him. "Please make a call and hurry it up. I prefer going home to staying in a hotel."

"I think she means to leave." Peter gave the doctor a wry smile. "I'll make the call." He stepped into the hall and dialed the officers at the house. "Have forensics finished?"

"Yes, sir."

"Mrs. Caldwell is coming home with a friend. I want you two to take shifts and watch the front of the house."

"What about the back?"

"I'll take that." He'd need a change of clothes and some bug spray. Maybe he could borrow Grace's. He reentered the room.

"I'll prepare your discharge papers." The doctor gave a shake of his head and walked out.

"Peter." Grace reached for him. Her eyes begged for forgiveness. "I had to give that thug the keychains. I feel like a fool."

"It's okay." He placed a hand on her arm. "You did the right thing. Your safety is more important." He kicked himself for not insisting he take those little animals with him. On the other hand, if she hadn't had them, what would the guy have done to her? "We'll solve this and find Serenity without them."

"But, we don't have to. I copied them onto my own flash drives." Grace gave him her one-hundred-watt smile and winced.

Chapter Fifteen

Peter stared at the woman before him for a long moment. She'd tampered with evidence—again. Frustration and relief warred for dominance inside him.

"Are you mad at me?" Her face fell.

"I'm trying to decide if I should give you a lecture or ... kiss you." He ran a hand over his scalp.

"I vote for kiss," she said in a soft voice.

He raised a tentative hand to the cheek on the side of her face that wasn't bandaged. "I'm afraid of hurting you."

"It will be okay." She closed her eyes and tilted her face to his.

He brushed his lips against hers, and drank in the underlying smell of sage that even iodine couldn't completely drown. Her soft lips yielded to his, and he kissed her again with more urgency.

"I haven't kissed anyone like that since my late husband, John." Grace ran her tongue over her lips and smiled. "I never thought I would want to."

"I—"

"Okay." The nurse pushed through the door. "Here are your walking orders. If you experience any signs of a concussion or have any trouble with the pain meds, call an ambulance." She shoved a paper at Grace. "Please sign here."

"Grace." The door slammed open, and Olga rushed in. "How are you?"

"I'm fine."

Peter stepped out of the way of the female tornado.

The nurse threw the intruder an ugly look, but Olga was oblivious.

"You don't look fine." Olga waved a hand around her head. "You have a bandage on your head and a black eye."

The nurse handed Grace copies of the paperwork and left. That was when Olga noticed him.

"And who might you be?"

"Detective Peter Young." He gave her his best smile.

"Oh, you're the—"

"Olga." Grace's voice held a warning.

"What?" Her friend threw up her hands. "I was going to say this must be the detective you told me you'd met." She shrugged a shoulder in a what-else-would-I-have-said gesture.

Grace narrowed her eyes at her friend.

What was Grace afraid this woman was about to say to him? He liked her spunk. "You didn't tell me who you are."

"Olga Petrovich. I'm Grace's publisher and her best friend."

That answered one of his questions—how conservative Grace became friends with a woman who looked like a gypsy. "What's the plan?"

"Olga is driving me back to the island and staying with me for a couple of days until we're sure I'm okay." Grace moved to the edge of the bed.

"I'll follow you back." Peter moved closer to the women.

Grace stood and fainted.

Peter grabbed her before she hit the ground and maneuvered her to a chair.

She came to an instant later. "I don't know what happened."

"You passed out." Olga patted her hand. "I don't know if this is going to work. I believe you should stay here."

"No." Grace gritted her teeth. "I'll call a taxi if you won't take me."

Peter exchanged a look with Olga. "I think she means it."

"But Grace, what if you fall asleep? Or pass out again?" Olga folded her hands in front of her. "I don't know the way to your house."

"It'll be okay. You can follow me back to the island." Peter gave Grace a stern look. "But I'm not carrying you to the car. You'll need a wheelchair."

Grace grimaced.

He drove to Grace's house, making sure Olga was behind him. The night sky had lightened to gray by the time Peter crossed the bridge to the island. Two hours to official sunrise.

Grace's kiss lingered on his lips. He'd been attracted to her from the first time he met her, but he couldn't read her. Was their kiss at the hospital more to do with pain meds than interest?

An officer met them in the driveway and helped Grace into the house. Peter carried in Olga's suitcase.

"They'll be an officer out front all night." Peter nodded toward the officer. "And I'll be out back."

"On the deck?" Concern filled Grace's voice. "You'll get eaten up out there."

"Nonsense." Olga shook her head. "I will be in the guest

room. There's no reason you shouldn't be in here on the couch. Yes, Grace?"

Grace nodded and yawned. "I'll see you in the morning."

"Let me help Grace to bed, and then I will find a blanket and pillow for you, Detective." Olga bustled her friend down the hall.

Peter crossed the room to the windows overlooking the ocean. Morning was almost here. It had been a long time since he'd pulled an all-nighter. He yawned and rubbed his stomach.

"I found an extra pillow and blanket in the closet." Olga handed them to him. "Try to get some sleep. I am not an early riser, and I doubt if Grace will be up soon either."

"Thanks." He plopped the bedding on the sofa and took off his tie and holster. The belt and shoes were the next to go, and he pulled his shirt outside his pants.

Finally, as comfortable as he could get, he positioned the pillow at one end of the sofa. He placed his phone and his gun on the floor where he could reach them and scooted down on the sofa in an unintentional mimicking of Grace.

Not that he intended to sleep. He'd just rest his eyes for a bit.

* * *

What was that incessant tapping? Peter pried his eyes open. Two men stood at the sliding doors, looking in at him. Adrenaline jammed his heart into overdrive. He grabbed his gun and shot off the sofa.

It took a moment for his brain to process that the two men were in uniform. He laid down his gun and tromped over to the back door. "What do you want?"

"Sir, we've been calling but you didn't answer." One officer glanced inside. "So, we came around back."

Peter held a hand up to his forehead. The sun glared in his eyes, and it felt like a giant was pressing in on his temples. "What is it?" He tried to take the edge out of his voice.

"We've got a witness for Mrs. Caldwell's attack."

295

Chapter Sixteen

Grace rolled over, and pain brought tears to her eyes. She pushed herself up in bed and raised her fingers to the bandage on her head. The aroma of coffee and toast made her stomach growl. With slow movements, she swung her legs out and eased herself upright.

"What are you doing?" Olga rushed in. "You should have called me to help you. Sit, and I will help you get dressed."

"I thought I was dressed." Grace furrowed her brow and drew in a breath at the pain.

"If you call a T-shirt and panties dressed. I thought you might want to be properly dressed when your detective returns." She held up a pair of capris and a cotton blouse. "Yes?"

She'd forgotten about Peter. How could she after that kiss? She raised a finger to her lips. Wait. "Peter's not here?" Did she come on too strong? Was he joking, and she roped him into kissing her? Misery swelled inside her.

"He had to leave, but he said he'd be back as soon as possible." Olga thrust the outfit at her once more.

Grace nodded. "I'd like to clean up first. Will you help me?"

"Of course."

By the time Grace had finished getting dressed, with Olga's help, and was sitting at the table, she was exhausted. "I'm so thankful you're here. I don't know what I would have done without you."

"You would have had to stay at the hospital." Olga sat a plate of eggs, bacon, and toast in front of her. "I'll pour you some orange juice."

Grace raised a hand to stop her. Their eyes linked. "You know I could never do that. Not after John." Oh, John. Why did he have to leave her? She laid her head in her hands. And now, when she'd been given the promise of a new relationship with Peter, she'd blown it.

"I know, my friend." Olga patted her shoulder. "But I think you should tell your detective why." She straightened.

"I suppose you're right." Grace sighed. "I'll tell him the next chance I get." If he still was *her detective*.

"Good. Now, you must finish your breakfast so you can catch me up on what has been happening."

"I can talk while I eat. Get some coffee and join me." Grace took a deep breath. She had to put her worries about Peter aside and concentrate on Serenity.

Grace told Olga about finding the key chain flash drives, her chat with Maude, and the night on Serenity's deck. Her friend got more and more excited, and Grace knew what that gleam in her eye meant. She was a book publisher, after all.

"This is wonderful." Olga couldn't contain herself any longer. "Tell me you are writing all of this down somewhere. A journal, perhaps? What a book this would make."

"Olga." Grace adopted the stern tone she used with her children at times. "Serenity is missing. She is my first priority.

And I do not intend to use her disappearance as the plot for my next book."

"I am sorry. Sometimes I get carried away." She grasped Grace's hands in hers. "Please forgive me. Of course, your friend's safety must come first. What can I do to help?"

"You already are. Helping me now is exactly what I need."

"What about the speedy drives? Maybe if I looked at them ..."

Speedy drives? "Flash drives." Another set of eyes might be a good thing. And Olga did see things differently. "Okay. I'll tell you where they are." Her shoulders fell. "But I don't have my computer. The police took it as evidence."

"I have mine."

"You brought it with you?"

"I go nowhere without it." She shrugged. "It has become like a part of my body."

"You are marvelous."

"I know." Olga grinned at her. "I will clean up the dishes and then we begin our own investigation." She rubbed her hands together. "I have never done this before. It is exciting." She held up her hands palms out. "I know. It is serious, but ... I can't help it."

Grace shook her head, but secretly, she understood. And then she remembered Elizabeth. "I need to make a call."

"Mom." The frantic voice of her daughter answered before it rang. "Are you okay? They called me from the hospital in Destin, but when I called back, they said you'd been released. But you never called me."

Grace's heart ached as she heard the tears in her daughter's voice.

"Chase convinced me you must be okay or they wouldn't have released you, and to wait for you to call."

"I'm fine. I fell and hit my head. You know how head wounds bleed. A couple of stitches and a bandage is all it needed." She couldn't tell her daughter she fell because a bad guy had knocked her out. Not yet. "Olga is here with me for a couple of days."

"Olga? Why?"

"You know how doctors always worry about concussions. So, I asked her to come stay. But I'm fine. We just finished a yummy breakfast of eggs, bacon, and toast, and we're about to work on my book."

"I was so worried."

"I'm sorry. I didn't know they'd call you, honey."

"Please call me tonight."

"I will. Promise. I love you. Love to all the guys too."

"I love you too, mom. Call."

Olga stood nearby. "So, you do not want your daughter to know the truth?"

"She'd be down here in a heartbeat and insist I return with her." Grace tapped her phone. "She thinks I'm old and frail. Maybe I am, and I'm just fooling myself."

"Nonsense." Olga tossed a hand in the air as if batting the idea away. "You are a vital capable woman."

"Would you put that on a coffee cup for me?"

"Sometimes Grace, I do not understand you. Put what on a coffee cup?" Olga opened her computer and powered it up.

"Never mind." Grace laughed and winced. "Let's do some detecting." She chose one of the flash drives and inserted it into Olga's computer. It was one she hadn't seen before. Files labeled Strange Cargo with dates appeared on the screen. She clicked on one.

Photos taken at night with a telescopic lens showed two people unloading what looked like a body from an SUV and taking it inside a house. It was wrapped in a diamond-patterned blanket. The picture was blurry, but that much was clear. The house looked familiar somehow.

"Is that a body?" Olga leaned in closer. "Try to make the picture bigger."

"When I do, it gets grainier. Watch."

"No good. You are right. Let's see what the other files look like."

The next one was a short video. This time, two people carried something between them that was shorter. At one point, the object jerked and one of people almost lost his grip.

"It's alive." Grace blinked and ran the video again. "Did you see that?"

"Yes," Olga said in a low voice.

The third and fourth files contained photos of the same quality of similar packages being brought into the same house. What was going on, and why had Serenity filmed them?

Grace ejected the flash drive. She labeled it and made a few notes. "What do you think?"

"I think your friend liked to stick her nose into other peoples' business, and it got her in serious trouble." Olga's tone no longer held a note of exhilaration.

Olga's use of the past tense sent a chill through Grace's blood.

Chapter Seventeen

Peter closed and locked Grace's back slider. After he had a chance to change clothes, he would join his men at the station and interview the witness. As much as he liked wearing suits, they didn't work in the Florida heat. Back to khakis and a polo shirt. He lifted an arm and took a whiff of his pit. But he'd need a shower first.

A woman's chuckle sounded behind him. He swung around to see Olga dressed in orange with her dangly earrings and an impish gleam in her eye.

"I need to go." He slipped on his shoes and holster, and jammed his phone and tie into his pockets.

"I will make you breakfast before you go." She marched into the kitchen and opened the refrigerator.

"Thanks, but I haven't got time."

"Nonsense." She stepped into the hall and blocked his exit. "Breakfast is the most important meal of the day. It feeds your brain cells so they can work best." She tapped him on the chest. "Besides, they will not start without you."

She had a point. He placed his holster on the table. "What can I do to help?"

"You make the toast."

As Peter ate, Olga bustled around, humming to herself. He liked this woman. She would take good care of Grace.

And she was right about breakfast. He stood and took his plate into the kitchen. "Thanks. I feel much smarter now."

She laughed and patted his arm. "Have a good day, Detective."

"Tell Grace I'll be back as soon as I can."

"I will."

Peter's bungalow sat in a cul-de-sac one block off the beach in a quiet part of the club. Five tall palms shaded the small house. He fell in love with it the moment he saw it, and the corners of his mouth lifted every time he pulled into the driveway.

Once inside, it was all he could do not to pull on some shorts and head for his hammock on the screened porch out back. But he had a witness to interview, and the guys were waiting on him. A quick shower, change of clothes, a pinch of fish food in his aquarium, and he was out the door again.

The police station sat on the main drag in Trinity Sands Village in an old Florida house that had been renovated. Peter entered through the front door. "Good morning." He waved at the sour woman at the desk. "Are they ready for me?"

"It's afternoon, Detective Young." She peered at him over her glasses. "And yes, they've been here about an hour."

Peter started to run a hand down his tie but caught himself. No tie. "Thank you." He gave her a brilliant smile. "You look lovely in that color, by the way."

A smile flashed on her lips before she got herself under control. "Thank you."

Kill them with kindness. That's what his mother always said.

Peter strode down the hall to the one interview room in the back wired for audio and video. As he opened the door, the unmistakable sound of a baseball game reached his ears.

"What's going on?" He scanned the room. The two officers and a third man were sitting at the small table. Each held a sandwich and had a soft drink and a bag of chips nearby. A computer was open on the table.

"Detective." One of the officers jumped up. "We got hungry." He closed the computer. "And we thought we might as well watch the game while we ate."

A hush fell over the room.

"I'm glad you got our witness something to eat." Peter pulled up a chair.

The release of tension was palpable.

"I'm sorry it took me so long to get here. I had some things to take care of." He waved a hand in their direction. "Finish your lunch, and then we'll talk."

"I think we're done." The officer looked at the other two, who hurriedly stuffed their last bites of sandwiches in their mouths and gulped their drinks. "I'll clean this up."

Peter propped his ankle on his knee and studied the witness. He was an older man with unruly white hair and a full white beard and mustache. His skin was bronze, and he had deep wrinkles around his eyes like he'd spent his days squinting into the sun. He looked like a sea captain—or what Peter thought a sea captain should look like.

"I'd like to record this if you don't mind." Peter hovered his hand over the green button.

"Fine with me."

"I'm Detective Peter Young. With me are ..." Peter turned

to the two officers who stated their names for the tape. "We are interviewing Mr. ...?"

"Dr. Roger Tisdale," the man said.

"Dr. Tisdale. Sorry." Peter made a quick note on his pad. "I understand you're a witness to the robbery and assault that happened last night at Grace Caldwell's home. Please tell me what you saw."

"I didn't see the robbery or the assault, but at about eleven, my dog started to bark, and my motion-activated light in the back went off."

"You're sure it was eleven?"

"I believe so." He ran a hand over his beard.

"What did you do?"

"I have to admit, I thought it might be a deer. We get them sometimes late at night, and my dog goes nuts." He shook his head. "But something told me to get up and look outside. And there he was."

Peter waited for Dr. Tisdale to go on.

"He was dressed all in black, and when I came to the window, he pointed a gun at me."

"What did you do then?"

"I stepped out of sight. In a hurry." He gave a mirthless laugh.

"Can you describe the man? Was he tall or short? Slim or fat?"

"Medium."

"Anything else?" Peter looked at his meager notes. The doctor hadn't given them anything they didn't already know.

"When I got out of his line of sight, I went into my bedroom. It was dark in there and I could watch him without him seeing me. The street curves past my neighbor's yard, and so after he crossed their property, I could see a light-colored van or SUV pick him up at the curb."

"By light-colored, do you mean white?"

"No. It wasn't white. Maybe silver? Or light gray?"

Now he had something to work with. "Anything else?"

"He was carrying a dark-colored bag. I hadn't seen it until he got to the van."

"You think it was a van?" Peter put his foot on the floor and leaned forward. "Not an SUV?"

"Van, SUV." Dr. Tisdale waved his hand in the air. "I don't know anything about cars. All I know is it was bigger than my sedan, and it wasn't a pickup." He rubbed the back of his neck. "Are we about done here? I've got a poker game this afternoon."

"We're good." Peter stood and offered his hand. "If you think of anything else, please get in touch. Thanks for coming in. You've been a big help."

"I'll give you a ride back to your house," One of the policemen said.

After Dr. Tisdale left, Peter turned to the other officer. "Check out who in Trinity Sands Beach Club drives a silver or light gray van or SUV. Don't forget renters. Get it to me as soon as possible."

"Yes, sir."

"And get forensics over behind Dr. Tisdale's house and the neighbor's too."

"What do you expect them to find? It's all sand and brush over there."

"I don't *expect* them to find anything." Peter glared at him. "But they might just discover something that helps the case. Now do what I asked you to do."

"Yes, sir."

Peter pushed the door open to the men's room. He laid his files aside, splashed water on his face, and dried it with a paper towel. Maybe he should have stayed retired. He owed the officer an apology.

The policeman sat at his desk with his phone to his ear. Peter took a seat and waited.

"Okay. Give me a call when you're finished." He hung up and turned to Peter. "Was there something else you wanted?" His tone was frosty.

"Yes. I want to apologize for snapping at you." Peter looked him in the eye. "No excuses. Just I'm sorry."

The man's eyes held a surprised look before he dropped his gaze to his hands. "I'm not used to my superiors apologizing to me." He pulled on his ear. "Thanks."

"I wouldn't recommend questioning orders the way you did. I'm not crazy about it, but I tolerate it better than most. Usually." Peter stood. "Today, I reacted and I'm not proud of it."

"I understand." The officer lifted his gaze to Peter. "I'll have that list for you ASAP."

Peter nodded. "Good work with the witness." He needed to do that. Now, he could move forward.

Next stop, Grace's place. The thought of her warmed his insides, and he had to know if their kiss was real or the pain meds talking.

Chapter Eighteen

Grace's gaze locked on the photos once more. Something about them struck a chord in her brain.

"What are you looking at?" Olga looked from the photos to Grace and back. "Which one has caught your attention?"

"It's something about the group ..." Grace gasped. "The dates. These were all taken around the time Serenity saw the strange lights."

"You think they must be connected?"

"I'm not sure how, but don't you think that's odd?"

"I think I am going crisscross." Olga rubbed her eyes. "Let's have lunch and get outside for a while."

At the mention of lunch, Grace's stomach rumbled. She closed the computer. "After lunch, you can help me retrieve my golf cart from Serenity's house. I left it there last night after we saw the lights." She handed Olga deli sliced ham and cheese. "Is this okay, or would you rather have turkey?"

"I prefer turkey."

Good thing she'd thought to buy some of each. Grace pulled out a tomato and lettuce. "Mayo or mustard?"

"Mayonnaise please." Olga took the jar from Grace.

The women ate their sandwiches while leaning against the kitchen counter in companionable silence. Grace grabbed two waters from the refrigerator and handed one to Olga. "I kissed Peter last night at the hospital."

Olga choked and spit water from her mouth. "You did what?"

"You heard me." Grace took a drink. "But I think it was a mistake. I think I kind of forced him into it, and now he may have changed his mind about me."

"Grace, my friend, I doubt very much you could make that dishy detective do anything he didn't want to do." Olga gave a hearty laugh. "Trust me. He is still very much interested in you."

"You think so?" Grace pressed her lips together. "I hate this. It's like being back in high school again, and I hated it then too."

"Then do not let it worry you. Let it flow naturally. Be yourself. You are—"

"A vital, capable woman." Grace chuckled. "So you told me." She pushed off the counter. "Do you want to drive my car home or the golf cart?"

"The golf cart, of course." Olga gave an elegant shrug. "I used to race carts."

"I think you're talking about go-carts." Grace slung her purse over her shoulder and ushered Olga to her car.

Seven minutes later, Grace pulled into Serenity's driveway. Her golf cart still stood in the shade under the house. As she exited the car, her heart climbed into her throat, and she motioned Olga over. "Am I crazy, or is that the house from the photos we looked at this morning?" Grace inclined her head toward the house to the left of Serenity's.

"You are not crazy, my friend," Olga said in a low voice. "Look. That is the vehicle also."

A man barreled out the front door of the house and clambered down the stairs. He opened the back door of the SUV, rooted around inside, and scrambled back up carrying a large wrench without a glance in their direction. Grace and Olga breathed out in unison.

"Let's move over in the shadows and think about what to do." Grace eased her car door shut and led Olga to a spot under the house.

"What do you mean? We call your detective." The urgency in Olga's voice came out as a hiss.

"Of course." Grace pulled her phone from her shoulder bag. But what if they had Serenity tied up in that house somewhere? Shouldn't she try to get to her? She dialed Peter's number. It went to voicemail. She left a message explaining where they were and what they suspected, and then she looked at her friend. "I've got to know if Serenity is inside that house."

"Nonsense." Olga grasped her arm. "You are not the police. You are a writer."

"Here's the keys to my car. Go get help. But I'm going to try to get into that house." Grace inclined her head next door.

"How can I leave? You are my friend." Olga threw up her hands. "But if I am killed, I will never forgive you."

"Okay. We need a good reason to go to the door." Grace squinted off into the distance. "How about we're the neighborhood welcoming committee?"

Olga surveyed the yard and house. "I don't think they will want to be welcomed."

"Collecting for something?"

Olga shook her head.

"Do you have any ideas?" Grace arched her brows at her friend.

"You are the writer. What would you have us do in a book?"

"We would go up to the door, and something crazy would happen to get us in."

"Then let us see if that works." Olga smoothed her orange top and motioned for Grace to take the lead.

Grace and Olga trudged up the stairs to the front door where Grace hesitated. Olga reached around her and rang the doorbell.

"Be brave, my friend," she whispered in Grace's ear.

The door flew open, and a short, thick woman stood there staring at them. She blinked twice. "Olga? Olga Petrovich?"

"Nadia?" Olga stepped around Grace. "I thought you were ..."

"Yes, yes." The woman nodded. "Come in. It has been a long time. I'm no longer Nadia. Now I go by Wanda Hopper."

"Ah." Olga tapped the side of her nose with her finger.

As they followed Wanda down the hall, Olga turned her head and winked at Grace.

Grace couldn't believe it. This chance meeting could have come straight from one of her books.

"What are you doing here?" Wanda motioned them to sit. "Can I get you something to drink?"

"No. We just had lunch." Olga smiled. "My friend, Grace, is looking for her friend, Serenity James, and I told her I would help."

"Oh, that crazy woman from next door. A policeman was here the other day about her." Wranda rolled her eyes. "That woman bugged me about some lights in the marsh out back. Asked if I'd seen them. I told her I didn't spend my time looking at muddy grass."

A loud thumping noise sounded above their heads. Grace exchanged a quick look with Olga.

"We're having plumbing problems." Wanda clasped white-knuckled hands in her lap. "My husband's upstairs taking care of them."

What was she so anxious about? Could Serenity be locked in a closet, struggling to get free? "May I use your restroom?"

Wanda's eyes shot up toward the ceiling. "Our bathrooms are a mess. Plumbing, you know."

"But I really need to go." Grace hugged her stomach and grimaced.

Wanda looked around as if the answer was hiding in the room. "Let me go clean one out for you." She disappeared through a doorway opposite the one they'd come in.

"If you are having problems, we should leave." Olga touched her arm.

"I'm okay." Grace leaned close to her friend. "I want a chance to look around. You keep her talking while I'm gone."

"No. I forbid it," Olga hissed. "You—"

"You can use the half bath off the kitchen. I'll show you." Wanda narrowed her eyes at them. "Is something wrong?"

"No." Olga waved a hand in the air. "Grace is an author, and I am her publisher. We were having a disagreement over a stunt she wants to do to promote her books." Olga glared at Grace.

"Oh." Wanda blinked. "What do you write?"

"I'll let Olga tell you, if you don't mind. Where's the bathroom?"

Wanda led her to a small powder room off the kitchen with a toilet and a sink.

"Thanks." Grace hurried inside and closed the door. A strong fish odor pervaded the space and almost made her gag.

After a long moment, she cracked the door and listened. Olga laughed at something Wanda had said. No doubt some comment about the friends she kept these days. Grace tiptoed around the kitchen, quietly opening drawers and cupboard doors. She found nothing out of the ordinary.

Next to the bathroom was another closed door. When she opened it, the fishy smell almost knocked her over. Laundry covered the floor and the tops of the washer and dryer. She backed out and started to pull it closed. *Wait a minute.*

A diamond-patterned blanket lay in a heap on the floor. The same blanket they'd seen in the photo. The one wrapped around the body.

Chapter Nineteen

Peter's phone vibrated with a text as Grace's house came into view. He ignored it. Olga's car sat in the driveway, but where was Grace's? In the garage? He parked and strode up to the house. Unease inched along his skin.

The doorbell echoed through the house. No sound of feet coming to answer. His phone continued to vibrate. He ignored it and rang the doorbell again. Nothing. Maybe they were on the deck.

As he strode around to the back, he pulled his phone from his pocket. The first text was the list of van and SUV owners in the club. He rounded the garage and looked up. The deck was empty.

The second text stopped him in his tracks. The runner lady across from Serenity called to report that the nosey woman was back at Serenity's house, and she had a friend with her. His unease turned to alarm that sat like a stone in his stomach. Grace and Olga.

He jogged back to his car and jumped behind the wheel. A third text came through. The runner lady again. She'd seen the women enter the nutcases's house. Peter grabbed the mic and called dispatch. "I need backup at 27 Suncatcher Drive. No sirens or lights. Repeat. Backup at 27 Suncatcher Drive. No sirens or lights. May have a hostage situation."

The first thing that caught his eye was the silver SUV parked in the driveway. Grace may have unwittingly walked into her attacker's hands and taken Olga with her. He rolled closer. Out of the corner of his eye, he saw runner lady exit her house and head for his car. "Oh, man."

"I wondered if you got my texts." She tried to open the passenger side door of his car. "Let me in."

"Ma'am, you need to go back inside. This is a police operation. We can't have any civilians around."

"But I gave you the information." She stuck her hands on her hips. "I should be able to see what happens."

"Watch from your house where you can't get hurt." Peter used his most persuasive tone.

"I'll sit on the porch."

He stepped out and approached her. "I'd hate to have to arrest you for obstructing justice." His icy gaze and voice cut the air between them.

"Okayyy." She huffed away and slammed her door.

He scanned the two-story house with the van. No change. Hopefully, they hadn't seen the exchange. He'd give back-up five more minutes, and then he'd go in alone.

* * *

A loud cough roused Grace into action. She'd get a knife and cut a piece from the blanket for evidence.

"What are you doing?" Wanda's angry voice sounded behind her.

"I, uh ..."

"You were snooping. Who are you really? What are you doing here?" The woman grabbed Grace by her arms and dragged her out of the laundry room.

"Leave my friend alone." Olga's tone was commanding, and for a second, the woman's grip loosened. But then she clamped down even harder. "Are you from the government?"

"What are you talking about?" Olga slapped Wanda on the back. "Let go of her this instant."

"Then why?" Wanda growled at Olga. "Why are you here?"

"We think you have kidnapped Serenity James because she discovered you are up to your old tricks." Olga wagged a finger at her.

Wanda flushed a deep scarlet. "Not the old tricks, as you call them."

"Then some new ones." Olga skewered her with an accusing look.

A muscle twitched under Wanda's right eye. "What business is it of yours?"

"It is, if you kidnapped my friend." Grace struggled in the woman's grasp. "Let go of me."

"Why do you think we have her?" Wanda gave them a puzzled look.

"We saw it on film. You were carrying a body into this house wrapped in that blanket." Grace inclined her head toward the laundry room.

The creases in Wanda's face deepened, and she chewed her lower lip. "Ah, yes." She scowled at Grace. "Not a body. And we don't know where your friend is."

"Then let us search the house."

"Not possible." Wanda shook her head. "You will have to take my word for it."

The loud thumping noise sounded above their heads once

more. Wanda loosened her grip, and Grace yanked her arms away. She ran for the staircase.

As she reached the bottom step, she heard a crash and loud cursing.

"Go," Olga called out. "I will take care of Nadia—Wanda."

Grace took the stairs two at a time. At the top, she paused. The doors in both directions were closed. Which way should she go?

She turned right and opened the first door. The room was empty except for a children's swimming pool in the middle. Odd. She continued down the hall. They were the same— including a small pool in each.

Except for the corner room. It had a bath attached. She opened the door and screamed.

Chapter Twenty

Peter wasn't waiting any longer. He drove up to the house, climbed the stairs, and banged on the door. "Police. Open up." Thumps and bangs sounded from within.

"I am coming." Olga threw open the door, her chest heaving as if she'd been running. "Detective, you are here at last."

A scream came from upstairs.

"Excuse me." Peter pushed past the woman and flew up the staircase. Where was she?

"What are you doing?" Grace's strident voice sounded from the end of the hall.

He drew his weapon. At the doorway, he pressed his back against the wall to hazard a glance inside. Grace was staring through another door from inside the room. He eased into the bedroom and held his finger to his lips to keep Grace quiet.

She glanced at him as if she didn't see him.

The voice of a man came from inside the smaller room. "I'm trying to calm him down. You're not helping."

Calm who down? Peter moved along the wall until he was

next to Grace. He motioned her to move out of the way. He spun into the doorway and dropped into a crouch, his gun extended. "Police. Drop your weapons and put your hands in the air."

"You don't want me to put my hands up," the man said.

It took a moment for Peter's brain to register what his eyes were seeing. A heavy-set man was leaning over a bathtub, pressing on an alligator. Water flowed over the edges of the tub onto the tile floor.

"He's not happy." Sweat beaded the man's brow. "And I've been trying to calm him down for about half an hour now."

Peter holstered his gun. Shouts came from below. Boots tramped up the stairs.

"Sir, are you up here?"

"Everything's under control, Officer." Peter kept his eyes on the prehistoric-looking beast in the tub and the man wrestling with it.

"Move slow and hand me that tranquilizer shot over there." The man held out his right hand.

Peter did as he asked.

"Now stand back." He plunged the syringe into the animal and pressed the plunger.

The alligator pushed up on his legs and threw the man to the floor. But the sides of the tub were too slippery and it slipped back into the water. The man scrambled up ready to do battle once more.

Everyone in the room held their breath. The drenched man hovered over the primitive animal until he was sure the sedative had taken effect. Then he leveraged himself to his feet using the side of the tub.

"There's got to be a better way to make a living." He ran a hand through his hair.

"Than the illegal catching and selling of wildlife, you mean?" Peter asked.

The man looked at him with a sorrowful expression. "Yes, sir."

"And kidnapping, Mr. Hopper?"

The man's knees gave way. "Kidnapping? No, sir. We ain't no kidnappers."

"Then you won't mind if we search your property."

"You go ahead and search." He waved his arms. "Animals are one thing, but people ... No way."

Peter nodded at the officer who read Hopper his rights, handcuffed him, and led him away. Afterward, he turned to Grace. "You could have been killed. Frank Hopper could have been the man who broke into your house last night with a gun." Anger and gratitude warred within him. Was it always going to be this way with her?

"I had to know if they had Serenity." She raised sad eyes to his and gave a shuddering sigh. "I was so sure I'd find her."

The lecture he planned to give her died on his lips. The despair in her voice hurt his heart. "I'll find her. I promise." He cringed inside. That was a mistake.

"No." She shook her head. "I know how hard it is. It's been three years, and the police aren't any closer to finding John's killer."

"Let's get out of here and let the guys do their search." Peter took her arm and guided her down the steps and outside. Somehow, he felt like he'd let Grace down. He glanced at the SUV. At least this was one vehicle he could mark off the list the officer sent him.

"Praise God you're okay." Olga pressed her hands together. "Wanda told me all about their business." She made air quotes around the word business and rolled her eyes. "I am not surprised. The woman has been in and out of prison many times."

"You know her?" Peter asked.

"We grew up together in the old country. She was always in trouble then too."

"What made you suspicious of the Hoppers in the first place?" Peter walked with them across the yard toward Grace's car.

"We'd seen photos and video of them taking big bundles into their house."

"Where?"

"On one of Serenity's flash drives." Grace leaned against her car. "But we didn't realize it was the Hopper's house until we got here. We came to get my golf cart."

Peter swiveled his gaze from where they stood toward the house. "You recognized it when you got out of the car."

Grace nodded.

"And the rest is history. As they say." Olga sighed. "Now I suppose we will retrieve the golf cart as we planned and ..." She turned her head to the right. "What are you looking at, Detective?"

"What color would you call their van?" Peter lifted his chin in the direction of the driveway to the right of Serenity's bungalow.

Grace glanced over her shoulder. "Ice blue?"

"I agree." Olga nodded.

"Do you think it could be mistaken for silver at night?"

"Yes, I think so."

"Me too." Peter furrowed his brow. "Did Serenity take any photos of her neighbors in that house?"

Grace pushed off her car and turned. "I think there were some, but I didn't spend much time looking at them. Why?"

"So, there are files you haven't seen yet?" That familiar twinge plucked his detective nerve.

"Yes. What are you thinking?"

"I'm thinking it's time for another talk with David and Ann Williams. You stay here." Peter sidled across the yard as if he wasn't interested in more than a pleasant chat about the weather. The double doors at the back of the van were open, and luggage filled half the space.

Grace and Olga followed him. He wasn't surprised.

David came out of the door and paused on the landing before descending the steps. "Detective. Ladies." He nodded at them.

"I thought you were staying until Labor Day." Peter took one of the bags from David's hands and carried it to the van.

"Change of plans." David wiped his palms on his shorts and charged up the stairs.

Peter surveyed the suitcases and other luggage inside the van. He sniffed. Was that the faint odor of marijuana? Was it enough to order a search?

Ann came out with the children. She held the little girl's hand as they took the steps one at a time. The older boy raced down and jumped off the second from the last step. Olga applauded, and he gave her a side-eyed look.

"He's my daredevil." Ann ruffled his hair. "Aren't you? Get in the car."

"I'm sorry you have to leave before the summer is over." Grace gave her a warm smile.

"Daddy's got busyness." The little girl skipped around the area. "So, we have to go home."

"That is too bad." Olga squatted down and grinned at her. "Where is home?"

The little girl tilted her head. "It's far away."

"Mine too," Olga said.

"Honey, it's time to get in the car." Ann held out her hand. "Come."

"I wish the lady could come with us, but Daddy says—"

"Get in the car." Ann grabbed her daughter and lifted her into the van. She turned back to Grace and Olga with a smile. "She has an imaginary friend. We're trying to break her of it. So, we told her the lady has to stay here." Ann rolled her eyes. "You know kids."

"I understand. My son had an imaginary friend called Johnson and Johnson." Grace laughed. "Maybe I used too much baby shampoo on him."

Olga gave a hearty laugh. Ann looked at Grace like she was crazy.

But Peter wanted to know where this imaginary friend was now. His twinge had turned into a full-blown alarm bell in his head. He opened the door on the other side of the van. "What does your daddy say about the lady, sweetie?"

Thrilled to have a new audience, the little girl grinned at Peter, but then her face fell. "He says she's too old to make the trip. She'll be dead soon."

Chapter Twenty-One

Grace moved closer to the van. What was the little girl telling Peter? Something about being too old to make the trip. Dead soon? The blood froze in her veins.

Ann Williams pushed past her and reached in to fasten her daughter's safety belt.

Peter came around the van. "Where is she?"

"Where's who?" Ann continued what she was doing.

"Step away from the van, Mrs. Williams."

"I don't think I will."

"Don't force me to drag you away in front of your children." Peter kept his voice low, but stone cold.

A little yappy dog rushed down the steps ahead of David. "What's going on?"

"Nothing." Ann stepped back and closed the door. "We're ready to rock and roll."

Peter took her by the arm and guided her behind the van, where he shut the back doors. Grace followed.

"Hey. What are you doing?" David reached for Peter.

Peter twisted David's arm around behind him and placed him in handcuffs. "Olga, get the officers to come up here now."

Olga took off at a fast pace.

"What have you done with Serenity?" Grace took a step toward David.

"You stupid witch." David Williams sneered at her. "This is all you and your idiot friend's fault. If you'd minded your own business, none of this would have happened."

His voice. "*You're* the one who broke into my house." Grace touched her scalp. "And hit me on the head."

"I would have done worse if your boyfriend here hadn't shown up." David jerked his head at Peter.

The rage that erupted inside her frightened her.

The man leered at her as if daring her to touch him.

"Leave him to us, Grace." Peter stepped between her and David. "We'll find out where she is."

She searched Peter's dark eyes. Would he be willing to do what was necessary to get David to talk?

Police officers arrived to search the house and surrounding area.

"Look through the van too," Peter said. "I smelled marijuana."

Once again, she was left waiting for results. How many times would this happen before Serenity would be found? Grace sat on a bench under the house. The little brown and white dog trotted over and put a paw on her leg. She stroked his wiry fur and wondered what would happen to him and the children if both their parents went to prison.

The dog got down and started pawing at something sticking out from under the door of the shed at the end of the driveway. Grace rose and went to see what he was so interested in. For the second time that day, she screamed at the top of her lungs.

Peter raced to her side. "What?"

She pointed down. A fingertip stuck out from under the shed door.

Peter looked around frantically. "I need something to force the lock."

"Maybe David has the key on his ring."

"Good thinking." Peter searched David for his keys and rushed back to the storage shed. The fourth key he tried opened the lock. He flung the doors open. "Call an ambulance."

Grace dropped to the ground next to her friend. Serenity's eyes were sunken, and her shriveled body was curled into a fetal position. She was barely breathing.

"I'm here, my friend. Help is on the way." Grace continued to talk to Serenity, telling her how the photos on her flash drives provided the clues needed to catch two criminals. "You are so smart and strong, and I know you're going to get better so we can celebrate." She slid her hand over and touched the woman's wrist.

Serenity's little finger moved, and hope surged in her chest. "Where's the ambulance?" She called over her shoulder.

"It's pulling in now." Peter appeared by her side and helped her up. "Let's get out of the way."

The EMTs were efficient but gentle. Soon, Serenity was wrapped in a blanket and strapped to a gurney with an IV started in her arm. "We're taking her to Destin, where she'll be airlifted to Ascension Sacred Heart Pensacola. They have a level one trauma center."

Grace gulped down a steadying breath, and Peter slid his arm around her. Olga came up on her other side, and Grace reached for her hand.

After the ambulance raced out of sight, Grace let go of Olga and stepped away from Peter. Now what? She surveyed the scene. "What happened to the Williams? And their children?"

"David and Ann are in custody at the police station. Family services came for the children." Peter rubbed a hand over his head. "We've called the grandparents, and they're on their way here to get them. Poor kids."

"Do we know what David and Ann were up to?"

"Ann told me it was all her husband." Olga raised an eyebrow. "I don't believe her. She said he got involved with drug dealers."

"Drugs?" Grace asked.

"Pills." Olga held a hand up with a finger and thumb, making a circle. "The lights at night? They were ... what do you call them? Crones?"

"Drones," Peter said.

"Yes, drones. Bringing the drugs. Then David would get them and pass them on to the next person."

"Did she know who the next person was?" Peter placed his hands on his hips.

"She says not." Olga shrugged. "But I think she knows more than she is telling me."

"You got more than I did." Peter gave her a wry smile. "I may have to put you on the payroll."

"No, no, no." Olga raised her hands. "I am a simple publisher. Nothing more."

"Who knew Wanda Hopper and helped with that case too."

"Pfft." Olga brushed that away. "That was luck."

"Or a blessing." Grace turned to gaze at the house on the other side of Serenity's bungalow. "What will happen to the Hoppers?"

"I've turned that one over to Florida Fish and Wildlife."

"What about the alligator in the bathtub?"

"Turns out that was Annie." Peter pressed the bridge of his

nose. "I convinced Wildlife to return her to our lake. Even though I'm not crazy about the idea."

"I guess we can go." Grace bit her lip to keep it from quivering. Why did she feel so deflated? She'd kept her promise to Serenity.

"I agree. Time to go home and get something to eat." Olga threaded her arm through Grace's. "I will finally get to drive your cart."

"I need to get to the station, but I'd like to come over later." Peter turned his gaze on her.

A breath of joy raised her spirits. "We'd like that." *She'd* like that.

Chapter Twenty-Two

G race never tired of watching the sun arc toward the sea. Every night, it was a different experience, each a reminder of God's glory in its unique beauty. She and Olga had eaten a good dinner, and the deflated feeling of earlier had passed—a combination of hunger, fatigue, and adrenaline let-down, most likely.

"You have a lovely home here." Olga stood beside her at the windows overlooking the ocean. "It will be hard to return to Memphis."

"I know." Grace turned and crossed to her chair. "But Elizabeth and Chase and the boys are there." She pulled a leg under her. "And you. Besides, I'm not going back for a week or so."

"I will be returning to my sister's place tomorrow." Olga settled on the sofa. "You do not need me any longer, and I want a few more days with her before I travel home."

"Tell your sister how much I appreciate her sharing you with me for these last days." Grace blinked back tears.

"She was glad for the break." Olga snorted a laugh. "We can only stand to be around each other in spurts."

Grace smiled. "I'll miss you."

"We will see each other when you are home."

The doorbell rang, and Grace rose. She peered through the peephole before opening the door. A lesson she'd learned the hard way. "Peter, come in."

"I brought dessert." He placed a box on the kitchen counter. "Homemade cookies. I didn't make them. The chief's wife did. I just asked if I could bring some with me."

"Thanks." Grace got a plate from the cupboard and opened the box. "Chocolate chip. My favorite." She arranged the cookies on the plate and took them out to the family room along with napkins. "Have you heard anything about Serenity?"

"She's stable, and they think she'll make a full recovery."

His words filled Grace with joy.

"Praise God we found her in time," Olga said.

"Amen." Grace grinned at them. "Now. Who wants milk?"

Peter raised his hand, and so did Olga.

Olga scooted forward on the sofa and reached for a cookie. "Yum. You are a man among men."

"Here you go." Grace handed out glasses of milk, snatched a cookie from the plate, and sat in her chair once more. "These are really good."

Olga put two more cookies on a napkin, stood, and picked up her glass. "If you will excuse me, I must pack. I leave tomorrow."

Peter rose.

"It was nice to meet you, Detective. I hope to see you again sometime. Maybe you can come to Memphis and visit."

"I enjoyed getting to know you, Olga. As for Memphis, I might take you up on your offer."

Grace took a sip of her milk. Her heart thudded in her chest. She hadn't been alone with Peter since before the hospital, and somehow things had changed. She gathered her courage and lifted her gaze. The look in his intense brown eyes made her nerves hum.

He sat on the sofa and patted the spot next to him. "Why don't you come over here."

Oh, man. She sat her glass of milk on the table and rose. "I'm not sure this is a good idea."

"I am." The corners of his mouth lifted in a slow smile. "We need to clear the air."

"About what?" She perched on the edge of the sofa cushion next to him.

"Our kiss. I need to know if that was you or the pain meds?"

Grace swiveled to look him in the eye. "You mean I didn't put you on the spot? You didn't feel like you *had* to kiss me?"

He put his arm around her and scooted her closer to him. "Come here." He wove his other hand through her hair and brought his mouth so close she could feel his breath. His lips meshed with hers in a kiss that was at once soft and filled with passion.

"I've wanted to do that almost since the day I met you." He ran his lips along her jawline.

Tears ran down Grace's face. She couldn't stop them.

"What?" Peter wiped her cheeks with the backs of his fingers. "I'm sorry. I didn't mean to—"

"No." Grace caught his hands in hers. "It's not that. It's ... I never thought after John that I would ever feel this way again." She touched his cheek. "Don't get me wrong. I'm not declaring my undying love or anything like that, but I sure do like you, Peter Young."

"And I like you, Grace Caldwell. I think we need to investigate this further."

Grace chuckled and sighed. "Except you live here, and I live in Memphis."

"We'll make it work. You'll come down here, and I know where Memphis is." He placed a finger under her chin and raised her eyes to meet his. "Maybe someday, you'll tell me what happened to your husband. I'm a good listener."

Grace squeezed his hand before clasping hers in her lap. "Sometimes, it seems like it was so long ago, and then it's like it happened last week." She sighed. "John had gone to visit a friend in the hospital. He was on his way back to his car when he saw two men attacking a woman in the parking lot. You can guess what happened next." She raised her gaze to Peter's. "John pulled his gun and ran over to help."

"Did he always carry a gun?"

"Yes. He was part of the security team at our church, and he'd just come from there." Grace shook her head. "But he carried a gun most times anyway, and I can't help but think that's what got him killed." She covered her face with her hands.

"It's okay. You don't have to talk about it." Peter rubbed her shoulder.

"No." She dropped her hands to her lap. "It's good for me, and you should know. From what I was told, one of the men ran away, but the other drew a gun and shot John in the midsection. John managed to shoot him in the leg, and the police were able to catch him." She shuddered as she remembered the next part. "They got John into the emergency room, but it was too late. He'd lost too much blood. By the time I got there, he was gone."

"Grace, I'm sorry." Peter reached for her.

But she moved away. It was too soon after going back to that time to find comfort in the arms of another man. Even if it had been three years. "Give me a minute to bring myself back to the present." Grace got up and swiped at her cheeks. "I need a tissue." When she got back, Peter had his phone to his ear.

"Yeah. Get the details and tell her we'll be by in the morning." He hung up and turned to Grace. "When are you going home?"

"In about a week or so. Why?"

"I've got another case, and I could use your help. If you still—"

Grace grabbed Peter by the shirt with both hands and pulled him close. "I still." She pressed her lips to his and let out a contented sigh when he encircled her with his arms.

THE END

About Deborah Sprinkle

When Deborah Sprinkle retired from teaching in 2004, she had a plan for keeping busy. Attend the women's Bible study at her church, join a local book club, and write a mystery novel. She began going to Bible study on Wednesday mornings, and when her local library started a book club, she was one of the charter members.

One thing led to another—as they usually do—and pretty soon, she was a Bible study leader and facilitating the book club.

In 2009, she was asked to attend the She Speaks Christian Writers' Conference put on by Proverbs 31 Ministry, where she met Kendra Armstrong. It was their friendship that led to her first book, *Exploring the Faith of America's Presidents*, written in collaboration with Kendra. It was published in 2012 by Lighthouse of the Carolinas. This book is no longer in print.

After attending lots of conferences, taking many classes,

and sitting at the feet of a plethora of experienced writers, Deborah wrote her first novel. And, in 2019, her dream came true when *Deadly Guardian* made its debut. Three more novels rounded out the Trouble in Pleasant Valley series, and she now has a new set of mystery novels set in a small town in Missouri called Mac and Sam Mysteries. The first of these is *The Case of the Innocent Husband.*

Originally from St. Louis, Debbie received her bachelor's degree in chemistry from the University of Missouri-St. Louis. She worked as a research chemist for many years at both St. Louis University Medical School and Washington University Medical School. In 1991, she and her family moved to Memphis, where Deborah taught chemistry for ten years at a private girls' school before retiring.

You May Also Like ...

Sharktooth Island

A collection of Romantic Suspense novellas

A fabled island that no one dares to tame.

This collection contains four novellas:

Book 1 - Out of the Storm (1830) by Susan Page Davis

Laura Bryant sails with her father and his three-man crew on his small coastal trading schooner. After a short stay in Jamaica, where she meets Alex Dryden, an officer on another ship, the Bryants set out for their home in New England.

In a storm, they are blown off course east of Savannah, Georgia, to a foreboding island. Captain Bryant tells his daughter he's heard tales of that isle. It's impossible to land on, though it looks green and inviting from a distance. It has no harbor but is surrounded by dangerous rocks and cliffs.

Pirates outrun the storm and decide to bury a cache of treasure on this island and return for it later. On board is Alex, whom the cutthroats captured in Jamaica and forced to work for them. Alex risks his own life to escape the pirates and tries to help Laura and Captain Bryant outwit them. Beneath the deadly struggle, romance blossoms for Laura.

Book 2 - *A Passage of Chance* (1893) by Linda Fulkerson

Orphaned at a young age, Melody Lampert longs to escape the loveless home of the grandmother who begrudgingly raised her. Stripped of her inheritance due to her grandmother's resentments, Melody discovers her name remains on the deed of one property—an obscure island off the Georgia coast that she shares with her cousin. But when he learns the island may contain a hidden pirate treasure, he's determined to cheat her out of her share.

Ship's mechanic Padric Murphy made a vow to his dying father— break the curse that has plagued their family for generations. To do so, he must return what was taken from Sharktooth Island decades earlier —a pair of rare gold pieces. His opportunity to right the wrong arrives when his new employer sets sail to explore the island.

After a series of unexplainable mishaps occur, endangering Padric and his boss's beautiful cousin Melody, he fears his chance of breaking the curse may be ruined. But is the island's greed thwarting his plans? Or the greed of someone else?

Book 3 - *Island Mayhem* (1937) by Elena Hill

Louise Krause stopped piloting to pursue nursing, but when money got too tight, she was forced to give up her dreams and start ferrying around a playboy who managed to excel during the Great Depression. When a routine aerial tour turns south, Louise is unable to save the plane.

After crash landing, the cocky pilot is stranded. She longs to escape the uninhabited island, but her makeshift raft sinks, and she and her companions are in even worse trouble. Can Louise learn to trust the others in order to survive, or will the island's curse and potential sabotage lead to her demise?

Book 4 - *After the Storm* (*present day*) by Deborah Sprinkle

Mercedes Baxter inherited two passions from her father—a love for Sharktooth Island, a spit of land in the middle of the ocean left to her in his will, and a dedication to the study of flora and fauna on and around its rocky landscape.

For the last five years, since graduating from college, Mercy led a peaceful, simple life on the island with only her cat, Hawkeye, for company. Through grant money she obtained from a conservancy in Savannah, she could live on her island while studying and writing about the plants and animals there. Life was perfect.

But when a hurricane hits the island, Mercy's life changes for good. Her high school sweetheart, Liam Stewart, shows up to help her with repairs and ignites the flame that has never quite died away. And if that's not enough, while assessing the damage to the island, they make a discovery that puts both their lives in danger.

Get your copy here:

https://scrivenings.link/sharktoothisland

* * *

Stay up-to-date on your favorite books and authors with our free e-newsletters.

ScriveningsPress.com